The Cold Case
and the
Corpse

Books by Debra Sennefelder

Food Blogger Mysteries

The Uninvited Corpse
The Hidden Corpse
Three Widows and a Corpse
The Corpse Who Knew Too Much
The Corpse in the Gazebo
A Corpse at the Witching Hour
A Corpse Among the Carolers
The Cold Case and the Corpse

Resale Boutique Mysteries

Murder Wears a Little Black Dress
Silenced in Sequins
How to Frame a Fashionista
Beauty and the Deceased
Sleuthing in Stilettos
What Not to Wear to a Graveyard

Cookie Shop Mysteries

How the Murder Crumbles

The Cold Case and the Corpse

Debra Sennefelder

Chapter One

"Hope, I can't believe you're actually going through with it," Sally Merrifield muttered, breaking the serene hum of the Merrifield Inn's dining room. She plucked another sugar cube from the dish, dropping it into her tea with a decisive plunk. "A whole weekend trapped in a lodge with strangers, all in the name of self-improvement. Sounds like a nightmare."

Hope Early wrapped her fingers around her teacup, the rich scent of cinnamon tea and fresh scones wrapping around her like a familiar embrace. Outside, Jefferson's Main Street lay dusted in fresh snow, a postcard-perfect contrast to the tension at her table. Sunlight streamed through the inn's dining room windows, casting a golden glow over the polished wood and lace-trimmed tablecloths. But as Hope took a sip of tea, her thoughts drifted beyond the cozy charm of the moment toward the retreat she would be attending that weekend. Two days of "limitless living" awaited her, though it was clear not everyone shared her enthusiasm.

"I think it sounds incredible," Jane Merrifield countered, her eyes alight with anticipation. "Two days dedicated to personal growth? If we'd had something like this when we were younger, imagine where we'd be now."

"Well," Hope said, setting her cup down with a soft clink, "it's never too late."

Sally scoffed. "Sounds more like a load of nonsense to me. 'Discover a life without limits,' huh?" She rolled her eyes, her gaze fixed on the electronic tablet in her hands.

"Sally!" Jane admonished, her voice tinged with exasperation. "Don't be so cynical. This could be a wonderful opportunity for Hope." She shifted her attention to Hope, seated to her right. Jane's bright blue eyes sparkled with a youthful energy, and a hint of pink blush dusted her cheeks. Her short white hair, styled with a playful fringe, completed her vibrant look. "Don't pay her any mind, dear. This retreat sounds like an incredible opportunity. Be sure to make the most of it."

Hope smiled. She'd been looking forward to this afternoon tea, a rare moment of peace amid the chaos of finalizing her cookbook and working on her food blog, *Hope at Home*. For once, she was able to relax and enjoy the company of friends.

"Are you ready to break free from the invisible barriers holding you back?" Sally read aloud from the website, her voice dripping with sarcasm. "At Limitless Living, you'll embark on a transformative two-day retreat that will open your eyes to the true potential you've always had within you. This is more than just a weekend getaway—it's the beginning of your journey toward empowerment, success, and boundless living."

Hope set down her cup. "That's the thing. It's about pushing yourself to a new level. And I'm curious to see just how far this so-called limitless living can take me."

Before she'd arrived at the inn, those words Sally had just read from Maisie Cox's website had excited her, but now she questioned their sincerity and her decision to attend the two-day event at Jefferson Lodge. She fought the urge to snatch her tablet from Sally's hold.

Instead, she reached for the last crumb of her scone, chewing slowly to mask the wave of frustration creeping over her. Excitement for the weekend retreat with Maisie Cox, the self-help guru she'd discovered online last spring, had bubbled inside her for weeks. But now, as Sally's skeptical remarks echoed in her head, Hope couldn't help feeling a little foolish.

Sure, Sally wasn't the only one to scoff when she signed up for Maisie's coaching packages. Others had rolled their eyes too, but Hope had defended her choices. After all, thousands of readers had found her blog the same way, through online connections, and now she had a cookbook launch soon. If anyone doubted the power of the internet, Hope's success was proof enough.

Jane, always perceptive, must have sensed Hope's deflation. She patted her hand reassuringly. "I'm not as doubtful as Sally about the retreat. But I have to admit, I'm impressed you managed to get

Maretta to sign up."

Hope was shocked that Maretta Kingston agreed to join the retreat. Jefferson's no-nonsense mayor wasn't exactly the type to embrace self-help woo-woo, her words, not Hope's. Skeptical of everything, the only thing she was fiercely positive about was their hometown. So, the promise of bringing tourists to Jefferson through retreats had gotten her attention. And as mayor, she felt it was her duty to support anything that benefited the town, even if it meant enduring a weekend with a life coach.

"No doubt that was a tough one to cross off your to-do list, huh, Hope?" Sally added, glancing up from her tablet with a teasing smirk.

Hope pressed her lips together, trying to keep her cool. Sally's mood was wearing thin. Sure, Sally was known for her blunt honesty, but today it felt like she was pushing the limits of even that. What was going on with her?

Wiping her mouth with a napkin, Hope leaned forward. "Actually, I didn't have to do much convincing to get Maretta to sign up." The words came out with more bite than she'd intended, but for a brief moment, it felt satisfying to prove Sally wrong.

"Really? She signed up that easily?" Jane's surprise slipped through before she caught herself. Composing her expression, she reached for the teapot, her voice smooth again. "Would you like more tea, dear?" Hope nodded, grateful for the distraction. It had been a long time since she'd been able to relax like this, and she decided to savor it for just a little while longer. After all, once she left the inn, it was back to reality—making dinner for her fiancée, Ethan, and his daughters, and then packing for the retreat. She murmured her thanks as Jane topped off her cup, the warm steam rising to meet her.

Stirring her tea, Hope briefly considered indulging in another scone but resisted. Those extra holiday pounds and the countless taste tests for her upcoming cookbook were still lingering. No, she'd resist the temptation. For now, at least.

"Maretta's only going to support Henry Greenway's push for more retreats at the lodge," Hope said, lifting her teacup.

Jefferson's location, just two hours from New York City and not much farther from Boston, made it an ideal destination for corporate and wellness retreats. With its reputation as the antiques capital of Connecticut, its historic charm, and its scenic horse country, the town had all the makings of a sought-after getaway. Henry seemed to recognize the potential, and the mayor was just as eager to turn that vision into reality.

Hope glanced out the window just as the first delicate snowflakes began to fall, swirling lazily against the backdrop of Main Street. The weather forecast had been all over the place—snow on and off for the next week, but no one could seem to agree on how bad it would get. Typical.

"We were thrilled when we heard Henry bought that old lodge," Jane chimed in, her eyes twinkling at the mention. "It's such a stunning location, though that driveway . . ." She trailed off with a small chuckle. "It's a nightmare in the winter. Wouldn't you agree, Sally?"

"Hmm . . ." Sally barely looked up from the tablet as she reached for a blueberry muffin. "Awaken your mindset, elevate your life . . . I've read enough of this life-coach nonsense. Why anyone pays for that drivel is beyond me. If you want something done, you do it. Plain and simple." She took a defiant bite of the muffin.

Jane frowned, shaking her head gently. "Sally, we were talking about Henry and the lodge."

Sally swallowed her bite of the muffin and reached for her tea with a shrug. "I heard you. You're right, that driveway is brutal. It's got to be at least a half mile, all uphill. Gorgeous in the spring with all the trees around, but in winter? No, thank you."

Jane leaned in closer, her voice dropping to a conspiratorial whisper. "I have to agree with Sally on this one. That driveway? No thank you—I'd hate to use it every day."

Driveways weren't the most thrilling of topics, but living in the northwest hills of Connecticut made them a necessity. When Hope moved back to Jefferson after more than a decade in New York City, she knew exactly what she wanted: an old house with a covered porch, a barn, and most importantly, a short, flat driveway. She'd imagined herself diving into home improvement projects, but one thing she had never dreamed of was digging herself out of snowdrifts on a steep, icy hill.

"Oh, look who's here!" Jane perked up, waving toward the dining room's entrance.

Hope turned, her curiosity piqued, as a tall blond woman stepped into the dining room. She made her way gracefully across the room, her heels clicking softly on the polished wood floor. As she approached, Jane and Sally stood to greet her, their faces lighting up with smiles. The woman embraced each of them in turn, her gestures filled with genuine affection.

"Melanie, it's so wonderful to see you!" Jane beamed, gesturing to the empty chair. "Please, join us. Have you met Hope?"

Hope smiled as she sized up Melanie, who was a couple of inches shorter than her with a sleek bob that framed her face sharply and a pair of dangling earrings that glimmered beneath her hair. They exchanged polite shakes of the head.

"Of course, I know who you are!" Melanie's hands flew to her chest, her excitement palpable. "Who in Jefferson doesn't know you? I absolutely love your blog! I can't wait for your cookbook. When will it be available? Where do you get your recipe ideas? How long does it take to film your cooking videos? And how did you get so many followers?"

Melanie's rapid-fire questions left Hope momentarily speechless. She'd met plenty of enthusiastic fans, but Melanie's energy was on another level, bubbling over and contagious.

"Look at me, bombarding you with questions!" Melanie flashed an apologetic smile, though her excitement was still bubbling over. "I'm just so thrilled to finally meet you! In fact, because of you, I'm heading to the Limitless Living retreat this weekend." She clapped her hands together, her smile widening with enthusiasm.

"You are?" Jane chimed in, her eyes lighting up. "Well, that's wonderful! You know, if Maisie Cox holds another retreat here, I might just go myself."

Sally harrumphed.

Melanie nodded eagerly, practically vibrating with energy. "I can't wait. Hope shared Maisie Cox's services on her social media, and with all the effort I've been putting into getting my calligraphy business off the ground, it felt like fate!"

"Calligraphy?" Hope asked, intrigued. "How long have you been in business?"

"Not long at all," Melanie admitted, her tone upbeat despite the story. "The company I was with downsized, and I ended up being one of the unlucky ones. But I'd been doing calligraphy for years as a hobby, and when I lost my job, my husband and I figured it was the perfect time to finally launch Melanie Tucker Designs."

"She really does beautiful work, doesn't she, Sally?" Jane refilled her teacup with a warm smile.

"Top-notch quality," Sally agreed, though her focus shifted as she closed the tablet and handed it back to Hope. "But this Maisie character sure charges an arm and a leg for her coaching. Hope you both haven't sunk too much into this."

Hope hesitated, not quite ready to disclose just how much she'd spent on Maisie's services. While Maisie's rates were high, they weren't outrageous, at least, not compared to what Hope knew other food bloggers had paid for coaching. Still, before she could reassure Sally that she wasn't being taken for a ride, she noticed a flicker of something in Melanie's eyes. Was it doubt? Regret? And it made Hope wonder just how much Melanie had invested in Limitless Living and whether she was already starting to second-guess it.

• • •

When Hope arrived home from the Merrifield Inn, she immediately set to work, determined to clear her to-do list before heading to the weekend retreat. After a couple of productive hours spent on her blog, she finally felt ready to step away without any lingering tasks hanging over her head.

She stood in her kitchen, untied her apron and dropped it onto the granite countertop of the expansive island. The old farmhouse had required significant renovations, with the most substantial changes happening right there. Walls had been knocked down to create an open layout that seamlessly connected the kitchen to the dining and family rooms. The transformation had involved countless late nights, callouses, and moments of doubt, but the result was a space perfectly suited for family dinners and entertaining. That night, however, Hope's attention was solely focused on preparing for the weekend ahead.

Her gaze shifted to the oven timers. The bottom oven held a bubbling lasagna, while the upper one roasted a colorful array of vegetables. She'd made extra-large portions to ensure Ethan and his daughters would have leftovers while she was away. With a few minutes left until dinner was ready, Hope grabbed her tablet from the island and leaned against the counter.

Curiosity tugged at her, and she couldn't resist diving into Limitless Living's private online group. Tapping away, she searched for Melanie Tucker, hoping to get a sense of her involvement in Maisie's program. Something about their earlier encounter had felt . . . off. Melanie had been so enthusiastic about the retreat, but when Sally mentioned the cost of the coaching, Hope had noticed a brief flicker of hesitation in her eyes.

Hope wondered just how deep Melanie was into the program.

After some scrolling, Hope finally found a post from Melanie in the private group.

"I'm really struggling to manifest the life I want. I've been at it for months, but nothing has changed . . . If anything, it's gotten worse."

Hope's brow furrowed as she skimmed the replies, pausing when she saw one from Maisie.

"Don't give up, don't release your power. You may feel like things aren't improving, but sometimes the rocky path is the one we're meant to travel to reach our ideal life."

Melanie's response was brief—a single heart emoji.

Hope stared at the screen, feeling a pang of unease. There was something hollow in that heart emoji, as if Melanie was clinging to the words but not truly believing them.

Hope's thoughts were interrupted by the sound of rushed footsteps, followed by giggles. Molly and Becca skidded to a stop beside her, with Bigelow close behind. The spirited dog, with his glossy tricolor coat and enthusiastically wagging tail, bounded into the room.

"Look, Hope! I finished my to-do list!" Molly, who was almost seven, beamed proudly as she waved a sheet of paper in the air. "It's everything we're gonna do this weekend!"

"We're going sledding!" Becca, four years old and clutching her stuffed bunny tightly, chimed in excitedly. "And then we'll drink hot cocoa!"

Bigelow, determined not to be left out, woofed in agreement, sending the girls into another fit of giggles.

"Let me see." Hope set aside her tablet and took the paper from Molly's hand, scanning the child's neat little list. "Very impressive! You even included your morning routine. You're already a pro at this!"

"Wash my face, eat breakfast, brush my teeth, and then cartoons," Molly declared with authority. "Everything's easier when you've got a plan."

Hope recognized herself in Molly's words. She was never without her own to-do list and planner, sometimes even keeping a digital copy on her phone. The idea of not having a clear plan for the day made her uneasy because there was always so much to juggle.

"Everything's easier when you've got a plan. Where have I heard that before?" Ethan's voice echoed from the mudroom as he stepped inside, the sound of his boots hitting the floor punctuating his arrival. He crossed the kitchen, encircling his arm around Hope as he leaned in for a kiss on her cheek. "Sharing your list, Molls?" he asked, glancing at the paper with a curious smile.

Molly nodded enthusiastically.

Hope inhaled the woodsy scent of his cologne, tempted to lean into him more, but the girls were watching. Any snuggling would have to wait until later, when they were tucked into bed.

Ethan looked at the list and smirked, his eyes teasing as they flicked to Hope. "Looks like someone's got our entire weekend mapped out. Wonder where she got that from," he said, giving Hope a knowing look. "Good to see that we have a schedule for taking care of the chickens and Bigelow while Hope is away. I also like how you've scheduled plenty of hot cocoa breaks," he added with a grin.

Becca's small face fell as she hugged her bunny tighter. "But Hope won't be here to make the cocoa," she said, her voice tinged with worry.

Molly, ever the problem solver, didn't miss a beat. "Daddy can make it. He has Hope's recipe! And if he forgets it, I know where to find it on her blog."

Ethan raised a brow, half amused, half impressed. "You do, huh?"

Molly shot him a look, the kind only child her age can give. "I'm almost seven, Dad."

Hope chuckled as she met Ethan's gaze. "She's almost seven," she echoed playfully as she took the list from his hand and placed it on the island. "Now, how about we set the table? The lasagna's almost done."

The girls eagerly nodded and, with Ethan's help, took plates from the cabinet. As they worked together to set the table, the kitchen thrummed with contentment, the scent of dinner drifting through the room.

Hope served dinner as the girls excitedly chattered about the upcoming weekend, listing all the movies they wanted to watch after sledding and building snowmen, their debate over which movie would be first filling the room with lively energy.

Once the meal was finished, Hope began clearing the table while Ethan took charge of feeding Bigelow, who wagged his tail impatiently, and Princess, Hope's cat. The fluffy white feline watched them with regal disdain, her tail flicking in mild annoyance as she observed the lively chaos two little girls brought into her domain. Only when her bowl was placed on her mat did she deign to approach, her nose twitching with feigned indifference.

With the dishwasher humming softly in the background, Hope turned her attention to serving dessert. Earlier, she had whipped up an apple cobbler, its sweet, cinnamon-laced scent wafting through the kitchen after coming out of the oven's warming drawer. She topped each helping of the fresh out-of-the-oven cobbler with generous scoops of homemade vanilla ice cream, the creamy dollops melting gently into the fruity mixture.

The girls, wide-eyed with delight, sat at the table, their spoons clinking against the bowls as they savored their treat. Hope and Ethan lingered at the island, where they enjoyed their dessert.

"I've still got to finish packing tonight," Hope said, her spoon sinking into the cobbler's golden crust. She glanced out the window, noticing fresh snowflakes twirling in the air. "I didn't realize it was supposed to snow again."

Ethan nodded, taking another bite. "It started on my way home. They're saying it'll keep going on and off until morning, and we might be looking at six inches by then."

"Six inches?" Hope gasped, her hand pausing in midair as she reached for her tea, taken aback by the news. "Well, at least the retreat is nearby. And if this turns into a blizzard, I know I've got my knight in shining armor ready to come rescue me."

Ethan chuckled, leaning in with a playful grin. "Always."

Her heart swelled with gratitude. Ethan had been her steadfast support after her life had nearly crumbled following a divorce and a very public defeat on a television baking competition. Now they were engaged to be married. She still couldn't believe it.

"Given the weather is taking a turn for the worse," he said, pausing to scoop up a helping of his cobbler, "maybe you should reconsider going."

Hope set her spoon down and planted a hand on her hip, narrowing her eyes. "Okay, what's going on? You've been acting strange about this retreat for days. It's not the first time I've gone away for a couple of days. Remember the blogger conference last fall? Is it because we're engaged now?"

Ethan's eyebrows shot up. "Wait, you think I've turned possessive all of a sudden?"

She tilted her head, studying him closely. "I don't know, you tell me."

Ethan stepped closer, closing the space between them. His lips brushed her forehead in a tender kiss, then moved to capture hers softly. When he pulled back, she pressed her lips together, smiling faintly.

"Okay, that was very nice," she murmured, "but it still doesn't answer my question."

He exhaled, a long breath filled with hesitation. "What do you really know about this Maisie person? Is she who she claims to be?"

Hope blinked, surprised by the sudden turn. "What are you talking about? Do you know something I don't?" Her voice trembled slightly, concern creeping in.

"No, not really. But . . . there's a cold case I've been looking into. A woman went missing in Vermont after attending a retreat with a life coach. She disappeared right after a group hike. The truth is, people aren't always who they pretend to be online."

Hope crossed her arms, frustration rising. "But sometimes they are. Look at me—I'm exactly who I say I am online."

He met her gaze, but doubt still lingered in his eyes. "I just want you to be careful."

"Of course, I will." Hope grabbed the dish towel, ready to wipe the counter, but hesitated. "Tell me more about this cold case you're investigating. Is Matt representing someone connected to it?"

Last fall, Ethan resigned as Jefferson's police chief and went to work for their mutual friend, criminal defense attorney Matt Roydon. The driving factor in the career change was that he'd have more time to spend with his daughters while his ex-wife regained her health after battling an addiction.

Ethan, now facing the refrigerator, let out a chuckle as he pulled out a bottle of beer. "You know I can't talk about my cases."

She shrugged. "It was worth a try."

"You and that insatiable curiosity," Ethan teased, twisting off the cap as he turned to face her. "It's gotten you into more trouble than I can count."

"Believe me, I'm well aware." Hope carried the dishes to the sink, but there was a faint edge to her voice now, a hint of unease. Ethan met her gaze, concern flickering behind his smile. "But it's just two days at the lodge. Claire, Drew, Maretta, and Amy will be there too. What could possibly go wrong?"

Chapter Two

When Hope woke Saturday morning and looked out her bedroom window, the world outside was draped in a thick, white blanket of snow at least six inches deep. She sighed, acknowledging that Ethan had been right about the weather. Her first thoughts turned to the extra time her morning chores would take, as the path to the chicken coop would need to be cleared. But to her relief, Ethan had already taken care of it, ensuring her morning routine remained undisturbed.

After a refreshing shower and a hearty breakfast, Hope was ready to head out. She hugged the girls goodbye, promising Becca she'd be back soon. She also reminded them of the upcoming ski trip to Vermont in a couple of weeks, which brought smiles to their faces.

After pulling out of her driveway, Hope navigated the snow-covered roads toward Claire's house. The conditions were unpredictable as some roads had been fully plowed while others waited for attention. As she turned into Claire's cul-de-sac, Hope was relieved that the street was cleared and that her circular driveway was easily accessible.

To Hope's surprise, her sister was not only ready and waiting but had packed light. There was just one medium-sized suitcase. Hope raised an eyebrow at this unusual sight, as Claire Dixon was notorious for overpacking. However, she noticed that the overnight bag was stuffed to the brim, signaling that maybe her old habits weren't completely broken.

Claire climbed into the passenger seat, buckling her seat belt quickly. "Let's not dally, I want to get there before the snow starts again." She'd always been decisive, even a little bossy, but lately it had intensified to the point of being overbearing. She'd taken to barking orders and cutting people off mid-sentence. Hope knew they needed to talk about it eventually, but now wasn't the time. They had to pick up Drew on their way to the lodge, and with the snow starting again, they needed to keep moving.

"For the most part the roads are clear," Hope said as she shifted the car out of park.

Glancing down at her lug-soled designer combat boots, Claire said, "These aren't snow boots."

Hope chuckled, glancing at her sister's sleek winter outfit. She wore a slim-fitting puffer coat over black flared pants, topped off with a cashmere beanie. "You'll survive," she teased, pulling out of the driveway.

The rest of the drive passed in awkward silence, despite Hope's best efforts to spark a conversation. She started by mentioning her upcoming trip to Vermont with Ethan and the girls, sharing how they'd be stopping by Balsam Dell to visit her friend Carly Hale at her restaurant. "The next time you go up there, you must try Carly's grilled cheese sandwiches. They're the best in all of Vermont!" Hope added, hoping to elicit some response. But Claire remained glued to her phone, scrolling and typing without even a glance.

Undeterred, Hope switched topics. She talked about the progress on her cookbook, proudly mentioning how close she was to finishing it. Still, nothing from Claire, just the soft clicking of her fingers on the phone screen. Finally, as they neared Drew's house, Hope decided to test her sister's attentiveness with an outrageous claim. "You know," she said casually, "I read somewhere about a house fire being put out by a herd of elephants. Wild, right?"

"Huh," was Claire's only response.

Hope was about to press her sister about her obvious distraction when she caught sight of Drew standing at his front door with his cousin, Susan Porter. His home, an antique white Cape Cod that had been in his mother's family for generations, looked as timeless as ever. He bought it from his aunt just last fall and was in the middle of a major renovation.

By the looks of things, Drew was deep in conversation with Susan. She held a squirming Trixie, Drew's energetic Jack Russell puppy, who wore an adorable plaid sweater. Hope was certain that Drew was rattling off last-minute care instructions. She could relate, knowing she would do the same in his position. Susan nodded earnestly, listening intently before playfully shooing him off the front steps.

"For heaven's sake, he's only going away for two days," Claire muttered, reaching over to honk the horn. "I'm sure Susan can handle the dog."

Drew spun around, shooting a glare at the car.

Hope quickly swatted Claire's hand away. "Trixie's his first dog. It's normal for him to be nervous about leaving her."

Claire rolled her eyes in response, clearly unimpressed by Drew's fussing.

Drew gave Trixie one last affectionate kiss on the head, scratching her under the chin as the puppy wiggled happily. But when he lingered too long, Susan gently nudged him down the steps and slipped back inside, closing the door with a knowing smile.

His shoulders sagged. He was clearly reluctant to leave. He hefted his duffel bag and trudged toward Hope's car, his boots crunching softly on the newly fallen snow covering the brick walkway. By the time he reached the Explorer, a light dusting of snow had settled on his parka. Without a word, Hope popped the hatch, allowing him to slide his bag into the cargo space before climbing into the backseat and shaking off the cold.

Looking over her shoulder, Hope asked, "You're already missing her, aren't you?"

Drew gave a sheepish nod. "It's the first time we've been apart."

Claire let out a dramatic sigh, glancing back at Drew with a raised eyebrow. "You'll both survive two days." She shifted in her seat, staring out the window with little interest in the conversation.

Drew's mouth dropped open in surprise.

Hope gave him an apologetic look and mouthed, *Ignore her.*

He huffed, leaning back in his seat.

"Are we going, or are we just going to sit here?" Claire quipped, turning her gaze forward.

Drew buckled his seat belt. "Okay, Claire, who messed with your manicure this morning? Those nails are sharper than usual." He shot her a sideways glance, his smirk full of mischief.

"My nails are perfect, as always, thank you," Claire said.

Hope stifled a giggle but wasn't quick enough.

Claire turned her gaze toward her sister. "Something funny?"

Hope wiped the grin from her face in record time. "Not a thing."

She shifted the car into gear and eased out of the driveway. "How about we switch topics?"

"Fine," Claire and Drew replied in unison.

"Yesterday, I met Melanie Tucker at the Merrifield Inn. She has a calligraphy business and will be at the retreat." Hope flicked on the windshield wipers, clearing away the thickening snow. "She's local, lives in Jefferson. Maybe she's someone you'd want to interview for your article, Drew?"

"Probably. Thanks for the suggestion," Drew noted, glancing out at the snowy landscape.

He'd been assigned to write an article about the retreat for the *Gazette*, Jefferson's weekly newspaper. "I'll be there all weekend, so I'm sure we'll have time to chat. Henry Greenway's really banking on these retreats to make the lodge a success, and it seems like a solid idea."

"They would definitely bring in tourists," Hope agreed, slowing for a stop sign. "It's why Maretta's going. She wants to support the lodge."

"Still, I'm surprised she's staying at the lodge." Drew leaned forward.

"Why?" Claire glanced up from her phone.

"You don't know?" Drew asked.

Hope and Claire exchanged confused looks, both shaking their heads.

"He broke her heart," Drew said matter-of-factly.

Hope came to a full stop at the intersection, turning to stare at Drew in disbelief. "When?"

Claire shifted in her seat, visibly intrigued. "Are you sure?"

"How long are we sitting at this stop sign?" Drew quipped.

"Oh, right." Hope snapped back to reality, guiding the car through the intersection. The roads were unusually empty, but with the snow still falling, she guessed most people had decided to delay their errands. The town plows seemed to have made the same decision. At least an inch of snow already blanketed the road.

"While I was interviewing Gretchen Winnower for her spring gardening tips, she happened to mention something interesting. Henry's return to Jefferson last year didn't sit well with Maretta," Drew said.

Hope kept her eyes on the road but let out a small laugh.

"Maretta's feathers are pretty easy to ruffle. She's been prickly since we were kids."

Drew nodded. "True. But apparently, this runs deeper. Turns out, back in high school they were an item. According to Gretchen, Maretta was head over heels for Henry. That is, until she found out he ditched a date with her to go out with another girl. Someone snitched on Henry, and Maretta was crushed."

Claire, who had been silent up until then, finally chimed in with a flat tone, "Hard to imagine Maretta even has a heart to break."

"We all know she's the queen of holding grudges," Drew added with a smirk.

Hope nodded, her grip tightening on the steering wheel as she navigated a sharp curve. "Oh, absolutely. This weekend could get interesting."

The GPS indicated that they were nearing the lodge, and Hope's attention shifted from the conversation to the road ahead. She knew what was coming and didn't like it one bit—a long stretch of road that was risky even on a clear day. With the snow coming down heavier now and the roads barely touched by plows, her nerves kicked in. The wind buffeted the car, and her muscles tensed, bracing for the next turn. It was time to stop thinking about Maretta and her past heartbreak. All of Hope's focus had to be on the weather and the slippery, treacherous road ahead.

Grateful she had shifted her focus to driving instead of reminiscing about Maretta's high school drama, Hope spotted the sign for the lodge just in time. It was barely visible behind overgrown evergreen bushes, and the sharp turn onto the narrow, elevated road came up fast. The snowfall had thickened, reducing visibility and forcing her windshield wipers to work overtime. Finally, a more prominent sign for the lodge appeared, and her GPS confirmed it. She turned onto the dirt road leading to the lodge.

She remembered that the driveway stretched a half mile and climbed sharply. With a steady breath, she tightened her grip on the wheel and started the ascent. The trees, dense evergreens and skeletal oaks draped in thick layers of snow, formed a canopy over the road, casting the path in a hushed, wintry gloom. The rutted driveway sent the Explorer bouncing along, its tires struggling for grip on patches of ice. Each slip made Hope's heart race, but she forced herself to stay calm and focused on the road ahead. There was no turning back now.

As Hope navigated the final stretch of the driveway, the lodge appeared through the falling snow like something from a winter postcard. The two-story structure loomed, a seamless blend of timber and stone, with large windows that reflected the gray sky. Snowflakes danced against the glass panes, some sticking to the edges, adding to the lodge's rustic charm. The wide, vaulted deck at the front was dusted in snow, while the wooden beams overhead provided shelter from the steady snowfall.

To the left, the covered carport offered a temporary refuge from the weather, though Hope could already see the wind swirling flakes underneath. At the far end, a second covered deck extended, offering an expansive view of the landscape beyond the lodge of dense trees outlined in white.

The lodge felt like a cozy sanctuary, but the sight of the towering trees and the unplowed drive reminded her that the world outside could be treacherous. She parked, taking in the view for a moment longer. The snow muffled everything, creating an eerie silence, broken only by the soft whoosh of her wipers.

The shrill ring of Hope's cell phone pierced the quiet inside the vehicle. She reached for it from the console between the front seats, glancing at the display—Amy Phelan.

"Hey, Amy," Hope answered, turning off the Explorer's ignition. "We just pulled up to the lodge."

"Great!" Amy's voice crackled through the speaker, barely audible over the background noise. "I'm running a little behind. My aunt fell, and we had to take her to the hospital. She's being released now, so after I drop her off at home, I'll head to the lodge."

Claire and Drew were already stepping out of the car, their doors closing with a muted thud as they moved to the back of the vehicle.

"I'm sorry to hear that. Is she okay?" Hope asked, pressing the button to pop the cargo door open.

"Yeah, just a bad sprain," Amy replied.

"Be careful driving. The roads aren't plowed yet," Hope warned.

"I'll be careful on the roads, don't worry. See you soon!" Amy's voice was light and quick, followed by the soft click of the call disconnecting.

Phone in hand, Hope stepped out of the vehicle and joined Drew and Claire, who were already pulling their luggage out from the back. She reached for her bags, slinging her tote over one shoulder and extending the telescoping handle of her suitcase. After closing the cargo door, the three of them headed along the covered deck, casting curious glances through the lodge's massive windows as they made their way toward the entrance.

Hope appreciated the shelter of the deck. The wind had picked up, blowing icy flakes in swirling gusts. By the time they reached the front, she let out a breath in awe. The entry consisted of two towering, floor-to-ceiling glass doors, framed by wide glass panels on each side. Drew stepped ahead, holding one door open for her and Claire. They hurried inside without hesitation.

The interior was impressive. A vast room with high vaulted ceilings featured a commanding stone fireplace where a robust fire crackled. Inviting arrangements of leather furniture invited guests to sink in and stay awhile, the fire's radiance making the cold outside feel worlds away.

"This place is incredible," Claire exclaimed, her eyes sweeping the space with an appraising glance. As a former real estate agent turned home stager and home furnishings shop owner, Claire had developed a sharp eye for design. "And that fireplace! Wow!" She moved ahead of Hope and Drew.

Hope followed, pulling her suitcase behind her, pausing in the center of the great room. The leather sofas practically called her name, inviting her to sit and unwind. The lodge seemed like the perfect spot for the retreat.

"Henry Greenway has done wonders updating this place," Drew commented, dropping his duffel beside him as he joined Hope. "I'm going to get some amazing photos."

"We should check in," Hope suggested, leading the way to the registration desk, where the long, polished oak surface was pristine but unattended.

"I told you that room was off-limits!" a man's voice rang out, sharp and angry.

Hope froze, glancing around, but no one was in sight. Then she noticed the slightly ajar door behind the desk, likely leading to an office.

"What were you looking for?" the man demanded again.

Leaning toward Hope, Drew whispered, "Looks like we walked into something."

Hope nodded in agreement.

"I wasn't looking for anything!" came a high-pitched, defensive reply. "I don't know what you think you saw, but I wasn't snooping! I have work to do."

"They could use some serious Zen," Claire quipped, tapping her fingers on the counter.

The office door swung open, and a woman emerged, dressed in black slacks and a crisp white button-down shirt. Her glossy black hair was pulled into a tight ponytail, accentuating her sharp features and hollow cheeks. Wide, dark eyes locked onto the three of them, clearly taken aback that her argument had been overheard. She quickly composed herself, a strained smile forming on her lips.

"Good morning," she said, approaching the desk with forced cheerfulness. "Welcome to Jefferson Lodge. I'm Kit."

"Hello, we're here to check in," Hope said, reaching into her tote for her wallet. "We're with the Limitless Living retreat. I'm Hope Early, and this is my sister Claire Dixon, and Drew Adams."

Drew stepped forward, extending his hand with a smile. "I'm the reporter from the *Gazette*."

Kit shook his hand eagerly. "Nice to meet you! Henry's been looking forward to *your* arrival." She released his hand and turned toward Hope and Claire. "He's excited to have you both here as well. Maisie and her team arrived last night."

"I've been looking forward to this for months," Hope said, handing over her credit card. "I was thrilled when I heard it was going to be held right here in Jefferson."

"Oh, you're local?" Kit asked, processing their information.

"We all are," Claire added, handing over her card as well.

"Such a charming town," Kit remarked as she completed the first two registrations. She paused, waiting for Drew to hand over his card.

Hope smiled wistfully. Jefferson was more than home to her. It was part of her soul.

After leaving for the big city and enduring heartbreak and humiliation, she had learned the hard way how special her hometown truly was. Returning had felt like rediscovering herself.

"You should see it during the holidays," Hope added, adjusting her tote. "It's magical."

"And a little dangerous," Claire muttered, earning a sharp look from Hope. Unfortunately, there had been two murders over the Christmas holiday that Hope had gotten caught up in.

"Now that sounds like an interesting story," Kit replied, handing them their room keys. "Here you go. You're all set."

"Keys, not key cards?" Drew raised an eyebrow.

Kit smiled. "Nope, we kept the old-fashioned locks and keys as part of the lodge's history. Now, let me show you to your rooms. Once you're settled in, feel free to come back to the lobby for refreshments."

"I'd like to speak with Henry, if possible," Drew said, lifting his duffel.

Kit shot a quick, almost nervous glance toward the office behind her. "Of course." She stepped out from behind the counter. "He's a bit occupied right now, but I'll make sure he knows you've arrived."

As they followed Kit down the hallway, Hope leaned closer to Drew and whispered, "I wonder what's keeping him so busy, and what room Kit wasn't supposed to be in earlier."

Chapter Three

Hope stood in the lodge's lobby, pouring a cup of coffee as the snow outside continued falling even harder. This wasn't what the forecast had predicted two days ago. Deep down, she had a feeling the storm was going to be much worse than expected. After she'd unpacked, she sent Ethan a quick text to let him know she'd arrived safely. The plan was for him to stay at her house to take care of Bigelow, Princess and the chickens. Then she stopped by Claire's room on the way downstairs. Claire had been on the phone with her kids, Logan and Hannah, but seemed more relaxed when they met up with Drew on the way to the lobby. Maybe it was best to hold off on a serious conversation with Claire until after the retreat. Then again, Hope wondered if she was just overthinking it. Claire had a lot on her plate, with running a business and raising two teenagers. Those things could make anyone cranky and distracted.

"This storm's going to be worse than we thought, isn't it?" Claire asked as she settled into a chair near the fireplace, her chunky gray turtleneck providing a soft contrast to the flickering flames.

Hope sipped her coffee, savoring the rich, bold flavor. While she and Claire had gone straight for the coffee, Drew had wandered off in search of Henry.

"I think so." Hope watched a bundled-up woman speed-walk along the deck outside. "I wonder where Maisie is."

Just then, the front door burst open, and Melanie Tucker stumbled in, shaking snow from her coat. "Oh. My. Word. It's like a blizzard out there."

A sharp gust of wind fought against Melanie as she struggled to close the heavy door. After managing to shut it, she grabbed her suitcase with a sigh. "Thank goodness for all-wheel drive. I don't think I'd have made it otherwise."

"The roads have gotten that bad already?" Hope's gaze drifted toward the windows, her mind instantly going to Amy. She didn't have an all-wheel drive and would be driving alone. Maybe she should call and tell her not to risk it.

"I'm not used to this kind of weather." Melanie brushed the snow off her parka before lowering her hood. "And those winding roads? They're a nightmare even when it's clear out."

"You must be new to the area." Claire chuckled. "This terrain around here isn't exactly forgiving."

Melanie's eyes lit up as she glanced at Claire. "Wait, aren't you the owner of Staged with Style? I love that shop!" She dropped her suitcase and eagerly crossed the room, sinking into the chair beside Claire. "I'm Melanie Tucker, by the way. I've bought so many cute things from your store. Are you here for the retreat too?"

Before Hope could catch Claire's response, the door swung open again and Maretta Kingston rushed in, her shoulders hunched against the raging snowstorm outside. She brushed off the snow clinging to her coat, her breath visible in the cold air.

Hope quickly set her cup down on the coffee cart and hurried to close the door behind the older woman. The cold hit her immediately, sharp and biting, sending a shiver down her spine. That wasn't the only thing that made her shudder. Maretta's scowl could have frozen the air on its own.

"Tough drive?" Hope asked, trying to sound upbeat.

"What do you think? Just look outside." Maretta gestured toward the window, her irritation palpable. "I've been calling nonstop to make sure the plows are out on the roads."

Claire chimed in, "Several of the roads weren't plowed when we got here. Isn't that what our taxes are for, Madame Mayor?"

Maretta's scowl grew darker. She took a small step forward. Hope could see this conversation heading in the wrong direction.

"Claire, Drew and I already checked in and got settled in our rooms," Hope said, steering the topic toward safer ground. "Maybe you and Melanie should do the same?"

Claire nodded toward the registration desk. "Check-in's over there."

Melanie sprang up from her chair and dashed over. "Hi, I'm Melanie Tucker," she said brightly, extending a hand to Maretta. "It's a pleasure to finally meet the town's mayor. I can't imagine it's an easy job."

"No, it's not," Maretta replied, casting a sharp glance at Claire, who had once run against her and lost. "It's all-consuming. There's not a moment when I'm not thinking about what's best for our little hamlet."

"I'm sure everyone appreciates your hard work," Melanie said before returning to her suitcase. She then wheeled it across the wooden floor toward the registration desk. She gave the bell a gentle tap.

Maretta followed, her tone bitter. "It would be nice if everyone actually *did* appreciate it."

Hope carried her coffee toward the chair Melanie had vacated, and with Claire, she watched as Kit emerged from the office and quickly processed the check-ins. Within moments, the two women received their room keys and headed off to get settled.

"Well," Claire said, leaning back in her leather chair, "if we're going to be snowed in, I can't think of a cozier place to wait it out."

"It's starting to feel that way, isn't it?" Hope murmured, glancing out at the swirling snow. "Like we're going to get snowed in." A subtle unease crept over her, prickling at her skin. But it wasn't just the cold or Maretta's sour mood. No, this felt different. Something deeper. The unsettling part was, she couldn't quite figure out what it was.

• • •

At precisely ten o'clock, Maisie Cox swept into the lobby, clapping her hands with enthusiasm and praising the attendees for their bravery in stepping toward their future. She radiated confidence in a tailored red pantsuit adorned with gold jewelry, her raven-black hair loosely styled in an elegant bun. Her dark, piercing eyes scanned the room as she greeted each person by name, reaffirming their commitment to themselves while moving gracefully in her towering four-inch stilettos.

Hope caught Drew's eye from across the room, and his expression mirrored the skepticism she had expected. As a reporter, his job required a critical eye, so she shrugged it off. Meanwhile, Melanie was engaged in conversation with Maisie, looking like a mixture of nerves and relief. Nearby, Lorna Morgan, who had registered before Hope arrived and had stayed in her room until now, stood stiffly in a long black velour dress. Her exchange with Maisie was polite, but Hope caught the way Lorna snapped her hand back from Maisie's grasp.

Claire, on the other hand, seemed unsure. Unlike Hope, she hadn't worked with Maisie before, and this type of coaching wasn't her usual environment. When Maisie finished speaking with Melanie, she turned to greet Maretta.

"Welcome to Jefferson, Maisie." Maretta shook her hand firmly. "As the mayor of this historic town, we're honored you chose to hold your first retreat here. I hope it's the first of many."

"So do I," Maisie said, breaking away from Maretta and leading the group toward the library just off the lobby. "We're still waiting for one more, Amy Phelan."

"She had a family emergency this morning, but she's on her way," Hope said as she entered the library. The library held the kind of stillness that made voices drop to a murmur. A fire snapped in the corner hearth, its light flickering across walls of bookshelves, their oak frames groaning slightly under the weight of hundreds of volumes. Wide armchairs, their leather cracked with age, sat angled toward each other on Persian rugs, while a checkerboard table stood in the back, its pieces already set for the next match. The air carried the dry scent of old paper and the subtle warmth of burning applewood—just enough to take the edge off the autumn chill.

"Amy works at my husband's real estate agency," Maretta noted as the group gathered in the middle of the room.

"Is she an agent?" Maisie asked.

"No, she's the receptionist," Maretta replied. "And she has some kind of podcast she does on the side. A hobby, I guess."

"It's a true crime podcast," Hope interjected, offering a bit more detail. "In fact, since Amy took over the podcast, she's enhanced its production quality, secured new sponsors, and turned into a popular show. She has a knack for podcasting."

"True crime?" Maisie's confident demeanor wavered for a brief second, but she quickly recovered, her smile wide and practiced. "How . . . intriguing." She paused, her eyes sparkling with forced enthusiasm. "We all have mysteries inside of us, don't we? It's just a matter of unlocking the potential to discover the truth beneath. I'm sure Amy's journey will be transformative for her."

At that moment, a petite woman entered the library, carrying a metal box. She was dressed in a less-tailored gray suit, her movements not as assured as Maisie's.

"Maisie, are we ready to collect the devices?" the woman asked.

Maisie turned to her with an exaggerated gesture of warmth. "Ah, Talia! Perfect timing. Everyone, this is my assistant, Talia Johansen. Actually, she's more than an assistant. She's a beacon of possibility. Just like each of you will become by the end of this weekend. It's time to unlock that potential you've been holding on to."

"What does she mean by ready to collect the devices?" Maretta asked.

Maisie flashed the group a smile. "We need to let go of distractions, our phones and tablets, anything that pulls us out of this sacred space. Because remember, we're not just stepping into this retreat, we're stepping into our future. Let's make sure we give ourselves the full opportunity to be *present* for this life-changing experience."

Confusion rippled through the group as they exchanged uncertain glances. Like Hope, no one had expected Maisie to make such a bold request.

Claire was the first to speak, raising her hand slightly. "What if my kids need me? I can't just disconnect."

Maretta shook her head. "I'm the mayor, for heaven's sake. And there's a snowstorm raging. I can't afford to be out of touch."

Drew crossed his arms. "I need my camera. I'm covering this for the paper."

Hope jumped in. "What if we all agree to simply turn our phones off? Surely that would be enough."

Just as the idea hung in the air, Lorna stepped forward with purpose, pulling her phone from the pocket of her dress and dropping it into the metal box. "I came here for the *full Maisie Cox experience*," she said, her voice resolute. "If it means handing over my phone for the weekend, then I'm all in."

An uncomfortable silence settled over the room, tension hanging thick in the air.

"The lodge has a landline for emergencies," Maisie said, her tone designed to reassure. "Sometimes we need to feel uncomfortable in order to grow. That's why you're all here this weekend, isn't it?"

Hope let out a shaky breath, her unease still lingering. But deep down, she understood Lorna's perspective. It was only until Sunday, after all.

• • •

Once the phones had been collected, Hope made a quick dash to her room to grab her electronic tablet, then joined the others in the library for the retreat's first workshop. With the doors closed to ensure privacy, Maisie introduced the session, titled "Unmasking Your True Self." Talia handed out paper and pens to each participant, and as she gave Lorna her supplies, Hope noticed a fleeting, friendly glance pass between them.

When everyone was ready, Maisie returned to the center of the room, her voice filled with conviction. "Each of you is a powerful creator of your reality. What you begin here will set you on a path toward your incredible potential. Trust that greatness is your destiny."

She paused, letting her words settle before continuing. "Now, for our first exercise, I'd like you to reflect on a moment when you've hidden your true self. Be as honest as possible. Think of this as a *Release*, a way to free yourself from the weight of what no longer serves you. Write it down, without names, and let it go. Let's begin."

Hope wasn't sure how long she'd been writing when Maisie gently guided them from their assignment to drop their folded papers into a basket that Talia passed around. With the basket, Maisie, now seated on a chair beside the fireplace, pulled one paper out and read aloud.

"There's been so much change that I don't know who I am anymore." Maisie looked up from the paper, her eyes filled with compassion and understanding. "This is such powerful self-awareness," she said. "When we're brave enough to acknowledge feeling disconnected from ourselves, that's actually the first step toward discovery for us. What I'm hearing is someone ready to explore who they are becoming. This is exactly the kind of self-discovery that brings transformation."

Maisie drew another slip and read, "I want to get over my need for everyone to like me, but I'm scared."

Hope felt a jolt of discomfort but kept herself composed, resisting the urge to fidget and reveal herself. After giving it a second thought, she couldn't help wondering, who was she kidding? After all, she was surrounded by those who knew her best—Claire, Drew, and Maretta. They already understood her struggle with this fear, a weight she knew wouldn't vanish in just two days.

"What beautiful permission you're giving yourself here," Maisie said, returning the slip to the basket with deliberate care. "When you peel back those people-pleasing layers, we often discover that seeking everyone's approval has been blocking our authentic self from shining through. This is where real transformation begins. Understanding our own weaknesses and vulnerabilities is the first, most important step on the path to genuine self-awareness."

Hope let out a slow, measured breath. Something in the coach's words about "people-pleasing layers" had touched a nerve in her. She'd always thought of her need for approval as a character flaw, but maybe—just maybe—it was more like a protective shell she needed to grow out of. The tension in her shoulders loosened, just slightly, as this new perspective settled in.

"So, the first step is to face our flaws and own up to the mistakes we've made?" Lorna asked, her gaze lowered as if mulling over the idea.

Maisie's smile tightened as she nodded. "Exactly. It's the surest way to clear a path toward abundance."

Lorna looked up, a glint of skepticism in her eyes. "And what about those who avoid taking those steps altogether yet still seem to attract success? Doesn't that seem . . . a bit unfair?"

For an instant, Maisie's smile faded, her eyes betraying a flicker of something familiar and guarded. She took a beat too long to respond, and Hope glanced between the two, sensing a charged energy simmering beneath the surface, though she couldn't quite place it.

"Life doesn't always seem fair," Maisie finally said, her voice subdued as she reached for another paper. "But true fulfillment comes to those who are willing to look within." She unfolded the next slip and began reading aloud. "My secret is that I've been dreaming of you . . ." Her voice wavered, and she swallowed before continuing. "I'm sorry, I meant to say another . . . another life."

Hope noticed a brief look of concern pass over Talia's face. It seemed as if she wanted to rush to Maisie's side, but something held her back.

Maisie thrust the paper into the basket as if it burned her fingers, her face settling into a neutral mask. "Wonderful progress, everyone. We'll read a few more, and then we'll move on to building positive self-talk that will help us overcome these self-imposed limits."

· · ·

The session wrapped up at noon, and Kit swung open the library doors, announcing lunch was ready in the dining room.

Hope stood and stretched, feeling both enlightened and overwhelmed. Listening to Maisie dissect everyone's fears had led to some unexpected insights, one of which was clear: real imposters don't suffer from imposter syndrome. That alone was a takeaway she'd carry with her. Yet, the sheer volume of motivational slogans Maisie had shared left her feeling somewhat dazed. Meeting Maisie in person for the first time, she hadn't anticipated how clichéd the woman sounded. How had she missed that during the self-guided video series?

"I'm . . . not sure what to make of that session," Claire muttered, breaking into Hope's thoughts as she stretched her arms overhead.

"It was definitely a lot," Drew agreed, flipping through his notes. He'd had to sign confidentiality agreements not to divulge any of the participants' information to be allowed to sit in on the sessions, but he'd still managed to jot down a few things for his story. "Let's grab some lunch. I'm starving."

"Did you find the session helpful, Maretta?" Claire asked.

"A little over the top," Maretta replied, briskly making her way out of the library. "But I can see how Jefferson could benefit from retreats like this."

Hope, along with Claire and Drew, walked out of the library and headed for the dining room, while Maretta continued on to the registration desk. Inside the dining room, they found Lorna already at the buffet, plate in hand. Just as they were about to join her, a loud voice halted them in their tracks.

"This is an emergency!" Maretta's voice rang out from the lobby, catching Hope, Claire, and Drew's attention. They exchanged a glance before peering out from the dining room. They saw the mayor toe-to-toe with a tall man wearing black-rimmed glasses and sporting a hat with the lodge's logo on it.

"That's Henry Greenway," Claire whispered.

"Oh, boy," Hope muttered.

"You're being utterly unreasonable, Maretta. Nothing's changed with you," he replied, crossing his arms in a stance of defiance. "Ms. Cox has set strict terms on when the phone lines are accessible, and a little snowfall doesn't qualify as an emergency."

Maretta's face flushed with frustration. "Let me explain something to you, Henry. I'm the mayor of Jefferson, and I'll be the judge of what's an emergency. And it's not 'just a little snow' out there! For heaven's sake, use your eyes and look outside! I need to reach my public works department, and I need that line *now*!"

"Is something wrong?" Talia asked as she emerged from the library, clutching a file folder with a look of mild distress.

"I need to make a call now," Maretta replied. "Either on my cell or the lodge's landline. It's urgent town business that can't wait."

Henry adjusted his glasses, his voice a bit clipped. "I was reminding Mrs. Kingston of the retreat's policy."

Talia's face softened into a diplomatic smile. "Considering the circumstances, Mr. Greenway, I think it's fine. Would you mind showing her to the office?"

Henry hesitated, clearly debating, but then relented with a curt nod, gesturing toward the registration desk. "Right this way, Madame Mayor."

Maretta let out a huff, then strode toward the office with purpose.

Drew glanced over at Hope. "Well, that almost got ugly."

Hope nodded. "Good thing we're only here till tomorrow. I think I'll go rest in my room for a bit."

"What about lunch?" Drew asked, looking torn between following her or going back to the buffet.

"I'm not hungry. You two go on and have lunch. I'll be back for the next session." Hope gave Drew a pat on the shoulder and slipped away toward the elevator. As she walked down the hallway, she froze when she saw Maisie and Henry standing close in the doorway of what looked like a storage room. Maisie's face was tight with irritation, and their exchange, though inaudible to Hope, clearly wasn't pleasant. Henry jabbed a finger at her, and she batted it away sharply before turning to leave—nearly colliding into Hope.

"Oh, I'm sorry!" Maisie recovered quickly, flashing a polite smile. "I wasn't paying attention to where I was going."

"Are you okay?" Hope asked, glancing past her at Henry, who had already retreated into the storage room and closed the door behind him.

"I'm perfectly fine." Maisie smoothed her expression. "I was just heading to the dining room. Care to join me?"

"I'm going to my room," Hope replied. "The first session was a bit intense. I just need a breather."

"I understand and I applaud you for recognizing your need for solitude and honoring it." Maisie began to turn but stopped, her expression cooling. "I know you have a reputation for . . . investigating things. I hope you won't jump to conclusions about what you just saw with Mr. Greenway." Her voice had lost its usual soft lilt, replaced by a more unsettling tone.

Taken aback, Hope stammered, "I don't jump to conclusions."

"Good." Maisie's gaze held Hope's. "Enjoy your rest—you'll need all your energy for conquering that fear of not being universally liked."

With that, she walked away, leaving Hope speechless.

Chapter Four

When Hope returned to her room, her first instinct was to reach for her phone to check in with Ethan, to see how things were going with the girls and the animals. Then she remembered she'd handed her phone over to Talia. With a sigh, she headed to the small desk across the room, where an embossed journal and pen sat waiting as part of the retreat package. The accompanying card invited her to use the notebook for journaling thoughts, expressing gratitude, and scripting a future.

But Hope had another idea.

She pulled out the chair, opened the notebook, clicked the pen, and began writing her observations and suspicions rather than the prescribed self-reflection. Her notes quickly filled the page with her thoughts on the morning session, including the moment when Maisie had faltered over a particular *Release*. Hope was certain she'd caught Maisie hesitating, her reaction too strained, and she was positive Maisie hadn't told the truth when she read that *Release* aloud.

When she finished her notes, Hope closed the notebook and set down the pen. After stretching her arms, she dashed to the bathroom for a quick touch-up before heading back to the lobby for the next session. After grabbing her journal, she left her room. She strolled along the hallway, pausing when she noticed a door slightly ajar just two rooms over. Inside, she saw Lorna rummaging through her suitcase.

Hope knocked gently, causing Lorna to startle. She spun around, hand on her chest, and relaxed when she saw Hope.

"Oh, I'm sorry, I didn't mean to startle you," Hope said with a small smile. "I'm heading downstairs. Want to join me?"

Lorna took a breath, nodding. "Yes, thank you. That'd be nice." She zipped up her suitcase and glanced at Hope. "I noticed you didn't stay for lunch."

"I wasn't hungry," Hope replied, stepping into the room, which mirrored her own with a queen-sized bed, rich wood furniture, and exposed beams lending a rustic charm. Her gaze landed on a framed photo on the nightstand of two young girls beaming at the camera.

"Lovely photo," Hope remarked.

Lorna looked over, her expression softening. "My sister and me, back when life was simpler. There was quite an age gap between us." She moved her suitcase to the corner, giving the photo a wistful look.

"You two look happy," Hope noted, thinking of her own bond with Claire. "I'm lucky to be close with my sister."

"That must be wonderful." Lorna collected her journal and pen from the desk. "I hardly know mine anymore." She glanced back at Hope. "Come on, we don't want to be late."

Moments later, Hope and Lorna stepped off the elevator together. During the brief descent, Lorna mentioned that she worked as a marketing consultant and, like Hope, had come across Maisie's website last winter. As they walked down the hall, the hum of voices drifted from the lobby. When they reached the registration desk, Talia gestured toward the lounge.

"The next session's in there," Talia said with a broad smile that didn't quite reach her tired eyes. Her constant shifting on her feet hinted that the three-inch heels had been a poor choice for a day spent standing.

"This place is fabulous," Lorna said, striding off toward the lounge opposite the dining room.

Hope lingered, feeling the pull of a nagging thought. "I think I left my favorite pen in the library. I'll be quick," she said to Talia.

"Just don't be late," Talia replied, eyeing her watch. "It's almost two o'clock."

Hope nodded, then rushed to the empty library. She scanned the room, spotting the basket that held the group's *Releases* on a nearby table. Crossing over, she peered into the basket and began unfolding the slips of paper until she found the one she'd been looking for.

My secret is that I've been dreaming of your death.

A chill skittered down Hope's spine. No wonder Maisie had hesitated to share it with the group, because it was a threat.

"Who could have written this?" she murmured.

Just then, a gust of wind slammed against the windows, causing them to rattle and jolting her from her thoughts. She looked up, noticing snow clinging to the panes and thick flakes dancing outside, obscuring the view over the vast, wintry landscape surrounding the lodge.

Hope stepped out of the library, the ominous note burning a hole in her back pocket. She scanned the area, her pulse quickening, but Claire and Drew were nowhere in sight. Darn. She'd been counting on their insight. Maybe talking it through would help her make sense of what to do next. Now, she was on her own.

"Hope!" Melanie called from the dining room entrance, a coffee cup in hand.

"We'd better head into the lounge," Hope replied, picking up her pace.

"Maisie's not in there yet," Melanie said as she fell in step beside Hope. "So, what do you think of the retreat so far?"

Hope hesitated before answering. Maisie was nothing like the polished, insightful figure she portrayed online. Beneath the carefully curated persona, she seemed shallow, relying more on flashy buzzwords than genuine substance. Or maybe she was being too harsh. The relentless storm and the unsettling discovery of the *Release* had left her on edge, making it hard to think clearly. But still, what kind of person would go so far as to put their darkest wish for Maisie's death into words?

"I'm holding out until after the next session before deciding," she replied.

"Well, I think it's been a total waste. Just like all the coaching I paid for," Melanie grumbled. "My business hasn't gone anywhere, even though I followed Maisie's program to the letter."

Hope raised an eyebrow. "So why come to the retreat if the coaching wasn't helping?"

Melanie's expression darkened, a sharp edge creeping into her voice. "This is Maisie's last chance to make things right or deal with the consequences." Without another word, she marched into the lounge.

A sharp voice caught Hope's attention just outside the lounge. Maretta was striding briskly toward her, with Talia trailing close behind, looking frazzled.

"Oh, no," Hope muttered, moving forward to intercept them. "What's going on?"

Maretta's usual scowl had deepened, with the furrow between her brows more pronounced. "I cannot believe she thinks she can keep me here against my will," she declared.

"I think there's been some misunderstanding," Talia said, breathless after trying to keep up with Maretta in her heels. "It's not our intention to keep you here against your will."

"Thank you," Maretta said.

"Maisie just believes it's best not to make a rushed decision," Talia said. "She'll be discussing that topic tomorrow."

Fixing her with an icy stare, Maretta replied, "Young lady, I have *not* made this decision in haste. I'm needed back in town. The snowstorm is worsening by the minute. As I informed Maisie, my husband will pick me up after dinner. There's no more to discuss." With that, she breezed past Hope and entered the lounge.

Hope felt no discomfort with the exchange, having grown accustomed to Maretta's brash style over the years. However, it was evident that Talia, still standing there flustered, was not quite prepared for Maretta's strong personality.

"Her bark is worse than her bite," Hope said, aiming to soothe the assistant's worries.

Talia, looking doubtful, shook her head. "I'm not too sure about that."

• • •

At four o'clock, the second session, "Rewriting Your Inner Narrative," ended. As Hope left the lounge, she realized she needed a hit of caffeine despite the time of day. It didn't matter that it was late in the afternoon; coffee never seemed to disrupt her sleep. And for that she was grateful. She excused herself from Claire, who was chatting with Lorna, and headed toward the kitchen.

The two-hour session built onto the first session of the day. As Maisie guided the discussion and offered structured prompts that helped them rewrite their limiting beliefs into empowering affirmations, Hope's thoughts kept drifting off.

She found herself replaying the heated conversation she had overheard between Kit and Henry when she first checked in—Kit's sharp tone, Henry's clipped responses, the unmistakable tension crackling between them. What room had Kit been in that she shouldn't have?

Then there was the *Release* that contained a veiled threat. The words had been deliberately cruel, meant to unsettle. Hope couldn't shake the feeling that Maisie had been rattled by it.

And then, at lunch, that hushed but intense exchange between Henry and Maisie. Hope hadn't been able to make out their words, but their body language had said enough. Maisie had leaned in, her expression tight with frustration, while Henry's jaw had been set like stone. Whatever passed between them, it hadn't been pleasant.

Hope toyed with the corner of her notebook as she tried to refocus on the session, but a nagging feeling clung to her. Separate moments, scattered puzzle pieces, but were they connected?

When Hope pushed open the kitchen's swinging door in search of coffee, she found herself pleasantly surprised by the space. Though not large, it was impressively organized and efficient. Everything had its place: copper pots hanging in neat rows, utensils within arm's reach, a spotless countertop running the length of the room. The neat arrangement of everything pleased Hope's organization-loving heart. She moved along the counter, glancing at the large window overlooking the lodge grounds, where thick snowflakes still fell in a steady cascade, a reminder of the storm's unrelenting presence.

Spotting a coffeepot, she began the hunt for a mug. After a brief search, she found one and then filled it with the dark brew. As she went to the double-sided stainless-steel fridge for milk, her eyes drifted to a darkened hallway branching off the back of the kitchen. The unlit, narrow corridor seemed almost out of place in the otherwise bright and welcoming room.

Hope's interest sparked. What could be down that hallway? Perhaps storage rooms, maybe a pantry? She paused, her gaze lingering on the shadowed entrance. But the smell of fresh coffee brought her back to the reason she was there, and she took out the milk carton and poured a splash into her cup. With a quiet sense of satisfaction, she replaced the carton, took a careful sip of her coffee, and padded back toward the lounge, the mystery of the dark hallway tickling at the edge of her thoughts.

• • •

On her way back to the lobby, Hope mentally reviewed the upcoming schedule. Before the end of the weekend, each attendee would have a one-on-one session with Maisie, a private, twenty-minute conversation that seemed designed for personal growth or, as Maisie had hinted to Hope, for confronting deep-seated insecurities. Ever since Maisie had made that jab about Hope's fear of disappointing others, she dreaded the upcoming talk. But after some reflection, her dread had morphed into resolve. She decided that during their meeting, she'd confront Maisie about her remark and set a boundary around the types of comments she found unacceptable.

As she rounded a corner near the library, low voices caught her attention. The door on the far side of the room was open, and Hope recognized Maisie's voice drifting out into the hall, though the other voice—a man's—was unfamiliar. Curious, she approached quietly, slipping closer to the doorway.

Peering in, she saw Maisie standing close to a tall blond man who looked to be in his mid-thirties. He wore a leather bomber jacket that gave him a rugged air, his posture rigid and gaze locked on Maisie with a seriousness that caught Hope's attention. Maisie, her back to Hope, leaned in toward him, her voice low and sharp.

"Make sure those things are never found," Maisie was saying. Her words carried an urgency that sent a chill up Hope's spine. "Do whatever you have to do to make sure they disappear forever. We can't have any ties to that . . . well, you know."

The man nodded, his voice steady. "Not a problem."

He shifted as if to leave, his face turning slightly in Hope's direction. Heart pounding, Hope pulled back, retreating quickly down the hall before he could spot her. She steadied herself, pulse racing, questions swirling in her mind. What was Maisie hiding? And who was this man?

"Amy's here!" Claire's voice echoed from the lobby, catching Hope's attention.

"Hope!" Drew's voice followed as he exited the lounge, his quick wave catching her eye. "Come on, let's find out how the roads really are doing."

Hope hurried toward the lobby, leaving behind the weight of the hushed library and the conversation she wasn't meant to hear. As she arrived in the lobby, she saw Amy bundled in a parka with a faux-fur-lined hood, surrounded by Claire, Melanie, and Lorna. Drew, already in the thick of the group, set his camera down on an end table and leaned in to greet Amy.

Amy pulled down her hood and gave her boots a firm shake, sending flecks of snow scattering onto the lobby floor. She looked cold but relieved, pulling off her gloves and setting her well-worn duffel bag beside her.

"You must be Amy," Kit's voice chimed in as she inserted herself into the group. "Welcome to Jefferson Lodge! Let's get you settled so you can warm up. Dinner will be served in a couple of hours."

Amy's eyes flicked around, slightly taken aback by Kit's appearance, but she quickly recovered, her expression softening. "That sounds amazing. It's *freezing* out there."

Maretta, seated by the fireplace, asked, "What are the roads like?"

Amy grimaced. "Bad. Really bad. I think it's falling over an inch an hour. This isn't what was forecasted at all."

Maretta's expression grew tense. She pushed herself up from her chair with determination. "I need to call Alfred again. I *cannot* wait until after dinner to leave."

Kit nodded. "Of course, Mrs. Kingston. Why don't you both come with me?"

Amy grabbed her duffel bag, nodding to Kit.

As she passed, Hope leaned in with a curious smile and kept her voice low. "Do you know Kit?"

Amy's face gave away a hint of something unreadable, but she only murmured, "I'll tell you everything later," before following Kit and Maretta.

As Hope watched them cross the lobby to the registration desk, she as struck again with a sense of unease. This retreat was supposed to be about self-improvement, but something about it felt . . . off. Like there was more happening beneath the surface than anyone was letting on.

Chapter Five

Talia strode toward them, folio in one hand and pen in the other, her demeanor all business. She lifted her chin slightly as she addressed Melanie. "Alright, Melanie, you're up first with Maisie in the library. The rest of you will have a quiet journaling session here."

Hope's doubts about the retreat and the worsening weather were starting to take their toll. She was ready to call it quits. Maisie, who had seemed so promising, was turning out to be a disappointment. Ethan's words echoed in her mind, *People aren't always who they pretend to be online.* It seemed Maisie was just another illusion, a mirage that evaporated upon closer inspection.

"Come on," Claire said, linking her arm through Hope's with a playful tug. It appeared her sister's mood had improved since they arrived at the lodge. "Let's dive into our journals like we used to in high school." She guided Hope toward the lounge, where they settled side by side on the plush sofa.

Across the room, Lorna had nestled into a quiet corner, her pen moving across the page as she scribbled intently. Hope opened her journal, feeling Claire's curious gaze flickering over her shoulder, trying to catch a glimpse of the thoughts she had jotted down earlier about the retreat.

"We're supposed to be writing about our feelings, struggles . . . even dreams," Claire murmured, her voice barely above a whisper. With a quick, gentle motion, she plucked the journal from Hope's hands and scanned the page, her eyebrow arching in surprise. "So . . . you think Maisie lied about what was on that *Release?*"

"I do," Hope replied, her tone low.

Claire looked at her, surprised. "But how can you be sure?"

Hope shifted, reaching into her back pocket to retrieve the folded piece of paper. She held it up for Claire to see.

Claire's eyes widened. "How did you manage to get this?"

"I went back to the library after lunch and looked in the basket. The notes were still in there."

Claire took the note, scanning the words as she read aloud in a hushed whisper, "'My secret is that I've been dreaming of your death.'" She lowered the paper, her expression a mix of shock and disbelief. "Wow. Who would write something so chilling?"

"One of the people we're spending the weekend with," Hope replied, her gaze steady.

Just then, Talia stepped into the room, her heels clicking sharply on the hardwood. "Ladies, is there a problem?" Her eyes narrowed as she looked from one to the other. "Maisie gave specific instructions that this is meant to be a quiet session."

Quickly, Claire slipped the paper back into Hope's hand and turned to Talia. "No problem. I think we're all just a little on edge with the storm intensifying."

Talia waved off the concern. "It's not as if we're isolated; the town is just a short drive away. Even if it gets worse, we'll be perfectly safe. Now, let's stick to our task. I'll go find Maretta and Drew so they can join you."

She gave them one last look before stepping out, leaving Hope and Claire in tense silence. But not for long.

"What are we going to do?" Claire set her journal aside, her expression tense. "This is not what I signed up for."

Hope leaned closer. "After I went to grab coffee in the kitchen, I overheard Maisie talking to some guy . . ."

"Tall, intense-looking, and a bit on the angry side?" Claire asked.

"Yes. Do you know who he is?"

Claire shook her head. "No, but I saw him talking with Talia earlier. What did you hear them say?"

"Maisie told him, 'Make sure those things are never found, and do whatever you have to.' She also told him that there cannot be any loose ends. He just nodded and said, 'No problem.'"

Claire's eyes widened. "Oh, my word. This weekend is turning into a nightmare. We need to get out of here. First, we have to get our phones, pack our bags, and leave while there's still some light."

Hope closed her journal and stood. "You know, that sounds like the best idea I've heard all day." But just as they prepared to leave, Maretta stormed into the room, her posture unyielding.

"Hope! You need to drive me back to town immediately!" she demanded.

"That's exactly what Claire and I were just discussing," Hope said. She gestured for Claire to join her, and they walked toward Maretta.

Across the room, Lorna looked up, a flicker of confusion in her eyes. "What's going on?"

"We're leaving, that's what's going on." Maretta spun around and marched out of the lounge.

Hope and Claire hurried after her into the lobby. Drew stood by the front doors, camera bag slung over one shoulder and a worried look in his eyes.

"Everything alright?" Drew asked. "You all seem ready to hightail it out of here."

"Very observant," Maretta replied dryly.

Hope paused, considering their options. "We were thinking of cutting out early. This storm's got us on edge."

Drew's brow furrowed. "I just heard from Kit that the power's flickering. Winds are really picking up out there." He glanced between them. "You sure you want to risk the drive?"

Just then Henry emerged from his office, a solemn expression painted across his face. All eyes turned to the lodge owner as he spoke.

"I have some unpleasant news," he announced, his voice low yet commanding enough to capture everyone's attention. "I just received an update from Alden, the town's emergency services manager. The main roads are impassable and have been shut down until the plow crews can clear them. It's likely this won't happen until tomorrow at the earliest."

Maretta's eyes narrowed. "I spoke to Alden a few minutes ago and he told me I had time. That the closure wasn't imminent."

"I don't know what to tell you." Henry shook his head slowly. "Looks like things have taken a turn. You'd better give Alden a call back to sort this out. For now, it seems we're all stranded here until this storm lets up."

The group fell silent as Henry's words settled over them. Hope felt her pulse quicken. "So we're stuck here?"

Henry nodded. "Afraid so. Though the generator will kick in if the power cuts, so we shouldn't lack for power at least. Or food, since there's plenty."

Maretta's irritation boiled over. "I told you I needed to leave." She turned to Henry, frustrated. "There must be some way to get back to town."

Henry laid a gentle hand on her shoulder. "Unless you can fly or have a broom, I wouldn't count on it," he said. "We're going to have to settle in and ride this out."

Drew chuckled wryly, but his eyes didn't have their usual sparkle. "Sounds like we're in for an interesting night."

An uneasy hush fell as the realization set in. Until the storm lightened up, they were stranded there. Drew broke the silence, keeping his tone light.

"Well, I don't know about you all, but I could use a stiff drink right about now. Who's with me?" He glanced around the group, his gaze finally settling on Henry. "There is a bar here, right?"

Indeed, there was a bar. Henry guided them to the library—Maisie's one-on-one with Melanie in there had already ended—and paused before a paneled section of the wall. With a twinkle of mischief, he nudged the panel, and a concealed door gave way to a secret hideaway. Hope gasped as she peered into the bar.

"Ladies first," Henry said.

The moment Hope stepped into the hidden bar, she felt as if she'd slipped into another era. The room's vintage charm and the air of secrecy evoked the clandestine allure of a speakeasy from the 1920s. She took in the polished wood, the gleaming glassware, and the soft amber light that bathed the space in a golden haze, making every detail feel alive with history.

The further into the room she went, the more it felt like a sanctuary, the perfect spot to unwind—at least for Hope, Drew, and Claire. Maretta had returned to her room, while Melanie and Lorna opted for the sauna. Maisie and Talia had excused themselves and huddled in the lounge for work. Before leaving the lobby, Hope asked Kit to inform Amy of their whereabouts when she updated her about the road closures.

Henry took his place behind the bar, happily pouring drinks for his guests. Hope and Claire each ordered a glass of red wine, while Drew asked for a beer. The innkeeper approached their table with a tray and set each drink down with a cocktail napkin.

"So, Henry," Drew began, a mischievous smile creeping onto his face, "what was Maretta like back in the day?"

Hope smiled at Drew's inquisitiveness, a trait honed by his years as a reporter. It came as no surprise that he was eager to delve into the old romance. Henry paused, giving a small, nostalgic smile as he straightened up. "She hasn't changed a bit."

Claire lifted her wineglass. "So she's always been, what . . . like a bull in a China shop?"

"Claire!" Hope scolded, but Claire only shrugged with a helpless grin.

Henry chuckled, his eyes glinting. "That about sums her up. But she was also beautiful, smart . . . always had a fire in her." A dreamy look crossed his wrinkled face, clearly seeing Maretta from decades past.

Hope caught his gaze and softened her voice. "Sounds like you really liked her."

"Liked?" Henry's voice turned wistful. "I loved her."

"Then why did you go out with another girl?" Claire asked, leaning in with curiosity.

He sighed, shaking his head. "I was young and stupid. We both were. But that was a lifetime ago."

Hope's voice was gentle. "Still, it seems like you still care."

Henry's smile was tinged with a mix of affection and resignation. "I do. But she's always been a hard one to care about." He glanced at his watch, as if bringing himself back to the present. "Anyway, I should get back to the office. Dinner will be served soon. Enjoy your drinks." With a polite nod, he set down the tray and left the bar, leaving the three of them to digest his story.

Hope swirled her wine, her thoughts racing as she processed the day's events. She had already confided in Claire, and now it was time to bring Drew up to speed. Over the next few minutes, she laid out all the unsettling pieces: the ominous note that Maisie had manipulated, the peculiar conversation she had overheard between Henry and

Maisie, another between the mysterious man and the life coach, and Maisie's pointed, disconcerting remark about Hope's insecurities, seemingly aimed at controlling her.

"Do you think she plans to use everything we've shared as ammunition against us?" Claire asked, leaning in.

Hope set her glass down, considering the thought. "You mean, like blackmail?"

Claire nodded.

"It seems pretty far-fetched," Drew said, downing the last of his beer. "No offense, but there are bigger names out there if someone's angling for blackmail."

Hope glanced down at her notebook and wrote the word *blackmail.* "No offense taken. You have a point. Are we just overthinking this?"

Claire laughed. "Overthinking? Maybe. But let's not forget that wherever you go, Hope, a mystery seems to follow. It's like you're a magnet for mayhem."

• • •

After finishing their drinks, Hope and Claire left the bar while Drew stayed behind to snap a few photos of the hidden gem. In the lobby, Claire turned to Hope. "I think I'll head up and freshen up for dinner." Hope nodded, deciding to linger a moment longer, watching the snow drifting past the large windows. Each snowflake seemed to intensify the knot of tension in her stomach, the storm stirring something restless inside her.

Deciding it was best not to dwell on the storm, Hope turned toward the elevator, considering a quick stop by Amy's room to continue their earlier conversation. Before she could make up her mind, the elevator chimed, and as the doors slid open, there was Amy. Seizing the moment, Hope stepped forward before anyone else could draw her friend's attention. She gently steered Amy down a side hallway to a quiet nook just off the lounge, where a pair of high-backed armchairs sat near a tall, narrow window. As Amy settled into one of the chairs, she looked noticeably calmer and far more at ease than when she had first arrived.

She was dressed in a Fair Isle sweater paired with dark jeans with her blond hair pulled back in a loose ponytail and silver hoops glinting at her ears. A touch of red lipstick and a hint of blush on her cheekbones brightened her face, her energy now more composed.

"Is it true the roads are closed?" Amy asked, leaning in. "I can't believe we're trapped here with *her*."

"Who are you talking about? Kit?" Hope asked. "I got the feeling you two know each other."

Amy shook her head, giving a quick scan of the area, as if making sure no one could overhear. "No. Though I didn't expect to see Kit here, either. She didn't mention working here." She paused, dropping her voice. "Kit is actually connected to a new episode I'm working on for *Search for the Missing*."

"She's linked to a missing persons case?"

"Yes. And it's a big one," Amy replied, her eyes sharp with purpose. "But now it's feeling a little too close to home."

"How so?" Hope asked, leaning forward.

"Kit's sister, Penny Foster, vanished a few years ago during a self-improvement retreat, a lot like this one," Amy confided. "It happened in Vermont. Penny went on a group hike but never came back."

A lump caught in Hope's throat. She thought back to the conversation with Ethan last night. "Wait. Ethan mentioned something similar to me. He was talking about your case?"

Amy nodded, her expression serious. "He's been helping me with this case. When Penny vanished, she lived in Hartford, and Ethan was part of the local police. He was assigned to work with Vermont authorities on her disappearance. Once I learned that, I asked him to see if he could still get in touch with the detectives on the case, and he didn't hesitate. He's been a huge help, cutting through all that red tape. You know he hates unsolved cases."

"I know," Hope replied, though she felt a flicker of discomfort. Ethan hadn't mentioned his involvement in Penny's case. As police chief, confidentiality was part of his job, and even now, as an investigator for a criminal defense attorney, he was bound by similar rules. But this? A case for Amy's podcast? Shaking it off, she refocused. "So, Kit never mentioned working here? Did she say what she does for a living?"

"I had no idea I'd see her here," Amy replied. "She's an insurance agent. Or at least, she was."

"Then why is she working here at the lodge?" Hope asked, a sense of unease growing.

"Maybe it's because of the retreat's leader," Amy suggested.

"Maisie Cox?"

"Correction, Demi Covington."

"Who?"

"They're the same person. The retreat where Penny Foster disappeared was run by Demi Covington, who went completely off the radar afterward. I've been searching for her for ages, and it looks like you and Kit have found her."

Hope blinked, the implications sinking in. "So . . . Maisie Cox, who's leading this retreat, is actually Demi Covington, the woman connected to Penny's disappearance?"

"Exactly. Looks like Demi reinvented herself once again."

"Again? She's changed identities before?"

Amy nodded. "I looked into her background and found she was born Elaine Thompson. She has a history of fraud arrests. Somewhere along the way, she reinvented herself as Demi Covington, and that's when she perfected her act. She was holding retreats back-to-back. Her online coaching had taken off. She was the go-to self-help guru. And all you had to do to enter her world was to give a thumbs-up on a post. Once you did that, you were hooked."

Hope's stomach tightened. A person who cycled through identities like that had to be a skilled manipulator. Was that who Maisie really was? While her in-person tactics felt rehearsed, she didn't strike Hope as a con artist.

"When Penny disappeared from the retreat, it put unwanted scrutiny on her and her company, so Demi vanished from the public eye until now. I'm not surprised she rebranded herself as Maisie Cox. The question is why? She's either hiding or running from something."

Hope's pulse quickened. No wonder Ethan had been concerned. This retreat wasn't just about self-improvement. The woman running it had a secret past. And the threatening note . . . could Kit have left it? No. Kit wasn't in the library during the session. That meant someone else had. Her mind raced through the possibilities, each one more unsettling than the last.

"Does Ethan know that Maisie Cox is really Demi Covington?" Hope asked.

Amy shook her head. "I haven't had a chance to tell him yet."

"This is . . . a lot to process. But now, things are starting to make sense." Hope pulled the *Release* from her pocket, the one she'd taken from Talia's basket, and handed it to Amy. She filled her in on when it had been written and how she'd found it.

Amy scanned the note, her expression darkening. "If these confessions were supposed to be anonymous, there's no way to tell who wrote this."

"Exactly." Hope took the note back, folding it carefully before slipping it into her pocket. "Someone here knows Maisie's real identity."

Amy's expression darkened. "Hope, we need to get out of here. I have a really bad feeling about this." Her voice was barely above a whisper.

A prickle of unease ran down Hope's spine. "Agreed. But first, we need to call Ethan. Do you have your phone?"

Amy exhaled in frustration. "No. Talia confiscated my devices when I checked in."

"Then we need to get them back. Now." Hope spotted Claire approaching, she raised her hand to wave.

Hope spotted Claire approaching, her arm raised in a wave.

"There you are! I've been looking everywhere for you," Claire called, urgency in her voice. "You need to come, now! I think she's about to burst!"

"Who?" Hope asked, puzzled.

"Maretta!" Claire was already moving at a fast clip, beckoning her sister to follow.

"Oh boy," Hope muttered, glancing at Amy before the two jumped up and hurried to catch up. They arrived in the lobby to see Maretta pacing, her arms crossed tightly and her expression as stormy as the night.

Approach with caution, Hope thought wryly. She broke away from

Claire and Amy, bracing herself as she stepped forward. Somehow, she'd always managed to calm the prickly Maretta, even though the woman had a knack for blaming Hope for every unfortunate incident—and every suspicious death—that had occurred in town since she'd returned from New York.

"Maretta, I know being stranded here during the storm isn't what you planned, but your team is well-prepared to keep things running smoothly." Hope held her breath, hoping her reassurance would hit the mark.

Maretta stopped pacing, her arms dropping to her sides. "Prepared? Of course they are. But this whole thing is far from ideal," she grumbled. "I have no idea why I let you talk me into coming here."

Hope's mouth fell open, surprised. Before she could respond, Maretta pressed on.

"All this . . . journaling about your feelings and trying to unearth some hidden 'inner strength' nonsense." Maretta huffed. "Honestly, Hope, what were you thinking?"

Hope stammered, "I . . . I didn't talk you into coming."

"Not worth the fight," Claire muttered, appearing at her sister's side. "Trust me—you're not going to win."

"What are you doing?" Drew whispered, arriving at Hope's side and gently pulling her back. "Maretta's in no mood for reason right now."

"She's not the only one wound up by all this," Lorna said, slipping into the conversation. She'd changed into flowy, wide-legged pants and a fitted sweater, her dark hair framing her face, bangs brushing her brows. "It's surreal that we're actually trapped here."

"We're not trapped," Kit pointed out, entering the lobby. "Everyone planned to stay overnight for the retreat, so the storm hasn't changed anything except the view."

Maretta's scowl deepened. "Could you be more out of touch? This storm has changed everything."

"Well, I think Kit has a point," Lorna said, changing her tune. "We might as well make the best of it. And frankly, I'm starving. When's dinner?"

Kit looked relieved to have someone on her side and motioned toward the dining area. "Actually, the buffet is ready for everyone. Please, help yourselves."

Hope led the way, and when she stepped into the dining room she immediately noticed the tables had been pushed together into one long arrangement, encouraging a communal meal. Along the far wall, a buffet stretched out, laden with steaming dishes that sent her stomach into a riot of hunger. She'd skipped lunch, and now the rich aroma of baked ziti, thick slices of roast beef, and a crisp, vibrant salad made her mouth water.

"What were you and Amy talking about?" Claire asked, sliding up beside her sister and adding a slice of roast beef to her plate. "What's going on?"

Hope glanced over her shoulder, searching for Kit, but she was nowhere in sight. Keeping her voice low, she said, "After we eat, we need to get our devices and get out of here. Maisie isn't who she claims to be."

Claire's perfectly lined blue eyes widened. "What?"

"Shh." Hope shot her a warning look as Lorna's head snapped up, her gaze now fixed on them. "I'll explain later. For now, let's just eat and then figure out our next move."

Claire frowned. "But the roads are closed."

"I'll call Ethan," Hope said. "He can drive through anything."

"This all looks delicious," Lorna remarked as she moved along the buffet. "Though, I get the feeling you two aren't talking about the menu."

Hope and Claire flashed identical innocent smiles, the same ones they'd used on their mother when they'd been caught whispering about something they shouldn't.

"Can we move it along?" Drew called from the back of the line, waving his empty plate. "Some of us would like to eat."

Plate in hand, Hope claimed a seat at the table. The blood-red cloth draped across its length was set with polished silverware and sparkling glasses, all arranged with precise care.

Drew slid into the seat next to Claire, while Talia took her place at the end of the table. As everyone settled in, a quiet hush fell over the room, the clinking of utensils the only sound as they began to eat.

Across from Hope, Melanie, seated beside Maisie, turned to Amy with a curious smile. "I heard you have a podcast, Amy. I love podcasts. What's yours about?"

Amy speared a cherry tomato, her expression brightening. "It's a true crime podcast focused on missing persons cases."

At the far end of the table, Lorna frowned. "True crime? That's such a dark topic." She smoothed her napkin over her lap. "I prefer a bit of pop culture with my podcasts. You know, something light and fun."

"There's a massive audience for true crime," Drew said, slicing into his roast beef. "People can't seem to get enough of it."

"I just don't see the appeal," Maretta interjected, settling into her seat beside Claire. "Discussing tragedies like they're entertainment is unseemly."

Amy blinked, taken aback. "It's not entertainment. I tell these people's stories in the hope that they'll be reunited with their families—or at least get the justice they deserve."

Hope leaned forward. "Amy is very respectful in how she covers her cases."

Melanie tilted her head, intrigued. "How often do you release new episodes? And what are you working on now?"

Hope shot Amy a wary look, wondering how she'd navigate the question, especially with Maisie sitting at the table.

Amy dabbed her mouth with her napkin, then met Hope's gaze with a reassuring nod. "Right now I'm researching the case of a young woman named Penny Foster."

Across the table, Maisie stiffened, her complexion paling. Her fingers curled around the stem of her wineglass, shoulders taut.

Hope's pulse quickened. There was no doubt now, Amy was right. Maisie was not who she claimed to be.

Chapter Six

Maisie's grip on her wineglass tightened, the tension in her shoulders visible even in the flickering candlelight. Hope exchanged a glance with Amy, a silent confirmation passing between them. Whatever Maisie was hiding, she knew the name Penny Foster, and that knowledge terrified her.

Amy set down her fork deliberately, her voice even but edged with purpose. "Penny vanished while attending a retreat, one much like this. One of the activities was a group hike, but she didn't make it back to the inn."

Melanie's hand paused mid-reach for her water glass. "How horrifying . . . and so unsettling."

"One thing is for certain, we won't be going on any hikes during this retreat," Lorna added with a nervous chuckle.

"Oh, no, nothing like that," Talia assured her, though a slight furrow creased her brow. She turned to her employer, her expression shifting to concern. "Are you alright, Maisie?"

Maisie nodded, but the gesture was unconvincing. Her usual poise wavered as she gripped the edge of the table, her fingers pressing so hard against the linen that it wrinkled beneath her touch. Her throat bobbed in a tight swallow, and when she attempted to smile, it faltered at the corners.

"I'm fine," she murmured. A thin sheen of perspiration glistened at her temples, and her shoulders, normally squared with confidence, seemed to inch inward as if bracing against an unseen force.

Hope didn't buy it. Neither did Amy, judging by the way she studied Maisie like a hawk sizing up its prey.

"Are you sure?" Talia pressed gently. "You look a little pale."

Maisie exhaled, forcing a small laugh that didn't quite reach her eyes. "Just a little warm in here, that's all." She picked up her napkin, dabbing at the base of her throat, but her fingers trembled.

Hope exchanged another glance with Amy. Maisie wasn't just warm. She was unraveling.

Drew, who was buttering his roll, asked, "Tell us more about this retreat Penny Foster attended. Were there any suspects or clues to what happened to her?"

Amy set her fork down, her expression sharpening. "The police never identified any clear suspects. But shortly after Penny disappeared, the life coach who hosted the retreat at the Colbert Inn up in Vermont, Demi Covington, vanished as well." She tilted her head, watching the reactions around the table. "I haven't been able to track her down since."

Hope's grip tightened around her wineglass as she studied Maisie, who remained unnervingly still.

Amy let the moment stretch, then flashed a slow, knowing smile. "But I think I've finally found her."

Hope's pulse kicked up. *Yes, you have.*

Drew and Melanie spoke at once. "Really?"

Talia cleared her throat as she set down her fork. "Perhaps we should switch to a lighter topic," she suggested, her gaze flicking to Maisie. "What do you think?"

Maisie, still gripping her wineglass, blinked as if coming out of a daze. "Huh? Oh—yes, of course." She forced a tight smile. "Thank you, Amy, for sharing your podcast with us. I'm sure it will be . . . a success." Her voice wavered slightly, betraying the strain beneath her polished exterior.

Claire leaned into Hope, whispering, "What is going on?" Then she yelped as she rubbed her arm. "Ow!"

Hope glanced past her sister and caught Drew's pointed look.

"He elbowed me," Claire hissed, glaring at him. "What is wrong with you?"

"What are you two whispering about?" he asked.

Talia's head snapped up. "Is everything okay?"

Thinking fast, Hope reached for the saltshaker. She knew Drew sensed something was going on and that he was being left out of it. "Drew just wanted me to pass the salt." She handed it to Claire, who narrowed her eyes but played along, sliding it to Drew.

He muttered a quick "Thanks" and turned his attention back to his plate.

Seemingly satisfied, Talia shifted her focus to Amy. "Are you hoping to turn podcasting into a full-time career? Is that why you joined the retreat?"

Amy set down her napkin, her gaze never leaving Maisie. "That's the goal. I may never solve a missing persons case myself, but by sharing their stories, I hope to give the victims and their families a voice." She let the words linger, watching for a reaction. "And who knows? Maybe one day I'll help find answers for someone."

Maisie reached for her water, but her hand shook slightly as she lifted the glass. A single droplet splashed onto the tablecloth.

"Like Penny Foster?" Kit returned to the dining room with a pitcher of water. "Hard to believe someone could disappear like that, surrounded by so many people, and no one saw a thing."

"Fascinating," Melanie said, turning to Drew. "And you're a reporter. Have you ever covered cases like the ones on Amy's podcast?"

Drew dabbed his mouth with a napkin. "Now and then, but we haven't had a big missing person case since Joyce Markham vanished two decades ago. We've had a few murder cases, though." He grinned at Hope.

Melanie's eyes widened as she turned to Hope. "I heard about those! Are you some kind of detective?"

"Really?" Kit set down the pitcher, leaning in with interest.

Hope forced a light chuckle, waving off the idea. "Not exactly," she said, trying to deflect. The last thing she wanted was to be the center of attention, especially with Maisie sitting across from her. Discussing local murder cases wasn't an ideal dinner conversation, at least not for her tonight. She was far more interested in peeling back the layers of Maisie's carefully crafted persona.

Lorna leaned back in her chair, arms crossing slowly, a thoughtful gleam in her eyes. "You know, all this talk about missing people and mystery-solving makes me wonder, maybe there's something thrilling in the unknown. But really, isn't the reason we're all here at this retreat to focus on self-discovery and true authenticity?"

She turned to Maisie as a knowing smirk flickered across her lips, amusement dancing in her eyes like a cat toying with its prey. "It's not often you get the chance to dig deep and reveal your real self, especially around people you may not know that well. It's an opportunity to leave behind anything . . . untrue."

A muscle twitched in Maisie's jaw, and she forced a tight-lipped smile.

"I think that's what I look forward to the most, hearing everyone's real story. Isn't that the whole point, Maisie?" Lorna asked.

Maisie's breath hitched, and she set her glass down. She pressed her palms against her lap, as if grounding herself, but the color had drained from her face. Her throat bobbed with a forced swallow, and for the briefest second her gaze darted toward the door, as if weighing the possibility of escape.

"I've got it!" Melanie leaned forward with excitement. "What if we have our dessert in the library and share our stories there? A chance to talk and really get to know each other."

Maretta's eyes narrowed as she set down her flatware. "Haven't we been doing that all day?"

"Well, I think it's a wonderful suggestion," Maisie said, standing. She turned to Kit, her voice smoothing with authority. "Could you and Henry bring dessert to the library?"

Henry's head popped into the dining room, a puzzled look on his face. "Did I hear my name?"

"Yes," Kit said. "We're moving dessert to the library."

Henry's enthusiasm was clearly lacking, but he quickly masked it with a practiced smile. "If that's what Ms. Cox wants."

Maisie offered a smooth nod. "Thank you for accommodating us, Henry. Let's all head to the library and get settled."

Hope rose, pacing toward the window. The glass was cold beneath her fingertips as she brushed away a patch of fog to peer outside. Darkness had swallowed the landscape, and the snow continued its relentless assault on the lodge, thick flakes swirling in the wind. The storm showed no signs of easing.

Claire joined her, arms crossed tightly over her chest. "Are we really doing this?" she murmured. "How much more can we talk about? Besides, I thought we were calling Ethan and getting out of here."

Hope exhaled slowly, her reflection in the window a ghostly blur. "Trust me. There's a lot more for us to learn before we leave." She turned to Claire, her expression unwavering. "Give me a minute, I need to talk to Maisie alone."

Hope slipped past her sister, weaving through the maze of chairs until she reached Maisie's side. A tight knot coiled in her chest, her pulse thrumming in her ears. Maybe Amy should be the one to confront the professed life coach. Maybe it wasn't her place.

But she knew she couldn't sit back and let the charade continue. Maisie had to come clean about her identity, about Penny Foster, about everything. And if she wouldn't, Hope would make sure the truth came out.

She leaned in. "We need to talk. In private."

The room slowly emptied, the scrape of chairs and quiet murmurs fading as the others filed out. Amy hesitated near the doorway, casting a questioning glance over her shoulder. Hope met her gaze with a steady nod, signaling her to go.

Once they were alone, she turned back to Maisie, who sat unnervingly still, her fingers curled tightly around her napkin.

Maisie arched an eyebrow as she settled back into her chair, crossing her legs with an air of calm control. "So, Hope. What is it you want to discuss?"

Hope leaned forward, her gaze unwavering. "Who was that man you were speaking to earlier? The one you told to 'Make sure those things are never found, and do whatever you have to.'"

Maisie's expression faltered for a moment, her eyes widening as she processed her own words echoed back to her. "Austin," she said after a beat, regaining her composure. "He works for me."

"In what capacity?"

"Operations," Maisie replied coolly, tilting her head as if Hope's question was somehow trivial. "Why this sudden interest in my staff?"

"It's not about your staff, exactly. It's more about what you said in your emails about this being your *first* retreat."

Maisie's lips tightened as she considered her answer. "And it is our first retreat."

"Yes, under the name Maisie Cox and Limitless Living," Hope

pressed. "But how many retreats did you run when you were known as Demi Covington?"

Maisie's breath hitched, as if Hope's words had knocked the wind out of her. She quickly composed herself, uncrossing her legs and attempting to mask her unease. "I . . . I don't know what you're talking about."

Hope leaned in. "Oh, I think you do, Elaine."

Maisie's eyes went wide, shock flickering across her face.

"That's right," Hope pressed on. "I know your real name is Elaine Thompson. And I know about the fraud charges. So does Amy. It was your retreat where Penny Foster vanished. What happened? Why did you change your name and lie to everyone here?"

Maisie's gaze dropped, her shoulders sagged slightly, as if shedding a weight she'd carried for too long. She inhaled deeply, then lifted her head to meet Hope's eyes.

"You're right. I lied about my name." A flicker of resolve steadied her as she continued. "But I swear to you, I'm not here to con anyone. Not anymore."

Hope remained silent, waiting.

Maisie exhaled. "When I was Elaine Thompson, survival was all I knew. And maybe . . . maybe a part of that old self lingered when I became Demi. But for the first time, I was finding my purpose. My passion."

Hope's skepticism was evident. "Helping people?"

Maisie nodded. "Yes. I know how that sounds. But not many people know that I grew up in an unstable home. My parents were . . . con artists. That's the life I was born into. The only life I knew." Her voice wavered slightly before she pressed on. "Until I realized I was good at something real. I liked helping people. And I wasn't pretending." She swallowed hard, her gaze imploring. "You have to believe me, Hope. When Penny disappeared, the scrutiny was intense. I had no choice but to pull back in order to protect myself."

Hope's gaze sharpened. "If you did nothing wrong, then why did you need protection?"

"I . . . I couldn't let my past be exposed," Maisie admitted, her voice barely above a whisper.

"Correction, you couldn't risk being exposed as a fraud," Hope said, her voice hard. "I'll give you this, Maisie, you're convincing." The realization sank in, and her stomach twisted at the thought of all the time and money she'd poured into Maisie's program over the last few months. Even worse, she'd promoted Maisie's program to her friends and fellow bloggers, urging them to trust the woman she herself had trusted blindly.

Maisie's eyes filled with tears, her voice trembling. "I'm not that person anymore, Hope. I left Elaine Thompson behind a long time ago. Becoming Demi changed me. I actually saw that I helped people. Then something terrible happened . . . But I swear, this, right now, is real."

Maisie's sincerity almost seemed genuine, and the glistening tears added to her plea. But Hope's gut told her to stay wary. The strange exchange with Austin and the unsettling note hadn't been forgotten.

"I'm sorry, Maisie. I'm done with you and this retreat." Hope turned, her mind set on finding Talia to retrieve her phone and call Ethan. But before she could take a step, fingers closed around her arm in a desperate grip. She looked back. Maisie's hand clutched her forearm, her knuckles white. There was no practiced composure now, just raw panic flickering in her eyes.

Maisie's fingers unclasped, freeing Hope's arm. "Hope, please..." Her voice cracked. "I need your help."

Hope hesitated, the plea sending a shiver down her spine. "With what, exactly?" she asked.

Maisie's voice cracked as she spoke. "First, I need Amy to stop her podcast about Penny Foster." She swallowed hard, then added in a whisper, "And . . . I need your help finding out who's trying to kill me."

Hope's breath caught. Hearing Maisie say it out loud, admitting the danger, was jarring, even after seeing the threatening note.

"There's nothing I can do about Amy's podcast," Hope said. "And as for your second request . . . have you called the police?"

Maisie shook her head.

"You should. I'm not law enforcement. I can't help you with this."

Maisie's fingers clenched into fists on her lap. "But you have to," she urged, her voice low and insistent. "We're snowed in, trapped, and you have a reputation for solving cases." She leaned closer, her desperation palpable. "Please."

Hope hesitated. Could she really help someone she no longer trusted? The idea made her stomach twist. But then another thought struck her, a darker, more unsettling one. If Maisie was trapped here with a killer, then so was everyone else. Her pulse quickened as a chill settled over her.

No. It was just a note. A scare tactic. Nothing more.

"You've got Austin," she said, doing her best to keep her voice even. "He seems more than capable of handling security. My advice? Go to your room, lock your door, and stay put until morning." Without waiting for a response, she turned on her heel. "I'm going to find Talia and get my phone back." Of course, she'd tell Ethan everything that Maisie had just shared with her about her background and the threat.

She stepped into the empty lobby, scanning the space. The registration desk sat abandoned—no sign of Talia or anyone else. Frustration simmered beneath her skin as she moved past it, ready to keep searching.

Then, sharp voices cut through the silence.

Hope stopped in her tracks. The conversation wasn't hushed, it was tense, heated. The words weren't entirely clear from where she stood, but she could hear the edge in their tones.

Henry and Kit.

Heart pounding, she edged closer to the office doorway.

"What's gotten into you?" Henry's voice was sharp. "You need to back off."

Kit scoffed. "Back off? Not until you tell me why Austin was going through your things? What's he after?"

"That's none of your business," Henry said. "In fact, none of this is. You're fired!"

Kit's gasp was audible.

Hope's pulse quickened. Austin had searched Henry's room? Why? What was he looking for?

A light tap on her shoulder sent Hope spinning around. She pressed a hand to her chest, exhaling sharply when she saw Claire standing there.

Claire took a step back, eyes wide. "You nearly gave *me* a heart attack!"

"Me? What were you thinking, sneaking up on me like that?"

"What were *you* doing? Eavesdropping?" Claire whispered.

Hope nodded, guiding her sister a few steps away from the office door. "Henry just fired Kit."

"What? Why would he do that?"

"She questioned him about Austin. She caught him searching Henry's room."

"Austin? You mean that guy I saw earlier?" Claire frowned. "Why would he be going through Henry's things?"

"I don't know, but I have a feeling it's connected to Penny Foster's disappearance."

"The woman Amy's covering on her podcast? What does she have to do with Henry or Maisie?"

"Good question." Hope glanced back at the office, then refocused on Claire. "I'll explain everything . . . but first, I need to track down Talia and get our phones. Have you seen her?"

Claire shook her head, her brow creasing with worry. "No. She vanished after dinner. Hope, what is going on?"

"A lot, and none of it's good," Hope replied grimly. "Can you help me find Talia?"

"Of course. I'll check the kitchen. She might be making tea. I could use a cup myself." Claire offered a small smile before taking off.

"Thanks. I'll try upstairs," Hope said, glancing at her watch. "Let's meet back here in ten minutes."

Claire nodded as she headed toward the kitchen while Hope moved to the elevator. Raised voices echoed from the dining room, pulling her attention. She stepped inside to see Melanie squaring off with Maisie.

"You're nothing but a liar!" Melanie's voice trembled with anger, her finger stabbing the air accusingly. "No wonder none of your advice ever helped! Who are you, really?"

Maisie recoiled, her confident façade crumbling. "I . . . I can explain. Please, Melanie, just calm down."

"Don't tell me what to do!" Melanie snapped, her eyes blazing.

Hope swiftly stepped between them, her hands raised in a calming gesture. "Melanie, please, take a breath. I understand you're upset."

Melanie whirled on Hope, her voice sharp. "Do you? Have you drained your savings account, only to realize you've been conned?"

Hope swallowed hard, a knot forming in her stomach. She had invested more than she cared to admit, but she hadn't risked everything.

"All I wanted was to make my business successful." Melanie's voice wavered as her shoulders slumped. "Now I've got nothing. Everything she said . . . every word was a lie. Limitless Living. Just another scam, and I fell for it."

Hope's heart clenched for her. Melanie had only wanted a chance to build something for herself, to feel capable and confident. Instead, she'd been sold empty promises and lost so much in the process.

"We were all taken in," Hope said, her gaze locked onto Maisie. "It's time you gather everyone and come clean. Let them know who you really are and end this retreat now."

Maisie bit her lip, seeming to consider Hope's words, but then her expression hardened with defiance. She straightened her shoulders and met Hope's gaze with a cool stare.

"It's obvious you're not going to help me, Hope," Maisie said, her voice icy.

"What's she talking about?" Melanie turned to Hope, confusion etched on her face. "Why would you help her? Are you in on this too? Are you getting a kickback from all the suckers that signed up?"

"What? No," Hope exclaimed.

"It doesn't matter," Maisie shouted

"I refuse to let you, Hope, or Amy tear down everything I've built. I've sacrificed too much to lose it all again."

"Again?" Melanie's voice trembled with anger. "You've done this before? How many people have you conned? How many lives have you wrecked?"

Ignoring the question, Maisie strode past Hope and Melanie, her chin held high and her steps determined.

"You won't get away with this!" Melanie shouted after her. "You'll pay for everything you've done. Just wait—you'll pay!"

• • •

Just after eight p.m., Hope entered the library with Claire by her side. The room was lit, and the air was thick with unspoken anticipation. Drew sat on the sofa, engrossed in a book, while Maretta stood by the fireplace, her arms crossed and her gaze distant. At the game table, Lorna was deeply focused on a jigsaw puzzle, her brow furrowed in concentration. Melanie, who had stormed out of the dining room after her confrontation with Maisie, hadn't been seen since. Neither had Talia, as both Hope and Claire failed to find her. They crossed the room and sank onto the sofa with Drew.

Drew glanced up from his book, eyebrows raised. "Hey, where've you two been?"

"Looking for Talia," Hope replied. "The retreat is officially over."

Drew straightened, closing his book. "Wait, what? Clearly, I missed a lot. Someone catch me up."

"What on earth are you talking about, Hope?" Maretta said, uncrossing her arms as she moved to an armchair next to the sofa and sat.

"Maisie's not who she claims to be." Claire settled into the other armchair. "Hope's uncovered some . . . unsavory details."

"What details?" Lorna chimed in from the game table, her puzzle forgotten.

"The winds are kicking up," Amy announced as she burst into the room, making a beeline for the windows.

"Not now, Amy," Maretta admonished. "Hope is in the middle of telling us why the retreat is over."

"I'm not surprised, seeing as Maisie Cox is a fraud." Amy turned to face the group. "She's Demi Covington."

Drew's mouth gaped. "Are you serious?"

"Wasn't that the person you said hosted the retreat that young woman disappeared from?" Maretta asked, her voice rising with concern.

"One and the same," Amy answered.

Maretta's gaze returned to Hope. "Hope Early, what have you gotten us into this time?"

Chapter Seven

A deafening crack split the air. The room plunged into darkness, followed by the eerie silence of a world suddenly without power. Hope's breath hitched. Then came the wind, howling like a wounded animal, battering the windows with icy fury. Her pulse skittered, her nerves fraying with the sudden shift from unease to full-blown panic.

Claire's grip tightened on Hope's hand. "What the—" she whispered. "What just happened?"

Drew's voice cut through the dark. "We lost power. Let's not panic."

"Seriously?" Claire snapped. "We're trapped in a blizzard, and now we have no lights? This is *exactly* how horror movies start. And don't the stylish blonds get killed first?"

Ignoring her sister's dramatics, Hope said, "He's right. We don't need to panic—"

A sharp *crack* from outside made someone gasp. The wind continued to howl against the windows, shaking them violently.

Lorna's trembling voice broke the silence. "That sounded like a tree coming down."

"Great." Amy let out a nervous laugh. "So we're stuck *and* the trees are out to get us."

Maretta scoffed, her irritation clear. "There's a generator. Henry mentioned it earlier."

As if on cue, the lights flickered back on, casting eerie shadows along the walls.

Henry rushed into the room, his usual calm manner now tighter, more urgent.

"No need to worry," he announced. "The emergency generator kicked in. We'll have heat and light through the night. Everything should be fine until morning."

Hope slipped her hand from her sister's grip and stepped forward. "That's a relief. By morning, the roads should be cleared, and we can finally get out of here."

Henry gave a slow nod, but his expression remained grim. "There's just one problem."

Maretta folded her arms. "My town's public works team will have those roads cleared by dawn. I assure you."

"I'm sure they will," Henry said, "but the issue isn't the snow. A power line came down at the end of the driveway. It's completely blocking access. Until it's removed, no one's getting in or out."

Hope exchanged a look with Claire, a chill settling in her bones that had nothing to do with the storm.

Maretta huffed, pushing past Henry. "Then I'll call my office and get a crew out here first thing."

Henry hesitated. "That won't be possible. The phone lines are down too, and we haven't been able to get a cell signal."

Maretta halted mid-stride, eyes narrowing. "Excuse me?"

Lorna let out a shaky breath. "So . . . we're completely cut off?"

Silence settled over the room, heavier than the storm raging outside.

• • •

At eight fifteen, Hope left the library to check the dining and media rooms, and both were empty. Where had Talia disappeared to? Muttering under her breath, she made her way upstairs and knocked on Talia's door. No answer, just like earlier.

She hesitated, then glanced at the closed door across the hall. Maisie's room. Could Talia be in there?

Pivoting, she rapped her knuckles against the door. "Maisie, it's Hope. Can you open up? We need to talk." Silence. She blew out a frustrated breath. "Is Talia in there with you?"

Before she could knock again, the elevator dinged. The door slid open and Claire stepped out, taking in Hope's stance in front of Maisie's room.

"There you are! Any luck?"

Hope shook her head. "I'm running out of places to look."

"What about Kit? Seen her?"

Another head shake.

Claire sighed. "I'm sure they'll turn up. It's not like they went out into the storm. Come back downstairs. Everyone's getting hungry.

Think you could whip up something for us to nosh on?"

Hope arched a brow. "Nosh?"

Claire smirked. "Drew's word, not mine."

"Figures." Hope let out a small laugh.

"As much as I hate this whole situation, we might as well make the best of it." Claire looped her arm through Hope's and steered her toward the elevator.

Hope pressed the button for the first floor. "What about tonight having all the makings of a horror movie?"

Claire waved a hand and rolled her eyes. "Okay, maybe I was a tad dramatic."

"Really?" The elevator door whispered open when they reached the ground floor, and Hope stepped into the corridor. "After we eat, I think everyone should lock their doors for the night."

Claire frowned. "Why?"

Hope kept walking. "Because Maisie thinks someone wants to kill her, and that person could be here."

Claire's footsteps quickened behind her. "Wait, what? She actually said that? Those exact words?"

Hope entered the kitchen and yanked open the fridge. She scanned the shelves, an idea forming in her mind. A charcuterie board. It would be easy but satisfying.

"Hope! Stop menu planning and answer me. Is there a killer among us?" Claire's voice shot up a notch.

Hope glanced over her shoulder. "I don't know. But whoever wrote that note—"

"The one about dreaming of Maisie's death?"

"Yeah. It could be nothing. An empty threat."

"Or it could be real," Claire shot back. "Did Maisie say if there was an actual attempt on her life?"

"No," Hope admitted. "So we don't know for sure." She turned back to the fridge, pulling out cheese and meats. "Let's focus on what we can control. Can you grab a board and check the pantry for crackers and nuts?"

Claire exhaled sharply but did as asked. A few minutes later, they stood back, surveying the colorful, carefully arranged board.

"You know, we're sharing a room tonight." Claire popped a cube of cheddar cheese into her mouth.

Hope didn't argue. She just nodded. The idea of being alone in this lodge, with the storm howling outside and Maisie's warning hanging over them, was enough to make her agree without hesitation.

She just wished she believed that locking their door would be enough.

For a few blessed minutes, Hope forced the unsettling thoughts away and lost herself in the simple pleasure of arranging a charcuterie board that was almost too pretty to eat.

"Not bad, right? Perfect for some late-night noshing."

"Absolutely." Claire stowed a half-empty box of crackers back in a cabinet. "I can't believe how the day turned out, though. This morning, I had no idea we'd be trapped here . . . or that we'd be dealing with a not-so-reputable life coach."

"That's putting it kindly," Hope replied, filling a ramekin with olives. "I'm sorry for dragging you into this mess."

"Oh, don't be! I did my own research. Like you, I didn't pick up on the warning signs either." Claire plucked an olive from the bowl and popped it into her mouth.

After a pause, Hope wiped her hands on a towel, giving her sister a concerned look. "I wanted to ask you—maybe it's not the best time—but you seemed on edge this morning. Is everything okay?"

Claire sighed. "Sorry for snapping earlier. There's just a lot going on. Andy's been traveling more for work, the kids are full-blown teenagers now, and I somehow got roped into hosting a weekend for my sorority sisters in April." She let out a tired laugh. "Honestly, I was starting to feel better . . . until we found out Maisie was a liar and a con artist."

Hope studied her. "Are you sure that's all?" Their dynamic had shifted over the years. Claire had always been the steady one, the rock Hope could lean on. But now, with her own life in a good place, she wanted her sister to know she could be that person too, if needed.

Claire met her gaze and nodded. "I'm positive."

Hope let it go, picking up the charcuterie board, but as she began to turn her gaze drifted to the shadowy hallway at the back of the kitchen. It wasn't the pantry because she'd seen Claire retrieve crackers and nuts from the door across from the fridge. Maybe it led to a laundry room or Henry's private quarters. Older estates often had tucked-away servant quarters or hidden spaces, and it wouldn't be surprising if Henry had carved out a sanctuary for himself back there.

A chill prickled at the back of her neck.

"Come on," Claire said, nudging her toward the door. "We don't want Drew to waste away. Talk about dramatics!"

Hope snapped back to the moment. "What?"

"Were you even listening?" Claire tilted her head toward the hallway Hope had been staring at. "What's down there?"

"Good question." Hope set the charcuterie board down on the counter. "I think it's time to find out. And maybe I'll figure out what Maisie had Austin looking for." She turned and headed toward the doorway, curiosity pushing her forward.

"Maybe we'll find our three missing people," Claire quipped.

Hope stepped into the dim corridor, her fingers trailing along the wall until they found a switch. She flicked it on, and an overhead fixture buzzed to life, casting a muted glow over the narrow hallway. The black-and-white tiled floor stretched ahead like a checkerboard, each of Hope's steps sending a soft echo into the quiet.

She had just reached the first door on the left when Claire's soft footsteps sounded behind her. A firm hand clasped her shoulder.

"What are you doing? We shouldn't be here," Claire whispered.

"Maybe not, but you were right, we *are* looking for Talia, Maisie and Kit."

"I wasn't serious," Claire hissed. "If we get caught, don't blame me."

"We're just going to take a quick look. I think this is Henry's room." Hope wrapped her fingers around the doorknob and twisted. She half expected it to be locked, but the latch gave way easily. "He really should have locked this."

"Hope, we really *shouldn't* go in. If this is his room, we're invading his privacy."

"Austin wasn't concerned about that. And I need to know why." Hope nudged the door open and stepped inside. She found the light switch, and light filled the room, revealing small sitting area with a plush sofa, a small television, and a modest desk.

She moved farther in, taking in the details. The space wasn't ransacked, but something felt . . . off. It was as if Henry had left in a hurry, abandoning half-finished tasks. Papers teetered on the otherwise tidy desk, a single brochure peeking out from beneath the disarray.

Hope slid the papers aside, her breath catching as she read the bold lettering on the brochure: *Colbert Inn, Vermont.* A chill prickled her skin. She knew that name. It was the same inn where Penny Foster had vanished, the very place that had come up in her conversation with Amy over dinner.

Why did Henry have this?

She rifled through the scattered papers and a leather-bound journal caught her eye. The cover was well-worn and the pages filled with precise but hurried handwriting. Henry's? Perhaps. Flipping through, she found scattered notes on various guests, but one cryptic entry stood out:

Must stay alert. Not everyone is who they claim to be.

Claire leaned in over her shoulder, her voice barely above a whisper. "What does that mean?"

"I don't know," Hope murmured, scanning the desk again. More notes lay beneath the brochure—names and dates, some circled in red. A sense of unease tightened in her chest. She was about to point them out when a sound in the hall made her freeze.

A shadow flickered across the doorway. Footsteps approached.

"Someone's coming," Claire said, eyes wide.

Hope shoved the journal back onto the desk, but before she could make everything look undisturbed, Henry stormed in.

His gaze zeroed in on the brochure still clutched in her hand. In a flash, he snatched it away. "What do you think you're doing?" His voice was low, tight with anger. "Going through my things? What kind of guest does that?"

Hope held her ground. "Why do you have a brochure for the Colbert Inn?" She gestured toward the journal. "And this note. You *knew* Maisie wasn't who she claimed to be, didn't you?"

Henry's expression flickered. Guilt? Panic? But in an instant, it was gone. He tossed the brochure onto the desk and snapped the journal shut with a sharp *thud*.

"She's not the only one hiding things around here," he said coldly. "I thought you were a food blogger, not a darn snoop."

Claire crossed her arms. "You clearly don't know my sister. She's *very* curious."

Hope shot Claire a look before turning back to Henry. "I know Austin came in here and went through your things. I think Maisie sent him in for a reason. She had another name when she ran that retreat at the Colbert Inn, the same place where a young woman went missing. Were you there then? If Maisie believes you know something, it's no wonder she wants to find out what. So tell me, Henry, what do you know?"

For a moment, his mask slipped. His gaze darkened with something close to regret, his posture stiff with hesitation.

Then, just as quickly, the hardness returned.

He stalked to the door, yanked it fully open, and gestured for them to leave. "I suggest you both stay in your rooms until morning." His voice was like ice. "You're leaving then, *both of you*."

• • •

By ten o'clock, Hope was back in the library, curled into the corner of the sofa, though relaxation was a tall order after the night's events. She traced the edge of her glass with a fingertip, her mind replaying the confrontation with Henry.

Across from her, Drew and Amy sat hunched over a checkerboard, their game muted by exhaustion. They exchanged the occasional jab between quiet bites from the charcuterie board, the steady clack of checkers against wood the only real sign of movement in the room.

Claire had spent the better part of an hour pacing before finally sinking into a chair by the fireplace, arms crossed, gaze distant. Whatever was running through her mind, she wasn't sharing.

Maretta sat nearby, a novel open on her lap. Yet, every so often, her brow furrowed and her eyes lifted from the page, as if she were reading something far more troubling between the lines of their evening.

If not for the weight of the lies and secrets pressing down on all of them, the moment would've felt almost homey—the steady embers, the smell of well-loved books, and the remnants of their late-night snack. But beneath it all, the tension lingered, unshakable.

Lorna entered, her gaze sweeping the room before she settled onto the sofa beside Hope. Without the heavy eyeliner, her freshly washed face looked younger, though fatigue lingered in her eyes. A headband kept her hair off her face, and she pulled her legs beneath her, tucking into herself like she was trying to ward off a chill.

"My room's freezing," she murmured, wrapping her arms around herself. "I was looking for Henry, but he's nowhere to be found."

Hope resisted the urge to mention where she'd last seen Henry, deciding it was best to keep her earlier snooping under wraps. Instead, she kept her tone light. "Seems like a few people have gone missing tonight. Have you seen Talia or Maisie since dinner?"

Lorna shook her head. "No, and I haven't seen Kit either."

Hope frowned. "It's strange, isn't it? It's not like we're in a massive resort. People shouldn't just disappear."

Claire gave a mock shudder. "It's exactly what happens in horror movies."

Hope sighed. "You're not seriously going there again."

Claire lifted her hands. "I'm just saying."

Hope made the decision to do another sweep of the lodge. But first, she needed answers to a question that had been bothering her since the start. She turned back to Lorna. "How do you and Talia know each other?"

Lorna's expression remained neutral, but something flickered in her eyes. Wariness, maybe?

"She's a part of Maisie's team," Lorna said.

"I got the sense earlier that there was a connection between you two."

"A connection?" Lorna shook her head. "I'm not sure what you sensed but I think everyone's imagination is on overdrive tonight."

Hope let the silence stretch, watching Lorna carefully. She wasn't convinced she'd gotten the whole truth, but it had only been a fleeting look, hardly solid proof. Maybe Lorna was right. Still, the friction between her and Maisie during the "Unmasking Your True Self" session was harder to ignore.

"If you're hungry, I put together a charcuterie board," Hope said, gesturing to the tray on the coffee table. She picked up her own plate and leaned back into the sofa. "So, what brought you to the retreat? Are you starting a business? Expanding one?" If they could find common ground, she might finally get the answers she sought.

Lorna hesitated before answering, as if choosing her words carefully. "Maybe someday. Right now, I'm just . . . figuring things out." She toyed with the edge of her sleeve. "Maisie would call it a journey of self-discovery."

"Do you think Maisie actually helped? Even with her past coming to light?" Hope asked.

A pause. Lorna's lips pressed together, before she finally said, "Maisie is . . . complicated."

"That's one way to put it." Hope set down her plate. "You know, earlier it seemed like there was some tension between you two. Did you know her as Demi Covington? Is that why you pushed back on her 'authenticity' speech?"

Lorna stiffened, her expression hardening slightly as she looked away. "You misunderstood, again," she replied. "Maisie and I don't have any history. Whatever you think you felt or saw . . . it's not real."

Hope held her gaze, sensing Lorna's defensiveness. "I didn't mean to imply anything, Lorna. I just thought maybe you'd known each other before. Sometimes, events like this retreat bring people together in surprising ways."

"You seem to observe a lot, don't you? Well, I hate to be the one to tell you that you should get your eyes checked." She stood. "Maisie and I don't have any history."

She strode out of the library, leaving Hope staring after her, more convinced than ever that Lorna was hiding something.

"Looks like she's not Maisie's biggest fan," Drew remarked as he flopped onto the sofa beside Hope, stretching his arms out along the back.

"Can't blame her," Maretta muttered, barely glancing up from her book. "She doesn't seem to be a fan of yours either, Hope."

Hope resisted rolling her eyes; there were bigger things to worry about than Maretta's barbs. "You're right, Drew. And I'm determined to find out why."

Maretta closed her book. "Just how do you intend to do that? She made it clear she didn't want to talk to you."

Hope pressed her lips together, sighing inwardly. She hated it when Maretta was right. "I'll figure something out."

Drew said, "I have to say, this isn't the story I pitched to my editor. I thought I'd be writing about self-discovery and 'limitless living'—but this? This is way juicier."

"Hold on!" Amy called from the game table. "Maisie's a part of my podcast series. I've been working on Penny Foster's story for weeks. You're not going to swoop in and steal this."

"I'm not 'swooping in,' Amy." Drew pulled his arms from the back of the sofa and folded them. "My editor expects a real story when we get out of here. After everything that's come out, I can't just hand in a fluff piece about a life coach's retreat."

Amy's cheeks puffed out as she shot back, "Oh, no, Drew Adams. You're not hijacking my podcast. I've put my heart into this. These bags under my eyes are from weeks of late-night research!"

Claire shifted in her chair. "Drew, she has a point. This was her story first, and without her none of us would know Maisie's real story."

Before the tension could boil over, Hope suggested, "What about a collaboration? The *Gazette* and Amy's podcast, covering the story together."

Drew and Amy exchanged glances, weighing the idea. Finally, Drew uncrossed his arms and nodded. "Actually . . . that could work. My editor's always looking for ways to boost readership, and a multimedia angle might just sell."

Amy's expression brightened. "A podcast-newspaper crossover could be huge for my show. We'd both benefit, right? It's worth a shot."

Hope exhaled in relief. "Perfect. You two can hash out the details while I track down Talia and Maisie. I still have questions for them." Deep down, she wasn't convinced Talia hadn't known Maisie's real identity. And if Talia had, then perhaps Lorna did too—especially if their connection predated the retreat.

"Bring her back when you do," Amy called after her. "We both want to hear what she has to say."

• • •

Hope navigated the silent corridors of the lodge, her eyes sweeping every shadowed corner for any sign of Maisie. Beyond the windows, the storm howled, wind rattling the panes—a relentless reminder that no one would willingly venture outside. That meant Maisie was still here. So were the others.

Talia. Kit. Henry. Melanie. Even Austin.

A tight coil of unease wound in her gut. It wasn't just Maisie's absence that set her on edge, it was the growing sense that the answers she needed were slipping further away with every empty hallway she passed.

Stop. Focus, Hope. Focus.

Kit was likely nursing her wounded pride after being fired. Henry could be tending to some lodge task—maybe checking on the generator, which, unfortunately, was outside.

That accounted for two people.

Which left four.

Maisie, Talia, Melanie, and Austin.

And still, no sign of any of them.

Then it hit her—Melanie and Lorna had spent time in the sauna earlier. What if that's where Maisie and Talia had gone? Hope pivoted, her pulse kicking up as she hurried toward the spa area. The sauna wasn't the most private spot for a secret conversation, but with the retreat buzzing with activity, maybe they thought it was their best chance to talk without interruption.

Or maybe they hadn't gone there willingly.

She made her way to the basement. The narrow staircase felt steeper as the cold from the stone walls pressed in on her. As she reached the dimly lit corridor, her gaze locked onto the sauna door at the far end. A faint glow slipped through the crack beneath it. But something was wrong.

Her breath caught as she took in the sight of the bench wedged beneath the sauna door's handle.

Someone had blocked it.

A stab of alarm pierced her, spurring her into motion. She closed the distance in a few quick strides, her pulse hammering in her ears. Bracing herself, she crouched, fingers fumbling as she yanked the bench away. Her hands shook as she straightened, grasped the door handle, and flung it open. A blast of scorching air erupted from within, slamming into her with suffocating force. She gasped, instinctively raising an arm to shield her face as the blistering heat seared her skin and clawed at her lungs, making it hard to breathe. A wave of dizziness washed over her, but she forced herself to steady, to focus on what—or who—was inside.

Maisie was slumped against the cedar bench. Her dark hair, pulled back into a ponytail, had come loose, stray strands clinging to her damp forehead. A thin cotton robe hung limply over her frame, the fabric darkened with sweat. Her skin was ghostly pale, her body unnervingly still, her eyes closed.

A bolt of panic shot through Hope as she lurched forward, her voice catching as she called Maisie's name. The suffocating heat pressed in, but the deeper silence was worse. Dread twisted in her gut as she reached out, her fingers trembling as they sought a pulse at Maisie's neck.

Nothing.

Hope's breath hitched as the truth crashed over her. Maisie was gone.

She staggered back, the room tilting as her mind struggled to catch up. A shaky inhale did little to steady her as she turned toward the empty hallway, as if expecting someone—anyone—to appear and make sense of what she'd just found. But there was no one. Just the oppressive heat, the deafening silence, and the chilling realization that she was now at the center of something far more dangerous than she'd ever imagined.

Chapter Eight

Hope stood in the outer room of the sauna, her pulse still hammering from the discovery. The air was thick with lingering heat, but a deep chill crawled through her limbs. Across the room, Drew paced, his movements sharp with agitation.

She barely remembered grabbing his arm upstairs, barely registered how breathless she'd been when she'd mumbled "found Maisie," barely recalled her return to the basement. Now, watching him run a hand through his hair, the reality of it all pressed down harder.

"Murdered?" Drew's voice was tight, disbelieving. "Are we sure? Maybe she just . . . dozed off, or took a sleeping pill with a glass of wine?"

Hope shook her head, pointing to the sauna. "There's no wine glass or pill bottle. Someone wedged a bench under the door handle. I had to move it to get in. Someone trapped her in there."

Drew exhaled sharply, dragging a hand through his hair. "So, what now? The roads are shut down, a power line's across the driveway—we're stuck here. *With a killer.*"

"A killer?"

Drew and Hope turned as Claire hurried down the staircase, a crease formed between her brows, her posture tense with worry.

"It's Maisie," Hope said.

"She's dead," Drew finished grimly.

"What?" Claire's gaze snapped to the sauna door. "That can't be possible!"

"Claire, trust me, you don't want to see her." Hope reached for her sister, and steered her back from the sauna's entry. "Let's step back and figure out what to do next."

As the sign at the sauna entrance indicated, this was the relaxation room, though its current atmosphere was anything but soothing. A narrow shelf held stacks of neatly folded towels, slippers, and robes. The seating area was empty, its bench now shoved aside and its cushion tossed near the wall hooks.

"We need to preserve the scene as much as possible for the police." Drew paced. "Hope, you already touched the doorknob and moved the bench."

"The bench? Why?" Claire echoed.

"It was wedged against the doorknob from the outside. Someone didn't want her getting out." Hope let the grim truth settle between them.

Claire swallowed hard, her gaze flicking between them. "That's . . . horrific."

"Indeed it is," Drew agreed. "We need a plan to get through the night, at least until we can reach the outside world."

Hope took a steadying breath. "First, we need to secure this area. No one should go near the sauna. Then we should gather everyone in the library and tell them what's happened."

Drew frowned. "Are you saying we should all camp out in the library? I don't love the idea of being stuck in a room with a potential killer."

Claire crossed her arms. "You'd rather be alone in your room with a murderer on the loose?"

"You're telling me you're not worried about that?" Drew asked.

Claire hesitated, then let out a sharp breath. "Actually, Hope and I already decided to share her room tonight."

Drew huffed. "And what about me?"

Hope smirked. "You can stay with us."

That earned a grateful smile from him.

"Okay," she continued, "let's go upstairs, find everyone, and make sure no one disturbs this area."

They hurried upstairs and into the library, where Maretta and Amy remained. At some point, Melanie had joined them and now sat across from Maretta, idly flipping through a magazine.

Maretta's fingers hovered over the charcuterie board, a cheese knife poised just above it. Her sharp gaze flicked up, her eyes narrowing as she took in the group.

"Where on earth have you all been?" she demanded, her tone cutting through the silence like the blade in her hand, more accusation than question.

"I'll get Lorna and see if I can track down Talia," Drew said, already heading for the door.

Amy's gaze followed him. "Why is he acting so weird? Something happened, didn't it?"

Melanie set down the magazine, her expression shifting to genuine concern. "Whatever it is, I can't imagine tonight getting any worse."

"You would think," Claire muttered under her breath, drawing a stern look from Hope.

Hope inhaled deeply, attempting to center herself. Her thoughts tumbled over one another, firing off in rapid succession. She needed to push through the chaos and stay focused because clarity and calm were her best allies tonight.

She leveled a look at Melanie and asked, "Where have you been?"

"In my room, of course," Melanie replied.

Hope hesitated a moment before saying, "There's something you all need to know. I found Maisie—"

"Well, finally," Maretta interrupted. "I hope she plans to give us an explanation and a refund for this ghastly weekend."

"She won't be doing that," Claire murmured.

Before anyone could respond, Kit appeared in the library, looking exhausted. "It's not my place to say anymore since I've been fired, but I suggest everyone call it a night."

"Kit! We've been looking for you." Hope crossed the library, weaving between the armchairs. "Where have you been?"

Kit fiddled with the cuff of her sleeve. "I needed a break after the blow-up with Henry, so I went to the wine cellar. It's quiet down there and there was a bottle of Bordeaux I've been dying to try. It's not like he can fire me since he already has."

Hope's stomach gave a jolt. The wine cellar was in the basement, not far from the sauna. Her pulse hammered. "Did you see anyone else down there?"

"Did you see anyone else down there?"

Kit shrugged. "Not when I went down there or when I finally left the wine cellar. Why?"

"What about Talia?" Hope pressed. "Have you seen her?"

Kit shook her head. "I've no idea where she is, and honestly, it's not my job anymore to worry about guests. If you all want to stay here, that's fine, I guess. But I would like to know what's going on."

Before Hope could tell Kit the news, Drew swept into the library, urgency in his step and triumph written across his grin.

"I found them," he declared, his voice urgent, stepping aside for Lorna to enter. She shuffled in reluctantly, her robe cinched tightly around her waist.

"Is this really necessary?" Lorna muttered, her gaze avoiding the others. "I was in bed."

Lagging behind them was Talia, who was dressed in a two-piece lounge set, and her annoyance was evident. "I finally get a little peace and quiet, and then this guy"—she jabbed a thumb toward Drew—"starts banging on my door. I had to deal with a freaking-out Maisie after dinner, and now I can't even sleep."

Drew's face remained grim. "You'll understand soon enough."

Hope rose to meet them. "Thanks for bringing them, Drew."

"So this was your idea?" Lorna snapped, her tone sharp. "What's your problem?"

Hope ignored the hostility, her voice softening as she said, "There's something everyone needs to know."

"What is it?" Lorna asked.

Hope hesitated before saying, "It's Maisie. She's dead."

Kit's hand flew to her mouth as she gasped, her eyes widening in what seemed like genuine shock.

Lorna froze, her face blank with shock. A trembling breath escaped her lips. "What?" she whispered. "No . . . no, that can't be true."

"I'm sorry," Hope said, stepping closer. "We found her in the sauna."

Lorna staggered, then gripped the back of a chair for support. "We weren't close, but . . . she still . . . how could this happen?" Tears filled her eyes as she sank into the chair.

"It wasn't an accident," Drew said. "Maisie was murdered."

Maretta bolted up from the sofa and surged forward. "There's a dead woman in the sauna?" Her glare pinned on Hope like a spotlight and her finger wagged accusatorially. "And yet again, you've managed to entangle yourself in the incident."

Hope sighed but kept her composure. "Trust me, I didn't go looking for it."

She wasn't surprised by Maretta's remark; the woman had a habit of blaming her for every murder that occurred. But Hope knew better than to waste energy defending herself to Maretta.

"What am I going to do now?" Talia crossed the room to the fireplace. She stretched out her arms, her hands gripping the mantel. "This can't be happening to me."

"What do you mean by that?" Hope asked the assistant.

Talia pulled back from the mantel and swung around, crossing her arms defensively. "What do you think? She was my boss! I needed Maisie, okay? This is going to ruin me, my career, my reputation. Who's going to hire me now?"

"Because she's been murdered?" Claire asked.

"No, of course not. Because of that one's podcast." Talia pointed at Amy. "Everything about Maisie will be revealed, and I'll be hung out to dry! Everyone will think I knew all about her past."

"You're telling us you didn't?" Amy asked.

Talia's eyes narrowed. "Don't you dare. I worked too hard for all this to fall apart because of her, or you."

"Can we please focus on the fact that Maisie is dead?" Maretta said. "Hope, how are you so certain that she was murdered?"

"That's enough." Drew stepped between them. "Right now, we need to focus on keeping everyone safe and figuring out what to do next. I'm open to ideas."

Before Hope could respond, Melanie's voice rang out from across the room. "Hey! Look outside! There are flashing lights coming this way!"

The group rushed to the window. Through the frost-covered glass, they saw a line of strobe lights slicing through the darkness, winding up the driveway toward the lodge.

As the vehicles drew closer, a wave of relief crashed over Hope. They were finally getting out of this ordeal. Then she spotted the vehicle trailing the police car, and her breath hitched. Her vision blurred with unshed tears.

"Ethan's here."

Without hesitation, Hope spun on her heel and charged from the library, footsteps pounding behind her as the others followed. She reached the lobby just as the front door swung open, letting in a blast of frigid air and swirling snow. Ethan stepped inside, his tall frame dusted with snow, followed by a uniformed officer Hope instantly recognized as Officer Roberts. Confident and efficient, he'd manage the situation now.

Hope took one look at Ethan and broke away from the group, rushing forward and throwing herself into his waiting arms. He caught her with steady hands, pulling her against his snow-covered jacket. His hold was solid, grounding, and she clung to him as if letting go would shatter her.

"It's so good to see you, babe," he murmured, his lips brushing her ear. "I'm sorry it took so long."

Hope shook her head, her voice trembling. "It's okay. The storm's awful. We're just . . . so relieved you're here. You and Officer Roberts." She swallowed hard, forcing herself to let go of him and step back. "Something terrible has happened. There's been a murder."

Maretta shoved her way to the front. With a none-too-gentle nudge, she edged Hope aside and planted herself in front of the newcomers. "You heard her—a murder! The body's downstairs in the sauna."

Drew stepped forward, his expression taut. "We haven't been able to find Henry Greenway, the lodge owner, or Austin, who works for Maisie. But everyone else is accounted for."

A hum of agreement rippled through the group.

Ethan's gaze locked onto Hope, his forehead creased. "What have you gotten yourself into this time?"

Hope exhaled, already bracing for the inevitable lecture. "I know, I know. You can say 'I told you so' later about this retreat being a bad idea. Right now, you and Officer Roberts need to get to the sauna. Maisie Cox is still there exactly where I found her."

"Maisie Cox?" Officer Roberts asked, flipping open his notepad. "Who is she?"

"The retreat host," Amy answered. "But her real name is Elaine Thompson. Or, as most people knew her, Demi Covington."

Ethan's posture stiffened. "Demi Covington? The life coach connected to the retreat where Penny Foster disappeared?"

Amy gave a grim nod.

"We all found out once Amy got here," Hope explained. She then recounted the evening's events from Maisie's sudden disappearance after dinner to the discovery of her body and everything in between. Officer Roberts's pen moved swiftly across his notepad, recording each detail.

"If you made it up the driveway, that means the driveway is cleared enough for us to leave, right?" Melanie asked, her voice tinged with hope. As she shifted, Lorna emerged from behind her, standing stiffly, as if unsure whether she belonged.

"I don't want to spend another second in this place," Lorna said, her voice tight with unease. "Please tell me we can leave."

Officer Roberts straightened, his tone assertive. "No one is leaving until we've secured the crime scene and taken statements. After that, you'll be free to go."

A ripple of murmured relief passed through the group.

"How long will that take?" Amy asked.

"As long as necessary, Ms. Phelan." His expression was apologetic, but his demeanor shifted to all-business when he turned to Hope. "Let's start with you, Ms. Early."

Drew leaned in slightly, his voice dry. "Guess he wants to kick things off with a seasoned pro."

• • •

Once Hope finished recounting the day's events to Officer Roberts as succinctly as possible, he radioed the dispatcher, requesting additional units, an ambulance, and a detective on scene. Then, with a sharp nod, he set off toward the sauna, his flashlight cutting through the dim corridor as he muttered about finding Henry and Austin.

Ethan remained behind with Hope and the others as they lingered in the lobby, their anxious voices rising in restless murmurs until he stepped in.

"I know you all want to leave," he said, his tone leaving no room for debate. "But Officer Roberts has a protocol to follow. He told each of you to return to your rooms. That means no wandering and no discussing the situation with each other."

Claire folded her arms. "I don't want to be alone. There's a killer on the loose."

"She's right," Melanie added, her voice tight with worry. "The cop is down in the basement and we'll be up in our rooms alone."

"I'll escort everyone upstairs and stay in the hall until more officers arrive," Ethan assured them. "You'll be safe."

Hope already felt safe the moment Ethan walked through the door. She'd faced her fair share of dangerous situations and managed to escape but having him here grounded her in a way she hadn't realized she needed.

"I think that will help all of us feel a little more at ease," Drew said, stepping toward the elevator with Amy at his side. Without a word, Maretta turned and followed.

"I won't feel safe until I'm home," Melanie muttered, marching ahead as well.

Lorna hesitated, then fell in line. When the elevator door slid open, they all stepped inside. The ride up to the second floor was silent, the weight of the evening pressing down on them. Once they exited, each retreated to their respective room without a word.

Once inside her room, Hope sagged against the door, releasing a slow breath as the weight of the evening lifted—just enough to remind her how utterly drained she was. Ethan lingered at the threshold, his stance solid.

"I'll be right here. No one's getting past me."

Hope nodded absently, her mind already shifting to the next task. Like everyone else, she wanted to be ready to leave as soon as possible. Grabbing her suitcase, she began packing with swift, purposeful movements.

"This doesn't feel real," she murmured, unzipping an inner compartment of her bag. "Why would Maisie go to the sauna?"

"To relax?" Ethan offered.

Hope shrugged. "Maybe. The night did take a downward turn. Her lies were exposed, and her world was crashing down around her."

"I'm sorry the retreat didn't turn out the way you expected."

"Me too." She exhaled, her thoughts circling back to the crime. "Do you think she was already dead when she was put in the sauna? Maybe knocked out and dragged in? Or did the killer confront her inside?" A realization gripped her. "If she was already dead, why jam the bench under the doorknob?" Her breath hitched. "Because she was alive . . ." Her voice faltered. It took a second before she could continue. "The medical examiner will be able to determine that, right?"

Ethan's expression darkened. "The Jefferson Police will investigate every angle."

"I'm sure they will. And I suppose Sam will get the case."

Detective Sam Reid always seemed to end up leading the investigations she found herself tangled in. At first, he'd bristled at her involvement. An amateur sleuth sticking her nose where it didn't belong. But over time, he'd come to appreciate her instincts and the way she got people to open up, sometimes uncovering leads he wouldn't have found otherwise.

Ethan smirked. "Whoever's on call gets assigned. But you and Sam seem to have a . . . productive arrangement."

"We do, actually." Hope reached for a folded sweater, but as her gaze flicked to the bedside table, she froze.

Her notebook lay open.

She was certain it was closed when she dropped it off when she was searching for Maisie. In fact, she'd tucked it beneath another book on the desk before heading downstairs.

The hairs on her neck stood on end as she moved nearer. She picked up the notebook and flipped through the pages. She scanned her notes, observations about Maisie, the retreat, and the tension that had pulsed since she'd arrived.

But beneath her neat handwriting, a new line had appeared.

The jagged, unfamiliar script cut across the page like a warning carved in stone:

You won't have limitless living if you keep asking questions.

Hope sucked in a sharp breath, the notebook slipping from her fingers and landing on the desk with a dull thud. "Ethan," she said, her voice low, urgent.

"What is it?"

She pointed to the desk, her hand unsteady. "Someone was in my room."

"Housekeeping?"

"No." Her pulse pounded. "I don't think it was housekeeping because someone wrote this." She gestured to the notebook, the ominous message glaring at her.

Ethan crossed the room in two swift strides, his expression darkening as he picked up the notebook. His jaw tightened. "When did this happen?"

"I don't know. Sometime between after dinner and now."

Ethan snapped the notebook shut, his gaze sweeping the room, body coiled with tension. "Don't touch anything else. Stay here," he ordered.

Hope nodded, her skin prickling. Someone had been there. Had rifled through her belongings. Had left her a message.

A warning.

Chapter Nine

Sunday morning, Hope woke in her own bed, the familiar surroundings a relief after the chaos of the lodge. It had been a long, grueling night. She and Ethan hadn't gotten home until just before five in the morning, delayed by hours of statements and dropping off Claire and Drew at their homes. Ethan had taken the wheel of her Explorer, promising to get a ride back to the lodge later to retrieve his truck. Despite having grown up navigating the winding roads of this part of the state, Hope was grateful Ethan drove. Exhaustion had hit her hard, and the icy, snow-covered roads had been treacherous.

Hope glanced at the alarm clock on her nightstand and sighed. Three hours of sleep weren't nearly enough to shake the fatigue weighing her down, but the day ahead wouldn't wait. Stretching her arms above her head, she stifled a yawn, already thinking about the chores waiting in the chicken coop. Every morning, she fed the hens, refreshed their water, and let them roam freely across her three acres if they chose to.

Before she could lower her arms, Bigelow sprang onto the bed, planting a slobbery kiss squarely on her cheek. Her pup had been fast asleep when she arrived home but sprang to life the moment he'd sensed her presence, erupting into an excited frenzy. It took several minutes to settle him down, giving her just enough time to exchange a quick farewell with Mitzi, her kindhearted neighbor across the street, who had watched over Molly and Becca while Ethan had rushed off to rescue Hope from the lodge.

On the drive home, Ethan admitted he'd been worried about her ever since she left for the retreat. But after dinner, the girls spiked fevers, and caring for them took all his attention until he got them tucked into bed. By that time, the storm had worsened, and she hadn't responded to his messages. When he discovered the lodge's landline was dead, his worry sharpened into urgency. A quick call to a friend in the police department confirmed his fear—a power line had gone down near the lodge. That was all he needed to know. Sitting at home, doing nothing, was no longer an option.

Gratitude bubbled up in Hope. How had she gotten so lucky to have him in her life? The bedroom door creaked open pulling her from her thoughts and Ethan entered, carrying a large mug of steaming coffee. The rich aroma filled the air, instantly perking her up. She nudged Bigelow aside and rearranged the pillows behind her to sit upright. Her bed was her sanctuary, with its plush linens, cloud-like pillows, and a down comforter she cherished but worried about when Bigelow strayed from the fleece blanket she'd designated for him.

Ethan leaned down and kissed her forehead. "It was a rough night," he murmured, scooting Bigelow out of the way and settling onto the bed, wrapping an arm around her shoulders.

"Tell me about it." Hope took another sip of coffee. "You must be wiped out too. Your night was just as long as mine."

"All I had to deal with was a moody Bigelow, two sick girls, and a blizzard," he said and chuckled.

"Was Bigelow really sad I was gone? What about Princess?" Hope glanced around for her fluffy white cat but didn't see her.

"What do you think?" Ethan grinned. "As long as she got fed, she couldn't care less."

Hope smiled. "Sounds about right." She returned to her coffee as her mind replayed the events of the past twenty-four hours. What had started as a promising retreat, intended to help her prepare for the next phase of her career as a published cookbook author, had spiraled into a deadly nightmare. To make matters worse, the killer had left her a chilling warning. When the notebook was turned over to Officer Roberts, she had no doubt Detective Sam Reid would be next to examine it. And like Ethan, his reaction would likely shift from concern to frustration as he read the ominous warning scrawled beneath her notes.

She had seen the emotions play out on Ethan's face—anger, worry, then exasperation—as he flipped through the pages, taking in her careful documentation of Maisie, the retreat, and the simmering tensions among the attendees. Instead of the self-reflection one might expect, she had chronicled her suspicions. To his credit, Ethan hadn't lectured her. He'd simply closed the notebook and handed it over to Officer Roberts, though the tightness in his jaw spoke volumes.

"As much as I'd love to stay here all day, I should probably head out to the chicken coop." Hope set her mug on the nightstand and snuggled deeper into Ethan's arms, savoring the warmth for just a few more moments before facing the cold air and deep snow outside.

"Not today," Ethan murmured, pulling her closer. "I took care of the chickens already. I think they're staying inside today anyway. I also cleared the paths to the coop, the garage, and the barn."

Hope blinked in surprise. "Wait, you did all that already? Did you get any sleep?"

Ethan shrugged casually. "I'll nap later. But first, I need to take the girls to Heather's place. She wants to take care of them until they're feeling better."

"Of course," Hope said, her tone softening. Her relationship with Ethan's ex-wife had improved significantly since Christmas. They'd spent New Year's Eve together and even gone on a day ski trip recently. Blended families came with their challenges, but she was determined to make things work for the girls' sake. "Are you planning to take the Explorer?"

"Is that okay?" Ethan asked, climbing out of bed. "I'll grab my truck later."

"Or I could pick it up for you," Hope offered, noticing the skeptical look on his face. "I've driven it before, remember? And the roads have probably been cleared by now."

"What are you up to?" he asked, his eyes narrowing suspiciously.

"Nothing," she said, flashing a sheepish smile. "Just trying to save you an extra trip." She didn't add that it would also give her a chance to visit the lodge again, maybe even track down Henry, who had been suspiciously missing when she left.

Ethan smirked. "You know, I *want* to believe you." Before he could say more, his phone buzzed. He grabbed it from its case on his belt and answered, his expression quickly growing serious. He listened intently, nodding and replying with the occasional "okay," while Hope practically vibrated with impatience.

Finally, he hung up. "That was Sam."

Hope threw back the covers and jumped out of bed. "Does he have an update on Maisie's murder?"

Ethan nodded solemnly. "After we left the lodge, they found Henry."

"Good!" Hope said, slipping into her oversized fuzzy robe. It was perfect for fending off the bedroom's chill, especially since the second floor was still waiting for its long-overdue renovation. "What did Sam say? Did Henry confess to killing Maisie?" She lifted her mug from the nightstand.

Ethan shook his head as he slid his phone back into its case. "He's in a coma."

Her coffee mug paused halfway to her lips. "A coma? What happened? Did someone try to kill him?"

"The investigation is ongoing." Ethan stepped closer, resting his hands lightly on her arms. "Let's not jump to conclusions."

She arched a brow. "I don't do that. Where did they find him?"

"Outside in the snow. Unconscious." He checked his watch, his expression tightening. "I've got to go, Heather's expecting us." Leaning in, he pressed a quick kiss to her cheek before heading for the door. "And don't forget your appointment with Sam to sign your statement."

His footsteps echoed down the hall, growing fainter until the house fell silent.

Hope sipped her coffee, her mind turning over Ethan's words.

Outside in the snow. Unconscious. Coma.

Sliding on her plush slippers, she tapped her thigh to summon Bigelow, who leapt off the bed and followed her out of the bedroom. "Why was he outside? How did he end up unconscious in the snow?" She had no answers, but one thing was clear: whatever happened to Henry had to be tied to Maisie's death. It couldn't be a coincidence.

• • •

Downstairs, Hope stood at the counter, the oven's heat already softening the morning chill as she sifted flour into a mixing bowl for a batch of cinnamon muffins.

The gentle melody of her favorite morning playlist blended with the rustling of Bigelow shifting in his bed in the family room. Now with his belly full of breakfast, he let out a contented sigh, resting his head on his paws.

She topped off her coffee and took a sip, glancing out the dining area windows. The snow from last night's storm lay untouched, a pristine blanket covering the patio and beyond. Everything looked peaceful now, but her thoughts churned with the events at the lodge.

She returned to her batter. The rhythm of her whisk slowed as her mind drifted back to Henry. Unconscious in the snow. Now in a coma. She wondered why he had gone outside. Had he gone out to the generator, or had someone been chasing him, or had he been trying to escape? And how did it all tie back to Maisie?

Hope set the bowl down and sprinkled cinnamon into the dry mix, the motion usually meditative, but today it failed to quiet her mind. A soft thud from the family room pulled her back to the present. She turned to find Bigelow watching her, ears perked, sensing her unease.

Hope smiled and wiped her hands on a dish towel. "You always know when something's on my mind, don't you?" she murmured. "I think it's time I figure out what's really going on."

She grabbed her phone and sent a text to Drew: *I need a ride to the lodge to pick up Ethan's truck. Interested in going?*

While waiting for a reply, she retrieved a muffin tin, lined it with paper cups, and divided the batter among them. Just as she scraped out the last bit, the oven beeped. Perfect timing. She slid the muffins in and set the timer.

As she rinsed out the mixing bowl, her mind rewound to her arrival at the lodge, then fast-forwarded through the chaos that followed until she remembered the ominous *Release* form she'd stuffed into her jeans pocket. Amid discovering Maisie's body and her escape from the lodge, she'd forgotten all about it.

Where was it?

"It has to be in my pocket."

She shut off the faucet and hurried upstairs to the laundry basket. Bigelow, jolted by her sudden movement, grabbed his tennis ball and bounded after her, tail wagging, convinced they were playing.

Hope zeroed in on the basket, dropped to her knees, and dug through yesterday's clothes looking for her jeans. Princess, her fluffy white cat, had been dozing on top, nestled contentedly. She lifted her head, emerald eyes narrowing in displeasure at the disturbance.

Hope barely noticed. She shoved aside shirts, searching for the jeans.

Bigelow nudged her arm, dropping the soggy tennis ball at her feet.

"Not now," she muttered, her pulse quickening as she tossed aside another sweater. *Please, please, be here.*

Finally, her fingers closed around denim. As she yanked the jeans free, Princess leaped to the floor with an indignant mewl. Hope plunged her hand into the pocket and exhaled when her fingers brushed against crumpled paper.

She pulled it out, smoothing it against her thigh. The words leaped off the page like a dark confession: *My secret is that I've been dreaming of your death.*

Bigelow barked, lunging for the paper in her hand, mistaking it for a new game. Hope twisted away just in time. "No, Bigelow," she warned, gripping the note tighter as he made another enthusiastic attempt.

Princess, still miffed at the earlier disturbance, flicked her tail and stalked off without a backward glance. Meanwhile, Bigelow, undeterred, nudged his tennis ball toward her and wagged his tail expectantly, oblivious to the weight of the words she held.

• • •

Drew arrived exactly an hour later, pulling up in his dad's truck. His own sporty car was useless in icy conditions, and the lodge's winding driveway was tricky even on a good day.

When he spotted the container in Hope's hands, his face lit up.

"For me?" he asked.

Hope nodded. "Cinnamon muffins. Freshly baked this morning," she said, buckling her seat belt before twisting to set the container on the bench seat. She knew he'd enjoy them later.

"You baked? Did you get any sleep?" He shot her a surprised, delighted look as he eased the truck into reverse. The neighborhood was still waking up. Snow blanketed the front yards, and thin plumes of smoke curled from chimneys, marking the quiet rhythm of a Sunday morning.

Hope glanced over at him, noticing the tired creases on his forehead, the slight dullness in his usually bright blue eyes. "A few hours. Same as you, I'm guessing."

He snorted. "Pretty much."

"I had to do something when I woke up. Ethan had already taken care of the chickens and shoveled. And, well, I was craving a muffin."

Drew smiled. "Well, I'm glad for that craving. Those muffins are going to hit the spot later with a cup of tea." He turned onto the main road, heading toward the lodge. "I spent most of the morning working on my story for the *Gazette*. Also pitched the idea of working with Amy's podcast."

Hope pulled a tube of lip balm from her tote. "How'd that go?"

After stopping at a four-way and rolling through the intersection, he said, "My editor's on board with the idea. He thinks it's a great angle. Amy and I already worked out how we'll handle it."

"Look at us being so productive after a night of murder and almost no sleep." She swiped the balm over her lips and dropped it back into her bag. "Ethan told me Henry was found outside in the snow and that he's in a coma."

Drew's hands tightened on the wheel. "I haven't been able to get an update yet."

The truck hit a slick patch on the next turn, fishtailing for a second before Drew regained control.

"Sorry about that," he mumbled.

Hope exhaled, peeling her fingers from the dashboard. "No worries." Settling back into her seat, she turned the conversation back to Henry. "Any idea why he was outside last night? Or how long he was out there?"

"From what I heard, it wasn't an accident," Drew said. "Someone hit him on the back of the head. He was found near the firewood pile."

Hope sucked in a sharp breath. "Someone tried to kill him?"

Drew shrugged, keeping his eyes on the road as he steered the truck up the treacherous driveway. Snapped branches littered the path, remnants of last night's storm. "Sounds like it."

A sudden weight pressed on Hope's chest as the lodge came into view. Yesterday, she'd arrived full of optimism, eager for a productive retreat. Now, she regretted ever stumbling across Maisie's social media page.

"Could someone outside the retreat have gotten inside yesterday?" she asked.

Drew flicked a glance at her before nodding toward the lodge. "You think someone hid out in there, waiting until nightfall to start killing?"

"Anything's possible. And the place is big enough for someone to hide. There were empty guest rooms, plus the whole basement. Henry's attack has to be connected to Maisie's murder. It just has to be."

"I agree. The timing is too suspicious. But figuring out the connection . . ." Drew let out a low whistle as he pulled into the lot and shut off the ignition.

Hope followed his gaze. She sighed at the sight of bright yellow crime scene tape cordoning off the entrance.

"Looks like we're not getting inside," Drew said.

Hope stepped out of the truck and into the frigid morning air. The wind nipped at her cheeks, and she pulled her scarf snugly around her neck. "So much for poking around. I wasn't even sure what I was looking for, but now I guess I'll never know."

Drew came around to her side, hands shoved deep into his jacket pockets. "Does Ethan know you're planning a little amateur sleuthing?"

Hope paused before answering. "I didn't exactly spell it out, but I'm pretty sure he figured it out when I offered to retrieve his truck."

Drew followed her gaze toward the far end of the lot, where Ethan's green pickup sat blanketed in a thin layer of snow. He tilted his head. "Same spot as last night."

Hope nodded, a flicker of disappointment settling in her chest. She'd been counting on the chance to explore the lodge, to look for whatever Maisie hadn't wanted anyone to find. But now, with the crime scene tape blocking her access, the opportunity felt further out of reach.

"What about Austin?" Hope asked.

"As far as I know, he still hasn't been found."

"Do you think he killed Maisie and attacked Henry?"

"It would explain why he disappeared."

Hope scanned the lot, eyes narrowing. "I wonder if Maisie's car is still here." She took a few steps, glancing around. Other than Ethan's truck, the lot was empty. "Do you remember if Maisie's car was here when Ethan and Officer Roberts arrived?"

Drew shrugged.

"You should check with your source at the PD," she said, returning to his side. "That could be important."

"I'll do that," Drew agreed. "But for now, we should get going. Go ahead and take Ethan's truck. I'll follow you back."

As she scanned the surroundings, something caught her eye. It was a cabin, partially obscured by a grove of trees, its chimney sending a delicate wisp of smoke into the cold air. "Sure, sounds like a plan," Hope replied absently, her focus fixed on the distant cabin.

"Then why aren't you walking to the truck?" he asked.

"Huh?" Hope turned to him, shaken from her thoughts. Drew knew her too well. They'd been through everything together since childhood: heartbreaks, triumphs, and, most recently, playing amateur detectives. She gestured toward the cabin. "What's that place?"

Drew followed her gaze. "Kit's cabin. Not sure for how much longer, since Henry fired her last night." His expression darkened. "You don't think she could've—"

"Had motive to kill them both?" Hope finished, lowering her voice. "It's possible, but I'm not convinced. Kit was working with Amy to discover the truth about her sister. She even tracked down Maisie. If revenge was her goal, why not let the justice system handle it?"

"Maybe she couldn't resist," Drew said. "Coming face-to-face with the person who might've been responsible for her sister's disappearance? That's not easy to walk away from."

Hope hesitated, then took a step toward the cabin. The shoveled path was uneven, snowdrifts lining the way. "Only one way to find out."

Drew sighed, trailing after her. "So, what's the plan? Knock on her door and casually ask if she murdered Maisie and attacked Henry? You think she'll just say, 'Oh, yeah, that was me'?"

Hope shot Drew a look, unfazed by his skepticism. "She probably won't admit anything, but I want to see her reaction."

The trek through the snow was tiring, but the cabin wasn't far. As Hope reached the porch, she knocked the snow from her boots, climbed the two wooden steps, and paused at the door. Her breath misted in the cold air as she raised her hand to knock.

"I'd like to see her reaction too," Drew muttered, stepping onto the welcome mat beside her. He eyed the door and lifted an eyebrow. "Maybe knock again. Louder this time?"

Hope rapped harder, the sound cutting through the silence. When no response came, she frowned. "Maybe she's already gone."

Drew rubbed his hands together, as if he could coax some heat back into them. . "Could be. We should call Amy, see if she knows how to reach her."

"If she took off after last night, that's suspicious," Hope murmured. "Hard to ignore the timing."

"No argument there." Drew shifted, his breath curling in the air. "But can we figure it out somewhere less frigid?"

"Agreed. Let's—"

"Uh-oh," Drew cut in, voice dropping.

Before Hope could turn, a hand clamped onto her shoulder. Her breath hitched, every muscle in her body locking in place.

Chapter Ten

"I wasn't expecting company," Kit said, releasing Hope's shoulder. "But if you want tea, I can put the kettle on."

Hope turned to face Kit. "Hey, we . . . we came to pick up Ethan's truck, but we also wanted to check on you."

"Check on me?" Kit scoffed, slipping between them to unlock her cabin door. "Sounded more like you're here to interrogate me. Lots of motives, right?" She swung the door open wide, her movement almost theatrical as she motioned them inside. "Well, come on in."

Hope's eyes met Drew's in a silent, shared moment of "we're so busted."

"No. We're not here to interrogate," Drew said as he followed Hope through the doorway. "Right, Hope? More like . . . an interview."

Hope shot him a look, her mouth twitching despite the tension. "Something like that."

The door clicked shut behind Kit as she peeled off her parka and unwound the thick scarf from her neck, tossing them both over a chair back along with her knit hat. Her boots came off next, left by the door as she padded in her socks toward the kitchen. The kettle clinked against the stove as she filled it with water and set it to heat.

Hope stepped inside, taking in the space. A well-worn gray sofa faced the wood stove, its cushions still dented from use. A bright knit throw was draped haphazardly over one arm, and two mismatched pillows leaned against the other—clear evidence of Kit's favorite spot. The kitchen, though small, was neatly organized. A butcher block counter held a coffee maker, toaster, and a bowl of fruit.

"This place is wonderful. Having it come with the job must make things easier," Hope said.

"This place was definitely a bonus." Kit pulled down a trio of mismatched mugs from an upper cabinet, her expression unreadable. She placed a tea bag in each one before retrieving a carton of milk from the refrigerator.

"Speaking of which, what made you want to work at the lodge?" Drew asked. "How exactly did you get the job? Amy said you worked in insurance."

"Insurance? You've had quite the career change," Hope said as she unzipped her jacket.

When the kettle whistled, Kit poured hot water into the mugs, a cloud of steam rising as the tea steeped.

"Come sit," Kit said, carrying the mugs to the small dining table. She added a splash of milk to her tea and gestured for them to prepare theirs. "I'll tell you everything you want to know."

Kit wrapped her hands around her mug, her gaze steady. "I'm not sure how much Amy told you about my sister's case."

"We know Penny vanished during the retreat Maisie held up in Vermont when she was going by the name Demi Covington." Hope took a sip of her tea, the bold flavor spreading through her, loosening the stiffness in her limbs. "How did your sister get involved with Maisie?"

Kit let out a heavy sigh. "Social media. Penny was always restless. Work, relationships, even where she lived. When she found Maisie's life-coaching program, she'd just started a travel blog. For the first time, it seemed like she was figuring things out. Travel blogging was perfect for her, and I believed Maisie's coaching would set her on the right path." She closed her eyes for a moment, regret softening her features. Her eyes then drifted to a framed photo on a nearby table of the two of them as little girls smiling, arms draped around each other. "I was wrong."

"What went wrong at the retreat?" Drew propped his elbow on the table and rested his chin in his hand, his expression keen with interest.

"When Penny called to tell me about the retreat, she was thrilled. Three days in Vermont in the dead of winter, so she expected activities like journaling sessions, meditation workshops, and life coaching, maybe with a short outdoor walk. It sounded perfect for her. But instead, Maisie arranged an 'empowerment hike' through the dense woods, despite the brutal cold. She framed it as a way for attendees to push their limits and unlock their true potential."

"Sounds more like a test of survival skills," Hope quipped.

"That's what I thought," Kit said. "Most of the participants were completely unprepared for the hike. The terrain was rough, the temperatures dropped lower than expected, and the conditions quickly became dangerous. Someone should have known better."

"How do you know all this?" Drew asked, studying her face. "You weren't even there, or were you?"

"I wish I had been there. I've spent months digging into the details of that retreat. I managed to track down three of the attendees, though it wasn't easy. A lot of time scouring social media paid off." Kit tapped her phone, a little too hard, as if daring it to contradict her. "From what they told me, one attendee had a preexisting medical condition. The combination of cold, exhaustion, and lack of medical support led to a serious health crisis while on the empowerment hike."

Drew nodded grimly. "Amy mentioned where the hike took place. I know the area well. They were miles from civilization, with no cell service, no way to call for help."

Kit rose and headed back to the stovetop. She refilled her tea and gestured to Hope and Drew's mugs; they both declined. "From what I've pieced together, my sister was the only one who became suspicious and questioned Maisie's manipulative tactics. The attendees I spoke with said Penny threatened to go public about what happened. That didn't sit well with Maisie. They said she lost it and lashed out at Penny."

"What happened to the participant who had the medical emergency?" Hope asked, taking a sip of her tea.

Kit returned to the table, her face etched with a new sadness. "He died. The local officials didn't want the bad press tarnishing the inn or the town because they rely on tourism for the local economy, so the circumstances around his death were quietly brushed under the rug. Business as usual, I suppose."

"And Penny disappeared during that hike, right?" Hope pressed.

Kit nodded, her jaw tight. "She and Maisie got into an argument. The others said Penny stormed off after that. And so did Austin. He'd been on the trail with the group. The next time they saw him was when they finally got back to the inn."

"Why didn't the others at the retreat go public with what happened?"

"It was like a cult," Kit said, her voice barely above a whisper.

"Maisie had this way about her, this charisma that just drew people in. You both saw it with your own two eyes. Hope, you were a client. She made them feel special, important."

"You mean like she brainwashed them?" Drew ventured, his expression skeptical.

Kit lifted her shoulders. "Maybe not brainwashed, but definitely influenced. And I'm sure some of them were afraid of losing their place in her inner circle, or afraid of what she would do to them if they betrayed her."

Inner circle. Those two words reverberated in Hope's mind, a cold wave of embarrassment washing over her. Last fall, she'd upgraded her membership in Maisie's coaching program—the MC Inner Circle. God, how naive had she been? She'd bought into the hype, the promises of transformation and success. It was all just a sales pitch, a carefully crafted illusion designed to prey on her insecurities.

"Anyway, when I didn't hear from Penny after the retreat, I panicked. While she was a free spirit, she never went long without calling or texting me. I reached out to the inn, and they told me Penny left right after the hike. They gave me Maisie's contact info, and her staff told the same story. I know she wouldn't have just taken off and not tell me."

A sinking feeling settled in Hope's chest. *I'd been looking forward to my retreat too. Look how that turned out.*

"You okay?" Drew reached out and touched Hope's arm. "You look a little pale."

"I . . . I'm fine. Please continue, Kit," Hope said, pulling away slightly.

"I immediately called the police but had to wait to officially report her missing. Believe me, that was agonizing. Then after they concluded their *investigation*, they told me that Penny had indeed left on her own. There wasn't anything to indicate foul play."

"You don't believe that," Hope observed quietly.

Kit slammed her hands on the table, the sound echoing in the sudden silence. "Absolutely not. It's been years, and I *know* my sister. Just like you know yours. Penny wouldn't have just vanished. She wouldn't have left me. Maisie had something to do with her disappearance. I feel it . . . a cold knot in my gut."

"We'll circle back to that," Hope said, cutting off Kit's protest with a raised hand. "Right now, we need to focus on how you found Maisie, despite the new identity. Time is of the essence." Because if Hope and Drew were right, and someone else was in that lodge last night, then they were dealing with a killer who was still out there.

"I didn't," Kit admitted. "Honestly, it was pure luck that I stumbled onto her at the lodge."

Drew let out a low whistle, a flicker of genuine admiration in his eyes. "Okay, but that brings us back to my earlier question. Why take this job at the lodge?"

Kit pushed her mug away, her expression darkening. "Over the years, I've learned a few detective tricks of my own. Those led me to Henry Greenway. He was working at the Colbert Inn when Penny disappeared."

Hope and Drew exchanged a glance. The brochure on Henry's desk . . . it all clicked into place. But what did Henry know? And did knowing it put him in a coma?

"When I spoke with the inn's owner," Kit continued, "she said Henry had been working as the assistant manager. I found out from one of the attendees I talked to that Henry was seen later on the day of the hike carrying a bag into the inn. The description sounded like Penny's duffel bag."

"What happened to it?" Hope asked.

Kit shook her head. "I don't know. That's what I've been trying to find at the lodge. As far as I know, he never turned it over to the police, which makes me think he kept it for a reason. And when Penny vanished, all her belongings were gone from the inn, too. Which I think is why the police didn't look very hard for her."

"They thought she went back to the inn and packed up her stuff and left. But you think Henry took the duffel bag." Hope's voice tightened. "But why?"

"Blackmail," Drew suggested.

The taste of bile rose in Hope's throat. The thought that Henry might have had information about Penny's disappearance, and chose to stay silent, was deeply unsettling, especially considering how much

Kit had sacrificed to find her sister.

"If you couldn't track down the life coach who ran the retreat, then Henry probably couldn't either," she said. "Maybe he planned to blackmail Demi Covington back then . . . but she vanished, too. Just like Penny."

"It makes sense," Kit said, her voice flat. "He didn't know Demi would disappear. And like me, he probably had no idea Demi had reinvented herself as Maisie."

Drew nodded. "Until she showed up for the retreat here."

"The moment Maisie and her team arrived, Henry changed." Kit's voice dropped to a whisper. "It was obvious he recognized her. And she recognized him, too."

"Last night in Henry's room, I saw notes on his desk with names and dates, some circled in red. Do you know what they mean?" Hope asked.

"You were in his private quarters?" Kit's jaw tightened, and she squared her shoulders. "Look, Hope, I know from Amy that you consider yourself some kind of amateur detective, but I've been working for years to figure out what happened to my sister. I don't need anyone's help." She glanced at her watch, a silver charm bracelet jingling softly on her wrist. "Henry might've fired me yesterday, but someone still must keep an eye on the lodge. I need to get back to work."

Hope's spine stiffened at Kit's dismissive tone. She hadn't meant to overstep. She genuinely wanted to help, but a seed of doubt had been planted. Did Kit know more than she was letting on?

Hope started to speak, but Drew was already on his feet, his hand resting on her arm. "We appreciate your time, Kit." He gave Hope a subtle nudge to follow his lead. She reluctantly stood and slipped on her jacket. Just as they reached the door, a question bubbled up that she couldn't suppress.

"When was the last time you saw Austin?" Hope asked, her voice carefully neutral.

Kit's expression remained guarded, her voice clipped. "Sometime after dinner, I think. I'm not sure."

"Thank you." With a curt nod, Hope turned and followed Drew

out of the cabin, convinced that Kit was holding something back from them.

As they descended the porch steps, Hope let out a frustrated huff. "I wasn't finished with her. Who does she think she is, telling me to back off?"

Drew's eyes gleamed with amusement. "Ooh, amateur sleuth showdown."

She elbowed him lightly in the ribs, but her heart wasn't in it. "Not helping."

"Hey, my money is on you."

"Thanks for the vote of confidence."

Swinging an arm around her shoulders, he guided her toward the parked vehicles. "Listen, I got us out of there for a reason. She's at the top of my suspect list. She had both motive and opportunity not just to kill Maisie, but maybe Henry too. And we don't know what happened with Austin as he seems to have vanished."

"I was thinking the same thing!" When they reached Ethan's truck, she paused. "So, you're planning on digging into all their pasts?"

"You bet I am," Drew replied, his voice firm. "I'm not trusting anyone's story. Not even a grieving sister."

• • •

Hope gave a quick wave to Drew through the rearview mirror as they reached the fork in the road. He turned toward the county's storm depot, eager to follow up on his story about the blizzard that had hammered the northwestern corner of the state. Hope, meanwhile, steered back toward town, the weight of the past twenty-four hours growing heavier with each mile.

Ethan's pickup truck handled the narrow snow-laden roads with ease as she navigated toward Jefferson. When she reached the intersection leading to Main Street, the familiar sight of her hometown offered a small measure of comfort. Jefferson, blanketed in fresh snow, was a tranquil wonderland. Rows of antique homes stood proudly, their roofs adorned with icy caps, while the quaint shops glowed softly under the afternoon sun. The pristine beauty almost made her forget the day's troubles.

She let herself indulge in the nostalgia of winters past—building snowmen, snowball fights with Claire, and endless sledding adventures. But the sweetness of those memories soured when they reached their favorite sledding hill near Jefferson Lodge. The image of Maisie's lifeless body flashed in her mind, a grim reminder that the magic of snow couldn't bury reality. Maisie had been murdered, and the unsettling feeling Hope had been carrying now gnawed at her like an unwelcome shadow.

The light ahead turned red, and she slowed to a stop, her fingers drumming lightly on the steering wheel. When the signal changed, she continued down Main Street. As she approached the Merrifield Inn, she decided to stop in. Jane and Sally would undoubtedly have questions about last night's events. Truthfully, Hope could use their steady presence and the soothing comfort of a cup of tea.

After parking, Hope carefully made her way to the inn's entrance, grateful for the freshly shoveled path. Clearly, the Merrifield Inn's caretaker was diligent. The sidewalk gleamed, and not a flake of snow remained on the steps leading to the stately front door. The inn itself, a cornerstone of Jefferson's charm. It had been in the Merrifield family for generations, evolving from a grand family home to a beloved inn sometime in the middle of the last century. Now, Sally and Jane ran it with the kind of care that only came from deep family pride. Just this past Christmas, their young niece Eliza had visited, lending a hand with the daily tasks. Jane had hinted to Hope that they hoped Eliza might one day take over the reins, though she'd quickly added that she and Sally weren't planning on retiring anytime soon.

As Hope stepped inside, the site of the familiar foyer was reassuring. The chandelier gave off a soft, easy light that stretched across the polished hardwood floor, while the fragrance of the vase of lilies on the registration desk drifted through the air. Behind the desk, Eliza meticulously arranged a stack of papers, her navy-blue velour dress catching the light. Her chestnut hair was pulled into a sleek ponytail, and a set of pearl earrings, paired with a matching necklace, shimmered softly under the chandelier's glow.

Eliza looked up, her face lighting up with a friendly grin. "Good morning, Hope. It's wonderful to see you." Her expression shifted to one of concern as she stepped out from behind the desk. "I heard about what happened at the lodge. How awful. Is it true you were the one who found that woman's body?"

"Who else would have?" Sally interjected, entering the foyer from the dining room. "Where there's a body, there's Hope Early."

"Aunt Sally, must you be so blunt?" Eliza chided lightly, reaching out to take Hope's jacket. "Go on into the parlor. Aunt Jane is in there. I'll bring in a tray of tea."

"That sounds wonderful." Hope offered a grateful smile as she shrugged off her jacket, the promise of tea already easing her tension. As Eliza disappeared toward the kitchen, Hope adjusted the strap of her tote bag and followed Sally into the parlor.

A fire crackled in the hearth, its flickering light casting soft, dancing shadows across the room. Near the fireplace, Jane sat on a sofa, a book open on her lap. The bright purple of her blouse and her bold red lipstick popped against her neatly styled white hair. She looked up with a welcoming smile.

"Good morning, dear."

Hope sank onto the opposite sofa with a sigh of relief, placing her tote at her feet and sinking back into the plush cushions.

"You've had quite an experience," Jane said, her tone sympathetic. "The retreat didn't turn out quite as you'd hoped."

"That's putting it mildly," Hope replied, letting out a small sigh.

Sally settled on the sofa next to her sister-in-law, folding her hands neatly in her lap with her characteristic precision. True to form, she was impeccably dressed in black slacks and a button-down shirt—this time in a soft shade of lilac that flattered her complexion. Jewelry wasn't Sally's style, save for the simple gold studs in her ears and the delicate gold necklace she'd received last Christmas from Jeffrey. The two had been inseparable since they started dating last year, and Hope had almost believed that Sally had mellowed with her late-in-life romance.

Or so she'd thought.

"Hate to say I told you so, Hope, but I told you so," Sally said, her tone brisk and unwavering.

Hope bit back a smile. Nope, definitely not mellowed.

"That retreat nonsense was bound to end in disaster," Sally continued, her voice matter-of-fact, as if she'd known all along what was to come.

"Now, Sally Merrifield, you know there's no way anyone could have predicted Maisie Cox would wind up dead," Jane interjected, her eyes narrowing at her sister-in-law. "By the way, two of the attendees checked in here this morning after they were allowed to leave the lodge."

"Talia Benson and Lorna Morgan," Sally added as she rose to her feet. Her sharp gaze softened slightly as Eliza appeared in the doorway with a tea tray in hand. "Thank you, dear."

Eliza stepped forward, carefully balancing the tray. "This is a soothing blend of chamomile and lavender with just a hint of green tea—calming, but with a gentle lift," she explained, setting the tray on the low table. Lately, she'd been experimenting for her tea sommelier certification, refining her craft one blend at a time. She had even introduced a Sunday Afternoon Tea service at the inn, a new offering that had quickly become a guest favorite.

"I'll leave you to enjoy." With a polite nod, she slipped out of the parlor.

Sally placed the tray on the coffee table and poured three cups of tea. Beside the teapot was a plate of shortbread cookies dusted with powdered sugar, their buttery scent mingling with the aroma of steeped herbs.

Hope accepted a cup with a quiet thanks and then picked up a shortbread cookie, its crumbs yielding beneath her fingers. As she took a bite, the buttery flavor melted on her tongue, perfectly crisp yet tender. She followed it with a sip of tea, the floral notes complementing the cookie's subtle sweetness.

"It's a good thing Ethan went to the lodge last night," Sally remarked, stirring a sugar cube into her tea. She'd returned to the sofa beside her sister-in-law. "Otherwise, you might have been stuck there for who knows how long with a dead body and a murderer lurking about. No question about it, he's a good man."

"I know," Hope agreed, pausing to take another sip. "I'm so

grateful he trusted his instincts and acted quickly. He managed to get the police out there and arranged for the power line to be cleared from the driveway. Without him, things could've been much worse." She glanced down at her teacup, the steam curling in front of her face. The gravity of what could have happened wasn't lost on her.

Jane leaned back into the sofa, her teacup balanced on its matching saucer. "I admit, I'm curious about what really happened there yesterday. Start at the beginning, dear, and don't leave out a single detail."

Hope nodded, shifting in her seat as she recounted the events from her arrival at the lodge to Ethan's arrival with the police in tow. Her voice wavered slightly when she described finding Maisie's body, though she was careful not to reveal too much. She knew the police preferred to keep certain details under wraps, and with Amy covering the case on her podcast, it seemed wise to exercise a bit of discretion.

Well, she tried to be discreet. But under the Merrifields' keen questioning, Hope found herself spilling far more than she intended. Fortunately, neither woman was known for fueling Jefferson's gossip mill. By the time she finished, her tea had gone cold, and Jane and Sally sat quietly, absorbing every word.

"There's no way this wasn't murder," Jane said with conviction. "Maisie couldn't have locked herself in that sauna. No doubt about it—someone you were with yesterday is the killer."

"Unless someone slipped into the lodge without anyone noticing." Sally set her cup and saucer on the tray and stood, moving to the desk across the room, where there was a laptop computer open.

"Drew and I considered that," Hope said. "With multiple entrances and so much activity during the retreat, it's possible. But something about the group's interactions—one person in particular— keeps nagging at me."

Refilling her cup, Jane asked, "Who?"

Hope set her teacup down with a quiet *clink*. "Kit is at the top of my list."

Her stomach grumbled, a reminder that she hadn't eaten since breakfast, aside from the shortbread cookie she'd just polished off. She reached for another, hoping it would hold her over until she got home for lunch. As she finished the last bite, she launched into a recap of her visit to Kit's cabin with Drew, recounting every detail of their conversation.

"Come," Sally said over her shoulder. "Look what I found on *ReadNow.*"

Hope hesitated before rising to join Sally at the desk. *ReadNow* had a notorious reputation. What started as lively discussions often spiraled into heated arguments, sometimes turning outright toxic under the veil of anonymity. Hope knew this all too well. She'd been the subject of a few unflattering viral posts, an experience that had made her swear off the site for good.

But today, she was willing to make an exception.

"Look at all these comments." Sally pointed to the screen, her voice sharp with disapproval. "People lost thousands of dollars. Some even lost their businesses because of her. They were in debt, depressed, and blamed Maisie—well, Demi Covington—for taking advantage of them."

Maybe Hope should have visited *ReadNow* more often. Then again, nowhere in the comments did she find a mention of the fact that Maisie and Demi Covington were one and the same.

"How could anyone do something so heartless?" Jane had joined them, leaning in to peer at the screen, her expression tight with dismay. "It's appalling. A sad commentary on our society."

Hope scanned the screen, her eyes catching on a particular comment that seemed eerily familiar.

"Wait," she said, her pulse quickening. She pointed to the post that was published two days ago. The username caught Hope's attention, a subtle nod to calligraphy that wasn't quite Melanie's name but close enough to raise suspicion. "This sounds a lot like Melanie's post she shared in Maisie's private forum . . . but there's more. It mentions financial problems in her marriage."

It seemed that Melanie lost a lot because of her investment in Maisie's program. Was it enough to kill for?

Chapter Eleven

Hope chewed her lower lip, her thoughts a tangled mess. Could that calligraphy-themed username truly belong to Melanie? If it did, perhaps Kit wasn't the only one who deserved a spot at the top of her suspect list.

Jane shifted beside her, arms crossed, her gaze bouncing between Hope and the screen. "You're making that face," she said, tilting her head. "The one that usually means you've connected some dots the rest of us haven't." She edged forward, her curiosity written all over her face. "So, what are you thinking?"

"No connections this time," Hope replied, returning to the sofa and picking up her tote. "Just more questions."

At the desk, Sally clicked through another page. "The complaints are endless. This Maisie person was quite the piece of work."

Hope couldn't dispute that assessment; it was spot-on and likely a more generous description than what others would say.

"You said that Talia and Lorna checked in," Hope said. "But what about Austin Dell? Has anyone heard from him?"

Jane turned to face her and rested her hands on her hips. "No, dear. Who is he?"

"He was Maisie's right-hand man," Hope explained. "No one has seen him since before I found Maisie in the sauna."

"Well, that's certainly suspicious." Sally stood from the desk and crossed her arms. "I'm sure Detective Reid is trying to track him down as we speak. In fact, I imagine he's handling the investigation quite capably."

"I appreciate your subtle way of telling me to stay out of it." Hope slung her tote over her shoulder. "Though, if I'm completely honest, I don't think I can. Just before finding Maisie's body, I confronted her with what Amy told me. Maisie swore up and down that she'd changed. That she'd given up scamming people and that she genuinely wanted to help."

"And you believed her?" Sally asked, raising an eyebrow.

"Yes . . . No . . . I don't know," Hope admitted, letting out a shaky breath. "What she did was awful, but she didn't deserve to be murdered."

"No one does," Jane said as she linked her arms with Hope and guided her to the lobby and toward the front door.

"Talia seemed utterly distraught when she arrived this morning," Jane said after she retrieved Hope's jacket. "She kept saying it was her dream job and how much she looked up to Maisie. The poor thing was still in shock."

With her jacket on, Hope's mind circled back to Talia's reaction when Maisie's corrupt past came to light. She'd been quick to express concern about how *her* career would be affected. From what Jane had said, the reaction she witnessed was far different. But then again, Talia's boss had just been murdered, and surely that would provoke a more complicated response. "You know, before I found Maisie, Talia wasn't with the group," Hope said.

Jane's blue eyes sparkled with curiosity. "So, she doesn't have an alibi?"

"Not that I know of," Hope replied. "What about Lorna Morgan? How did she seem when she checked in?"

"She was the complete opposite of Talia," Jane said. "Not a single tear. In fact, she seemed almost . . . detached. She rushed through the check-in process and went straight to her room. Then, about twenty minutes ago, she hurried out."

"You don't know where she went, do you?" Hope asked, just as Eliza stepped out of the dining room carrying an empty tray.

"Who are you talking about?" Eliza paused nearby.

"Lorna Morgan," Hope replied.

Eliza's brow furrowed. "She asked the oddest question. Wanted to know where the closest lawyer was."

Hope exchanged a quick look with Jane. It was definitely an unusual query—unless, of course, Lorna was guilty of something and preparing her defense.

"What did you tell her?" Jane asked her niece.

"I mentioned the only lawyer I know in town," Eliza replied. "Matt Roydon. His office is just down the street."

Last fall, Matt had relocated his law practice from the city to Jefferson, making the transition from weekend visitor to full-time resident. His office, located in a charming Federal-style building on Main Street, was just minutes from Hope's home and even closer to the inn. If Lorna was seeking legal advice, this would be the most logical place to start looking.

"His office is open today? I have to go," Hope said, pulling the door open. "Thanks for the tea and all the information." She hurried out, her mind racing. Finding Lorna wasn't guaranteed, and even if she was there, would she be willing to talk? There was only one way to find out.

Despite the sidewalks being shoveled and salted, Hope kept her pace measured. The last thing she needed was to take a spill on the pavement. By the time she reached the street corner, the traffic light had turned red and she was forced to wait, her breath forming soft clouds in the air. Once the light turned green, she crossed and continued to Matt's office.

When Hope arrived, she peered through the front windows of the office. Inside, Callie, Matt's legal secretary, was seated at her desk, engaged in a phone conversation. Hope pushed open the door and entered the office, where the aroma of freshly brewed coffee lingered. Callie glanced up, her smile quick and easy as she gestured for Hope to wait a moment.

Hope nodded in acknowledgment and pulled out her phone, quickly checking for any missed messages or updates from Drew or Detective Reid. There were none.

"Good morning, Hope," Callie said after she ended her call and rose from her desk. "If you're looking for Ethan, I'm afraid he's not here. Matt and I are the only ones in the office today. Prep for a big case this coming week. Though, we had an interruption."

"Actually, I'm not looking for Ethan." Hope slipped her phone back into her tote and turned her focus back to the ever-efficient Callie. Tall, with squared shoulders and a no-nonsense demeanor, Callie ran Matt's office with precision and discretion—qualities vital for her role but occasionally inconvenient for someone like Hope.

"I was just at the Merrifield Inn," Hope explained. "I know Lorna Morgan checked in there, and I wanted to talk to her. See how she's holding up after last night." And maybe figure out if she's a murderer,

Hope added silently.

"I've heard about what happened at the lodge." Callie moved to the waiting area, straightening magazines and inspecting a nearby plant. "Terrible. It must have been awful for you. I heard you found that poor woman's body. Have you heard anything about how Henry Greenway is doing?"

"No," Hope admitted.

"I'll keep him in my prayers." Callie straightened, her expression sympathetic, but her keen eyes remained alert and observant. "If you're not here to see Ethan, why are you here?" Directness was another one of Callie's traits, a quality Hope usually appreciated, but not so much today. She had hoped to bump into Lorna, not have to navigate Callie's pointed questions.

"As I said, I was looking for Lorna. Eliza mentioned she might be here." Hope's gaze shifted to Matt's closed office door, and she wondered if Lorna was in there or if she'd already left. She wouldn't get a straight answer from Callie.

"Hope, you know all of Matt's cases are confidential. That includes his clients and appointments." Callie returned to her desk, her tone firm but professional. "If you'd like to leave a message for Ethan, I'm happy to pass it along."

"No, no message," Hope said, feeling a pang of disappointment. She began to turn toward the door, resigned to trying to connect with Lorna later, when Matt's office door creaked open and out stepped Lorna.

Despite her flawless makeup, Lorna's oval face bore the unmistakable signs of weariness. The artful contours of her features couldn't hide the exhaustion that had settled into her expression after the deadly events at the lodge. She paused mid-step when her eyes met Hope's. Her black puffer coat hung loosely over her frame, paired with jeans and a gray sweater, while a knit cap covered her brown hair.

"Hope . . . what are you doing here?" Lorna's voice wavered, her confusion evident. "Are you also a client?"

"No. I heard you might be here and wanted to check in on you," Hope replied. "I'll admit, I was surprised to find you at Matt's office, given that he's a criminal defense attorney."

"I . . . I needed some advice," Lorna said, her tone guarded. "This is all so overwhelming for me. It's like I can't even think straight."

"Well, Matt's one of the best. You're in good hands," Hope offered with a reassuring smile.

Lorna shook her head lightly. "He's not my attorney. Like I said, I just needed some advice." Her hands fumbled in her purse before she produced a tissue and dabbed at her teary eyes.

Before Hope could respond, Matt stepped into view, his broad frame towering over Lorna. He was as tall as Ethan, with sandy blond hair neatly combed back. His navy suit fit to perfection, the paisley tie lending just a hint of flair.

"Hope, well, this is a surprise," Matt greeted her, his voice carrying a note of inquisitiveness. "What brings you by?"

"I'm guessing the nosy innkeepers told you where to find me, and you just couldn't resist discovering why I needed a lawyer." Lorna's eyes had dried up and the tissue had been discarded. "Am I right?"

"Hope knows our conversation is privileged," Matt interjected as he stepped around Lorna and moved into the waiting area of his office.

"Of course," Hope replied, though her inquisitiveness got the better of her. "Still, it does seem a little . . . unusual to consult an attorney so soon after Maisie's murder."

"Hope," Matt said, his tone low and firm, the subtle warning unmistakable. And Hope acquiesced. The last thing she wanted to do was to alienate Matt. He'd not only been a good friend, but he'd helped her and Claire out of legal jams in the past.

Lorna smirked. "I knew it. Small towns like this thrive on busybodies, always sniffing around for their next juicy tidbit."

"Ms. Morgan isn't obligated to explain herself to anyone." Matt walked to his secretary's desk. "And you shouldn't be here, Hope."

Hope blinked, stunned by his admonishment. "I—"

"Mr. Roydon is right," Lorna cut in. "But since you seem like a nice person, I'll put your curiosity to rest."

"I *am* a nice person," Hope replied, her shoulders squared.

"You're the kind who wants everyone to like her," Lorna said knowingly. "I could tell the moment Maisie read the *Release* that it was you who wrote it. Anyway, I didn't come to see Mr. Roydon because I'm guilty of murder. Far from it. I'm here to figure out what to do next . . . as Maisie's next of kin."

"Next of kin?" Hope echoed, her voice rising in surprise. "You're related to Maisie?"

Lorna nodded, her expression unreadable. "We were half-sisters."

Hope hadn't seen that revelation coming, and it almost rendered her speechless. "The photo from when you were children, that was you and Maisie, wasn't it?"

"Back then, she was Elaine. It feels like a lifetime ago," Lorna murmured, her voice carrying the weight of the past. She inhaled deeply, as if pulling herself back to the present. "I really must go. Thank you for your time and advice, Mr. Roydon." Without another word, she turned and slipped out the door, the soft click of the latch punctuating her exit.

Matt leaned against his desk, arms crossed over his chest, his expression a blend of exasperation and amusement. "What are we going to do with you, Hope?"

"For starters, you could help me—"

"Absolutely not."

Hope huffed. "How do you know she's telling the truth about being Maisie's half-sister? For all we know, she's the one who killed her."

Matt shrugged. "I don't have to know. That's for the police and the courts to sort out, if it even gets that far."

"Can't you at least tell me—"

"Don't even think about it."

Hope narrowed her eyes. "Fine. Then don't even think about cookies. Not even a crumb."

Callie's eyes widened in mock horror. "Boss, I think she's serious."

Matt studied Hope, as if assessing whether she'd actually enforce the cookie embargo. "I'm starting to get that impression."

"Glad we're on the same page." Hope pivoted on her heel, tossing a breezy "Bye!" over her shoulder.

She had taken only a couple of steps outside when a fierce gust of wind slammed into her, whipping her hair across her face and nearly toppling her. Muttering a rude word under her breath, she steadied herself against the chill and moved on.

Another frigid gust cut through her jacket as she headed for her vehicle. Main Street was usually a pleasant stroll, but not today—not with the wind gnawing at her resolve. The thought of a heated seat and a straight shot to her next stop felt far more appealing.

Hope quickly climbed into Ethan's truck and drove to the police department. After securing a parking space, she hurried inside the brick building. She checked in with the dispatcher, who directed her to take a seat while she waited for Detective Reid.

Settling into the chair, she loosened her scarf and rummaged through her tote in search of a mint. Her stomach grumbled with a not-so-subtle reminder that shortbread cookies at the inn weren't a proper meal. Hopefully, the mint would take the edge off. She unwrapped it and popped it into her mouth, the cool burst of peppermint sharpening her focus as she mulled over her conversation with Matt.

His refusal to help had stung, though in hindsight, she couldn't blame him. His hands were tied, and she respected that. Still, if there was one thing her grandmother had taught her, it was that where there was a will, there was a way. And Hope had plenty of will. Lorna Morgan wasn't off the hook just yet.

She bit down on the mint, the crisp snap resonating in her head. Of course, she wasn't going to enforce a cookie embargo on Matt. She wasn't heartless and he was a good friend.

Hope's name was called, and she glanced toward the door leading to the offices. Detective Sam Reid stood there, waiting. Tall and lean, with the coiled energy of a man always half a step from breaking into a run, he had the kind of presence that turned heads without trying. His dark hair was trimmed close, and his sharp brown eyes missed nothing, taking in everything and giving away very little in return. Hope rose and crossed the lobby, offering a polite smile as they exchanged pleasantries, and he led her deeper into the station.

Walking through the Jefferson Police Department felt strange now that Ethan was no longer chief. She'd been here countless times when he was in charge, and as they turned down the hallway leading to his old office, she half expected to see him step out of the doorway, coffee in hand. But the space belonged to someone else now.

"Have a seat," Reid said, stepping aside to let her enter his office first. "Coffee?" He moved around his desk and sat, flipping open a file and lifting a document from the stack.

Hope lowered herself onto one of the chairs opposite him, shaking her head. "No, thanks." If the coffee here was the same as she remembered, lukewarm and bitter, she'd pass. That was why she'd always stopped at the Coffee Clique to bring Ethan a cup when she'd visited.

"I appreciate you coming in to give your statement." Reid set the document down and clasped his hands together. His expression was unreadable, his tone mild. "I imagine last night wasn't pleasant for you. Did you get any sleep?"

"Not really."

Reid nodded, then reached for his reading glasses before glancing down at the paper in front of him. "I've reviewed the statement you gave to Officer Roberts. You and the others searched for Ms. Cox after dinner, following the revelation about her true identity. You ultimately found her in the sauna—deceased. Later, when you returned to your room to pack, you discovered a threatening message written in your journal." He looked up, meeting her gaze. "Everything I just said is accurate?"

"Yes." Hope shifted in her seat, tucking a lock of hair behind her ear with a restless hand. She hoped he wouldn't be too upset with her for withholding pertinent information in his case. "There's something else." She reached into her tote, and she pulled the folded paper out, holding it between them like a peace offering. "I forgot to mention to Officer Roberts. And I'm really sorry about it."

Reid lowered his glasses. "What's that? Is it connected to the case?"

"It most certainly is." Hope smoothed the creases between her fingers. "The retreat was divided into sessions, and in one of them we were asked to write about a time we hid our true selves. Maisie called this a *Release*."

Reid's brow lifted. "Your true self?"

To his credit, he didn't dismiss the exercise as feel-good nonsense. Instead, his focus remained unwavering as Hope explained the session and how she'd gone back for the dark confession. She unfolded the paper and handed it to him.

Reid slid his glasses back on and read in silence.

"You don't know who wrote this?" he asked.

"The whole point of the exercise was anonymity so we could be honest," Hope said. "I should have given this to you right away. I'm sorry."

Reid's expression relaxed. "You were under a lot of stress last night. It's understandable that you weren't thinking clearly. What matters is that I have the note now." He set it down on the desk.

Hope bit her lip, her mind already racing with new questions and theories. "I wonder if the handwriting matches Lorna's," she murmured, the thought forming even as she considered how she might get a sample of Lorna's writing. Sam now had the original, but she'd snapped a photo of it—just in case.

Reid gave her a knowing look. "Leave that to me, Hope. I mean it."

She held up her hands. "I hear you."

Reid studied her for a moment before removing his glasses and setting them on the desk, as if bracing for a long conversation. "I'm curious why you think the handwriting could be Lorna Morgan's? Is there something else you want to tell me?"

"She claims she's Maisie's half-sister. Think about it—an estranged sibling showing up just before Maisie's death? That's more than a little convenient. And from what I saw yesterday, their reunion was far from heartfelt. And Lorna doesn't seem all that grief-stricken."

Reid frowned. "You saw her today?"

"Yes. At Matt Roydon's office."

Reid let out a slow breath, his fingers pressing against the bridge of his nose. "I'm guessing that wasn't just a coincidence."

Hope folded her arms. "Does it really matter?"

"It does. In one scenario, you ran into her by chance. In the other, you're interfering in my investigation."

"I'm not interfering," she countered. "I spoke with Lorna, and I'm sharing what she told me with you. In a timely manner, I might add."

"Unlike this . . . what did you call it? A *Release*?" His tone was dry.

Hope opened her mouth to defend herself but shut it quickly at the sound of a knock on the door. Turning in her chair, she recognized Officer Stanton. The officer entered the office with a purposeful stride. Stanton had joined the department five months before Ethan resigned as Chief. Their interactions had been few, but Hope had found her professional, pleasant, and surprisingly funny.

"Sorry to interrupt, Detective, but I have a message for Hope."

"For me?" Hope reached into her tote, fumbling for her phone. Had she missed something important? A quick scroll through her texts revealed nothing. "Who's it from?"

"Mayor Kingston."

Hope stopped scrolling. Oh, boy. If Maretta had sent a message through the police department, it couldn't be good.

"She wants to see you in her office when you're done here," Stanton continued. "Oh, and she said—direct quote—don't dawdle, I'm very busy."

Reid looked amused, his mouth twitching as he held back a laugh. "Thank you, Officer Stanton."

"I'll do my best not to dawdle," Hope muttered, dropping her phone back into her tote.

"Good luck," Stanton whispered on her way out.

Reid smirked. "Well, looks like you've got your marching orders."

"But it's Sunday. Why is Maretta at Town Hall today?"

"Probably because of the storm and the next one that's coming in a few days. They need to review and make plans. You shouldn't keep the mayor waiting."

"That's it? We're finished?"

"Not quite. I still need to add the information about the note from the retreat to your statement. Come back later to sign it. I'll let you know when it's ready."

She gathered her belongings but hesitated before standing. She had planned on asking a few questions of her own, but being summoned by Maretta made her pause. The mayor wasn't known for her patience, and Hope could already hear the lecture about the value of Maretta's time. Still, this might be her only chance to get more information out of Reid. She shifted in her seat, her mind made up. "Just one more thing before I go. Did you find Penny Foster's belongings in the lodge? Kit mentioned that Henry found her bag after she disappeared from the hike."

Reid's expression became unreadable again. Gosh, he was good at that. "You know I can't comment on an ongoing investigation."

She understood, but that didn't mean she had to like it. "What about Henry? Is he still in a coma?"

"As far as I know, yes." Reid closed the file on his desk. "Thanks for coming in, Hope."

• • •

Hope pushed open the heavy wooden door of Town Hall, her footsteps echoing off the polished marble floor. She hadn't planned on stopping by, but Maretta's summons left her with little choice. While she disliked the mayor's abrupt request, Hope saw it as an opportunity to speak with Maretta without having to chase her down. The mayor's office was on the second floor, and Hope quickened her pace, determined not to keep Maretta waiting.

She passed by mostly quiet offices, the usual bustle replaced by the eerie stillness of a Sunday afternoon. A handful of employees remained, their hushed conversations and the occasional ringing phone the only signs of life as she made her way to the elevator.

When she stepped off the elevator, she saw the office door was wide open, revealing a reception area in the midst of renovation. A ladder stood on a drop cloth in one corner, while a slab of plywood rested on sawhorses nearby, accompanied by a bucket of tools.

"Hello," Hope called out as she stepped inside, her voice carrying slightly in the sparsely furnished room. The carpet beneath her feet was plush and newly installed, but the familiar paintings of Jefferson that had adorned the walls were conspicuously absent. Even the plaque on the mayor's door was missing. "Maretta?"

Hope crossed the room to the closed door of the inner office and rapped twice. No reply.

"Well, it's about time you got here." Maretta breezed into the office from the hallway, carrying a thick binder. Her glasses were perched atop her head of dull brown hair and she wore a dark plum shirtdress cinched with a narrow belt. Her black pumps were sensibly low-heeled, and her jewelry was minimal—just petite hoop earrings, a delicate necklace, and her gold wedding band. "I thought I was very clear when I spoke to Officer Stanton that I am extremely busy today and needed you here ASAP. My goodness, things have not been running smoothly at the PD since Ethan left."

"I came here as soon as I finished with Detective Reid," Hope said. "What did you want to see me about?"

Maretta dropped the binder on the desk with a thud. "What do you think? The murder, of course."

Hope blinked, letting Maretta's snarkiness roll off her back. "Right."

"The whole retreat thing has turned into a fiasco," Maretta continued. "I have local and regional media contacting my office nonstop. It's hard to fathom that Maisie Cox managed to fool hundreds of people. In this day and age, with social media, I would have thought her kind of con wouldn't exist any longer."

"I feel the same way," Hope agreed, nodding. "It's so hard to believe because nothing really disappears from the internet once it's out there." She knew that fact firsthand; there were still a few viral videos of her in less-than-flattering moments being liked and shared.

Maretta gave a dismissive wave. "That's very true. Just look at your videos. Especially that one last month when you used a giant candy cane as a weapon."

Hope paused, mentally counting to ten. She had explained the situation to Maretta when it happened, but the mayor seemed intent on bringing it up again. Hope knew from years of experience that Maretta Kingston could be exasperating, but having known her since childhood, she also knew it was often better to let the older woman's thoughtless comments slide.

"How about we focus on what happened at the lodge last night?" Hope suggested, trying to steer the conversation back on track.

Maretta glanced at her watch. "I have a Public Safety briefing in a few minutes. You'll need to walk with me."

"Walk with you?" Hope repeated, taken aback.

"Yes, yes." Maretta spun around and marched out of the office, her heels striking a quick staccato on the floor. "Come on, don't dawdle!"

"I . . . I don't dawdle," Hope stammered, scurrying after her into the hallway.

As they headed for the stairwell, Maretta filled Hope in on the town's response to yesterday's storm and shared the details about the next one forecasted to hit their region in a few days. Her voice was brisk and efficient, leaving Hope little room to do anything but listen and keep pace.

As they moved briskly down the hall, Maretta's coworkers instinctively stepped aside, clearing a path without hesitation. To an outsider, it might have seemed like a display of authority—the kind that came with holding office—but the truth was, everyone in town knew Maretta's personality. It wasn't respect that made them move. It was self-preservation.

"It sounds like your team is well-prepared for the next storm," Hope said, nodding at a few familiar faces as they passed. "Though, I doubt that's why you summoned me here."

Maretta slowed her pace slightly. "Correct. I wouldn't have asked you to come here to talk about the next storm."

Asked? It certainly hadn't felt like a request.

Maretta reached the stairwell and pushed the bar on the door, stepping inside. "I have no doubt you'll be poking around this murder like the others."

Hope's lips pressed into a thin line, but she said nothing.

Maretta continued, her tone matter-of-fact. "While I have full confidence in our police department, I don't believe our interim chief, Captain Ackerman, is anywhere near the caliber of Chief Cahill."

A familiar pang of pride swelled in Hope's chest. Ethan had been an outstanding chief—dedicated to the point of exhaustion. He'd sacrificed too much and knew that a change was necessary for his family.

"Now you understand my dilemma," she said as she descended the stairwell, her voice echoing slightly in the narrow space.

Hope followed, her footsteps soft but just as hurried. "No, I really don't."

Maretta let out an exasperated huff before pausing mid-step, glancing over her shoulder.

"I want you to do that thing you do with murders—within the bounds of the law, of course. I *am* the mayor, after all." Without waiting for a response, she snapped her head forward and continued downward.

Hope hesitated, the words catching her off guard. "What . . . what? That *thing* I do with murders?"

"Yes! You stick your nose where it doesn't belong, dig up clues, and find leads the police sometimes overlook." Maretta reached the landing, turned quickly, and planted her hands on her hips. The fluorescent light above flickered once before steadying, casting a stark glow over her no-nonsense expression. "Are you going to stand there all day?"

Hope shook off her surprise and picked up her pace. "You usually *discourage* me from getting involved. Why the change of heart?" She crossed her arms, narrowing her eyes. Then it hit her. "It's because of Henry, isn't it?"

Maretta sighed, the sound bouncing off the cinder-block walls.

Hope pressed on. "It *is*! You and Henry were very close in high school, weren't you?"

A wistful smile tugged at the corners of Maretta's mouth. "Close might be an overstatement."

"On the contrary, I think it's an understatement," Hope said gently. "He told me that he loved you back then."

For a split second, a trace of softness crossed Maretta's otherwise stoic face, a faint blush betraying feelings she'd long kept hidden. "We went to a few school dances, shared a milkshake or two at the soda fountain—but that was a lifetime ago. Ancient history, really."

"Whatever you say," Hope replied, choosing not to press further. Instead, she steered the conversation back to what mattered most. "Did you two stay in touch after he left Jefferson?"

Maretta shook her head, her gaze unfocused, as if sifting through old memories. "Not really. After graduation, Henry left town, and that was that. I didn't hear from him again until he bought the lodge." She exhaled, a hint of something unreadable in her expression. "I was surprised, honestly. I never thought he'd come back."

"So you haven't spoken to him until he came back to open the lodge?" Hope pressed, watching her closely.

Maretta's lips thinned. "The last time we spoke was the day we got our diplomas."

"Then you don't know where he's been or what he's been doing." Or, the type of man he turned out to be. But, Hope kept that last observation to herself. "I talked to Kit earlier when I went to pick up Ethan's truck, and she told me that she tracked Henry down after learning he worked at the Colbert Inn when her sister disappeared."

"That's quite an accusation," Maretta said. "Henry, involved in something nefarious? I just don't see it. He was always kind and respectful and honest."

Hope walked to the stairwell door and pushed it open. "But that was over forty years ago," she reminded her as they stepped into the first-floor hallway. "People change."

"I'm fully aware of that," Maretta snapped. Her pace slowed and her shoulders dipped slightly. For the first time, she looked like a woman whose carefully preserved memories were beginning to crack. "The last thing I want is for whoever killed Maisie Cox and hurt Henry to go unpunished. And I certainly don't want Henry's reputation ruined by Kit's claims or some sensationalized true crime podcast."

"Amy's podcast doesn't sensationalize crime," Hope said, standing firm.

Maretta raised a finger. "They all do. And in their wake, good people get caught in the crossfire. I don't want that to happen to Henry if he's innocent. But if he's guilty of any crime, then he should have to pay the price."

A man in a dark suit, balancing a stack of file folders and a laptop computer, strode past them. "Good afternoon, Mayor. Everyone is in the conference room, ready for the meeting."

Maretta nodded, then turned back to Hope, her gaze sharpening. "So, you'll help sort this mess out?"

Hope had little time to process the unexpected request from Maretta Kingston when a shrill alarm rang out, echoing down the hall.

Maretta jolted. "Good grief! A fire drill?"

Doors swung open as town employees emerged, shrugging on coats as they made their way toward the exits. Swept up in the exodus, Hope and Maretta followed the group outside.

As the cold air stung her cheeks, Hope watched Maretta hurry to her car, flipping on the engine to keep warm while they all waited for the all-clear to enter the building. Rather than stand around in the cold, Hope decided to head out and check in with Drew at his office.

• • •

Hope spotted a parking space in front of the *Gazette*'s historic brick building, which stood sentinel at the end of Main Street before it meandered onto Route 14 and into the heart of the state's most stunning horse country. She darted into the newspaper's lobby. The compact space paid tribute to the *Gazette*'s rich history, with exposed brick walls adorned with framed black-and-white photographs of former editors and memorable front pages. The worn wood floors bore the scuffs and scars of decades of use, while a sleek, modern reception desk at the center of the room provided a striking contrast.

Behind the desk sat Whitney Pelham, a harried yet cheerful receptionist who greeted Hope despite barely looking up from her duties. She juggled a telephone, computer keyboard, and notepad with ease.

"Good morning, Hope," Whitney said, hanging up the phone and pecking at her keyboard with a bit too much enthusiasm. "I didn't expect to be working today, but with what happened at the lodge . . . How are you holding up? Finding that woman in the sauna must have been utterly dreadful." She paused typing and swiveled her chair around to face Hope, her eyes bright with curiosity. "What was it like, seeing her . . . like that?"

Hope knew Whitney's eagerness wasn't born out of genuine concern or even a penchant for local gossip. She was an aspiring reporter, and it was clear that she was using this opportunity to sharpen her investigative skills. Hope understood the ambition but knew there was only one reporter she would trust with the information she had, and he was currently tucked away in his office upstairs.

Just beyond Whitney's desk, a staircase spiraled up to the editorial offices on the second floor. Among them was Drew's newly acquired space, an office with a view of Main Street. He had earned this prime location following his promotion to editor of the *Gazette*'s quarterly antiques and home edition.

"It was certainly a shock finding Maisie Cox's body in the sauna," Hope said, offering Whitney a tidbit that was true but revealed little.

"You mean Demi Covington." Whitney's smile remained in place, though a flicker of disappointment passed through her eyes at Hope's vague answer. She rested her chin in her hand. "I've always wondered how someone like that manages to pull off a scam in this day and age. But then, I guess there's a sucker born every—" She stopped herself with a wince. "Sorry. That came out wrong."

Hope's smile tightened. She didn't need reminding how easy it was to be duped. She had her bruised pride to prove it.

"I actually stopped by to see Drew."

"He's upstairs in his office. Go on up," she said, gesturing toward the staircase with a well-manicured hand.

Hope expressed her thanks and approached the staircase, her hand gliding along the smooth, sturdy wooden banister, worn by countless touches over two centuries. As she reached the landing, she paused to take in the blend of tradition and technology that filled the air, a testament to the enduring spirit of small-town journalism. The hum of activity and the clatter of keyboards reminded her that work never truly stopped at the newspaper.

She greeted Drew's colleagues with soft "hellos" as she walked along the carpeted corridor, finally arriving at his office. The door stood wide open, revealing Drew engrossed in his work. She rapped lightly on the doorframe as she stepped inside. He glanced up from his laptop computer, surprise flickering across his features.

"Hope," he said, leaning back in his chair and pushing away his laptop computer. "You won't believe the morning I've had."

"Oh, I think I can top it." Hope quickly shed her jacket and dropped her tote onto the chair in front of Drew's desk. Through the window behind him, a picture-postcard scene unfolded: snow-covered buildings, rising church steeples, and gentle rolling hills—a winter wonderland now marred by murder.

He gave her a "challenge-accepted" look as he steepled his fingers and grinned.

"Lorna Morgan claims that she's Maisie's half-sister," she said.

"What the . . . how did you find that out?"

Hope dropped onto the chair in front of the desk and returned his look with a "wouldn't you love to know" look.

"You went to the Merrifield Inn, didn't you?" He snapped his fingers. "That's where I planned on going, but it's been crazy here. On top of following up with my sources about the murder, I'm drowning in edits! I know we're knee-deep in snow right now, but I have to get this spring gardening special issue together. Between us, Libby is a nightmare writer to work with."

Hope laughed softly. She could relate to his pain. When she was a food magazine editor, she worked with a few of those writers.

"She believes that since she's the garden club vice president her work doesn't need to be edited." Drew shook his head in frustration. "Anyhoo, back to this bombshell you just dropped!"

"I did go to the inn. I found out that both Lorna and Talia checked in this morning. Eliza told me that Lorna asked about a lawyer and Eliza directed her to Matt."

"Seems like deception runs in the family." Drew pulled his computer closer and started typing furiously. "Maybe this explains why I found nothing on Lorna Morgan. Well, I did find a cellist from San Francisco and a bunch of others who aren't *our* Lorna Morgan."

"What are you searching now?" Hope asked, leaning in to get a glimpse of the screen.

"Half-sisters, huh? Let me start with Maisie's birth surname, Thompson." Drew's fingers danced over the keyboard. "Okay, here's an article." He scanned the document, clicking the keyboard repeatedly.

"What's taking so long?" Hope asked, her impatience growing.

Drew gave her a sidelong look. "What? You think this information magically appears?"

Hope shrugged, a small smile playing on her lips.

"While I research, why don't you tell me what else you've got?" Drew suggested, his eyes still glued to the screen.

"Not much. Matt wouldn't give me any details about why Lorna was there, but she did mention having questions about her role as the next of kin. Then I went to the police department to sign my statement and hand over the *Release* I forgot about last night. Sam wouldn't give me any more information on the investigation, other than Henry is still in a coma and they haven't found Penny's belongings at the lodge."

Drew looked up from his screen. "Actually, that's something, Hope. He's connected Penny's disappearance to the lodge and possibly to Henry." He returned his attention to the computer, tapping away.

"While I was there, Maretta sent a message for me to meet her at Town Hall," Hope continued.

"What did she want? Let me guess, lecture you about how you've brought another murder to Jefferson and insist you stay out of the case," Drew said, a hint of sarcasm in his voice.

"Just the opposite. She wants me 'to do that thing you do with murders.'"

Drew's head snapped up, his eyes wide with shock.

"Yeah, that was an exact quote."

"Whoa! I never saw that coming." He dragged his fingers through his blond hair, which had darkened slightly in the winter months. "I have to admit, the woman never ceases to amaze me."

They shared a quiet moment, both knowing that despite Maretta's tough exterior and blunt manner, she always had the best interests of their beloved town at heart.

"Drew!" Whitney appeared in the doorway. "There's a fire at Town Hall!"

"You mean it wasn't a drill?" Hope asked, her brow furrowing in confusion. When she got puzzled looks from both Whitney and Drew, she continued. "I was there when the fire alarm went off. Maretta thought it was a drill."

"It was no drill," Whitney assured. "Fire trucks have been dispatched."

"I'll go over and see what I can learn from the scene." Drew shot up and closed his laptop with a snap.

"Okay. I'll call Byron to see if he can also get on scene to cover it in case there are any injuries. He can go to the hospital," Whitney said, already dialing her phone as she spun around and disappeared from the office.

"Sorry, Hope. I'll have to look into Lorna Morgan later." Drew rushed out the door, leaving Hope alone in the office.

She stood, ready to leave as well, but lingered for a moment, staring at Drew's computer. Her mind buzzed with questions. One thought kept circling back—how many more secrets were going to come to light about Maisie Cox?

Chapter Twelve

The mudroom door had just clicked shut behind Hope when she stepped out of her boots, already calculating how quickly she could make tea. The day's events—that shocking secret, the favor that still made her question whether pigs were flying somewhere, and then the fire—had left her feeling like she'd run a marathon. All she craved was the simple comfort of her favorite mug and some ridiculous cat antics on her phone. But Bigelow, ever the opportunist, had other ideas. With perfect timing, he dropped his slobbery tennis ball precisely between her feet, his entire body quivering with anticipation as he fixed her with his most persuasive gaze.

She couldn't help but smile at the sight of his wagging tail and hopeful expression, despite the fatigue clinging to her. It had been a long day.

"All right, buddy," she said, scooping up the ball. "Let's go get some fresh air."

She bundled up again and stepped out onto the patio. The frigid air bit at her nose and stung her cheeks, seeping through her boots to nip at her toes. Bigelow, unfazed by the cold, dashed across the yard with the ball clutched proudly in his jaws. His energy was a stark contrast to hers, and a not-so-subtle reminder of the many morning runs she'd skipped lately.

Between recipe testing for her blog and rounds of cookbook edits, her once-regular fitness routine had slipped through the cracks, and her waistband was starting to show it.

As Bigelow trotted back toward her, triumphant and tail-wagging, Hope made a silent promise. Tomorrow morning, no matter how early or how cold, she'd lace up her sneakers and hit the pavement again. It was time to reclaim her mornings and her fitness.

Bigelow's energy waned after a few rounds of fetch, and they both retreated into the warmth of the house. After a drink from his bowl, he curled up on his bed in the family room. Hope made her tea and warmed a muffin in the microwave. Later, standing at the kitchen counter with the scent of cinnamon still lingering in the air, she sipped her tea and scrolled idly. Her phone rested beside her cup, speaker turned up. She'd gotten a notification that there was a new episode of *Search for the Missing*. Amy's voice poured out—calm, polished, and professional.

"A young woman disappears. A desperate sister searching for answers. A life coach that isn't who she claims to be."

Hope froze, her hand hovering above the tea towel. She was familiar with Amy's style—the dramatic opening, the deliberate pacing. But this time, it wasn't just another cold case.

Ethan stepped into the kitchen from the mudroom, his stride faltering. His shoulders squared, and his body went rigid as Amy's voice drifted from Hope's phone.

"Two self-improvement retreats. One during a nor'easter at an isolated lodge. Another during a bitter cold snap. One disappearance. One murder."

He moved closer, his gaze flicking to the phone, then to Hope. His jaw tightened slightly.

"Welcome to Search for the Missing, *the podcast where we discuss cold cases that may have been forgotten . . ."*

Hope watched him out of the corner of her eye, trying to gauge his reaction. He didn't say anything. Didn't need to. The slight crease forming between his brows was enough.

". . . When I arrived at the Jefferson lodge, I discovered that the self-help guru I was greeted by was indeed the same person who held the retreat from where Penny Foster went missing. That wasn't the only twist, my dear friends. By the end of the night, retreat attendee and food blogger Hope Early discovered the body of the life coach. Was it an accident or was it murder?"

Ethan crossed his arms, slow and deliberate. "Wow," he said, the word heavy with implication.

Hope flinched. Of course she'd known Amy was recording the episode, but she hadn't fully considered that her role in the story would be front and center—broadcast for everyone to dissect.

"And let me tell you, that isn't the only twist in this story . . ." Amy continued.

Hope reached for the phone and hit pause.

"I wasn't expecting it to sound so . . ." She trailed off, unsure of the right word. Invasive? Theatrical?

"Public," Ethan said flatly.

"Exactly." Hope lifted her cup and took a sip of tea, which was now lukewarm. "I get that it's a podcast and it's meant to be public. I just wasn't ready for it to feel *that* public. Anyway, did you hear about the fire at Town Hall?"

"I did. Turns out it was a small electrical fire," Ethan said, resting a hand on the counter. "We need to talk."

"You know I stopped by Matt's office today."

"I thought you were just picking up my truck, wrapping up your statement with Sam, then spending a quiet Sunday baking."

"I did all that and a few other errands, too." She moved past him toward the table, where her laptop and recipe drafts lay in disarray. A knot of worry tightened in her stomach. She already knew where this conversation was headed. "What did Matt tell you?"

"Everything," Ethan said, voice low and firm.

"I can explain," she replied, lowering herself into a chair.

Before he could respond, his phone buzzed. He pulled it from his pocket and glanced at the screen. "I need to take this. We'll finish this later," he said, walking out of the room.

Bigelow padded over and settled beside Hope's chair, gently placing a paw on her lap. She gave a small smile and scratched behind his ear. "Thanks, buddy. I think I might be in some serious trouble."

● ● ●

Monday morning greeted Hope with a windchill of five degrees, which sent a shiver through her as she bundled up and ventured out to the chicken coop. Beneath her parka, she wore layers of thermals and her thickest socks, but the cold still nipped at her nose, stung her cheeks, and seeped into her bones. Her breath misted in the frigid air as she made her way to the henhouse, the gravel crunching beneath her boots. After scattering feed and checking over each of her hens, her daily ritual no matter the weather, she tugged her fleece gaiter higher and braced herself for the dash back to the house.

Even Bigelow, her usually eager sidekick, had chosen to stay curled up by the fireplace. She couldn't blame him. He was clearly the wiser of the two that morning.

Yesterday, she'd told herself that today would be the day she reclaimed her mornings and her energy. A run had sounded ambitious, but a walk with Bigelow felt more manageable . . . until she'd checked the forecast. Five degrees? No, thank you. Instead, she'd pivoted to cooking.

After returning inside, she shrugged off her coat and swapped her boots for slippers. She tied on an apron, pulled her hair into a messy bun, and set about making chicken soup. Carrots, celery, and onions were chopped and swept into a large wooden bowl, followed by a few cloves of garlic and a handful of fresh thyme from the little pot on her windowsill. The rhythm of the knife against the cutting board was soothing, a welcome change from the tension of the past twenty-four hours. Once the vegetables were prepped, she set her Dutch oven on the six-burner stove, added a splash of olive oil, and began sautéing the mirepoix until the kitchen filled with the savory aroma. As the chicken browned and broth was added, the room warmed, not just from the heat of the stove but from the comfort of routine.

Next on her list was to bake a batch of her tried-and-true biscuits. The dough came together quickly, and by the time she cleared her work surface and wiped down the counters, the oven timer dinged to signal golden, flaky perfection.

The night before, she'd texted Heather, Ethan's ex-wife, and offered to drop off a care package for her and the girls. Hope understood how draining it could be to care for two sick little ones and wanted to help in whatever way she could. Heather had responded with sincere gratitude, letting her know she was welcome to stop by anytime.

While the soup bubbled gently on the stove and the biscuits cooled on the rack, Hope filled the teakettle and set it on the stove. She sliced a bagel and dropped the halves into the toaster.

Footsteps echoed from the foyer, giving Hope just enough warning before Ethan entered the kitchen. He appeared in the doorway dressed for the day—dark jeans, a soft gray sweater, his cashmere coat folded neatly over one arm.

Last night had been tense. After taking his work call, he'd kept his word and resumed their conversation about her visit to Matt's office.

Hope had tried to explain her reasoning, but Ethan had made it clear that she'd overstepped. Whether or not Lorna was technically Matt's client didn't seem to matter to him. The rest of the evening, including dinner, had been wrapped in silence. And judging by the tight line of his jaw this morning, his frostiness hadn't thawed overnight.

"Good morning," Hope said evenly, pouring hot water into her mug as the tea bag floated on the surface. "Would you like to review my agenda for the day before you leave for work?"

The words were out before she could stop them. Sharp. Unfair. But not entirely unearned, she thought as she set the kettle on the trivet.

Ethan sighed, then crossed the room and gently took her hands in his. "I'm sorry about last night," he said quietly. "I do understand why you did it, Hope. But that doesn't mean I wasn't right to be upset."

Hope glanced down at their entwined hands, her defenses slipping. She understood where he was coming from. In hindsight, confronting Lorna at Matt's office hadn't been her most thoughtful decision. She could've given herself more time to think it through and waited until Lorna returned to the inn.

"I know," she said quietly, meeting Ethan's gaze. "I could have handled it differently. I'm sorry too."

He gave her hands a gentle squeeze. "Let's just promise to communicate better next time, okay?"

"Deal." She nodded, feeling some of the tension begin to ease, like a window cracked open to let in fresh air.

Ethan looked around and smiled. "The kitchen smells amazing. All this is going to Heather's?"

"Chicken soup and biscuits," Hope said, her tone lightening. "I still need to make the banana bread. Do you want a cup of tea before heading out?"

"No. This is all I need to start the day." He pulled her into a hug, holding her close.

Wrapped in his arms, the kitchen warm and fragrant around them, Hope felt a sense of relief. The frost between them was melting, and she was grateful for the chance to start the day on a better note.

• • •

Despite the rocky start to her day, Hope's mood improved, and not too long after Ethan left for work she ventured out. While loading the dishwasher a text from Drew came in asking her to meet him at the Coffee Clique, the best coffee shop in town. He was vague but she hoped that he had an update since they last spoke. She replied that she'd meet him after dropping off a care package at Heather's house. The loaf of banana bread she had baked was packed up with the chicken soup and biscuits and ready for delivery.

When Hope arrived at Heather's house, the girls were still in bed, so she left the basket with Heather, politely declining the offer of coffee since she was planning to meet Drew. When she reached the Coffee Clique, she parked in the lot behind the coffee shop and hustled inside, grateful to escape the cold. The aroma of freshly brewed coffee and sweet pastries enveloped her. Just as she stepped through the door, her phone buzzed again with a text.

Sorry. Can't make coffee. On my way to Vermont. Fill you in later.

Hope frowned at the screen. So much for their catch-up. She glanced at the long line snaking toward the counter, debating whether to wait for caffeine or leave, and then a familiar voice called out.

"Hope!" She turned to see Elspeth Higgins waving from a corner table, impossible to miss in her bright fuchsia turtleneck and chunky silver jewelry. She looked like she'd stepped out of a fashion spread. The lime green cat-eye glasses perched on her nose sealed the deal. Jefferson's resident fashionista never failed to make a statement.

Elspeth owned EH Fashion and Accessories, just a few doors down from Claire's shop, and was known for her fearless approach to style and a wardrobe that could brighten even the gloomiest New England day.

"Good morning, Elspeth." Hope approached the table, unwrapping her scarf from around her neck. "Don't you look like the vision of cheerfulness."

Elspeth blushed as she accepted the compliment with a broad smile. "I feel it's my responsibility to spread a little fashion cheer to everyone. Dull clothes beget a dull mood."

"You're definitely anything but dull," Hope said with a soft laugh.

"And neither are you." Elspeth's oval-shaped face took on a more serious expression, her full red lips turning down into a frown. "I heard what happened Saturday night. What an awful experience you went through."

Hope braced herself. She knew she'd have to field plenty of questions in the days ahead, some well-meaning, others laced with gossip, and steer the narrative when necessary.

"When I heard Maisie Cox was hosting a retreat in Jefferson, I had no idea she was actually Demi Covington," Elspeth went on, shaking her head.

Hope prepared to give her usual polite-but-firm response—the kind she'd perfected for redirecting nosy conversations—when Elspeth's next words stopped her cold.

"I still can't believe Demi resurfaced after all this time," Elspeth continued. "You know, she had blood on her hands."

Elspeth lifted her coffee cup, taking a slow sip as her eyes locked onto Hope's.

Hope stared, caught off guard by the statement. "Blood on her hands? What do you mean by that?"

Elspeth leaned forward, resting her manicured hands lightly on the edge of the table, her voice dipping as if inviting Hope into a secret. "You don't know?" She glanced around, as if worried someone might overhear. "I was on that retreat up in Vermont. The one where Penny Foster disappeared."

Hope's breath caught. "You were there?"

"Of course, I had no idea that Demi was a con artist at the time, but yes, I was there." Elspeth paused and took another sip of coffee, her eyes distant for a moment. "To be honest, even though she was a fraud, I had a good experience. It was intense, yes, but I felt motivated."

She set her cup down with a gentle clink. "But there was a woman— Nina, I think her name was. She emptied her bank account to pay for the whole mentorship package. It was heartbreaking. She was fragile to begin with, and when the results didn't come quickly, she spiraled."

"That's awful," Hope said, her voice soft with sympathy.

Elspeth sighed. "It was hard to watch. Demi—Maisie—whatever— she was magnetic, but also . . . ruthless in her own way. You either thrived or floundered under her program."

She checked her watch and gasped. "Oh, drat. I've got to open the shop." She stood and gathered her things, pausing to give Hope a meaningful look. "Be careful poking around in all this. That woman left a trail of damage behind her, and not everyone walked away."

With that, she flashed a quick smile, slung her purse over one shoulder, and swept out of the coffee shop with her usual flair.

Hope stood still for a moment, her mind suddenly spinning with new questions.

Another customer brushed past, bumping Hope's shoulder and jolting her from her thoughts. She realized she still hadn't gotten the coffee she'd come in for. The line at the counter was shorter now, so she headed back and took her place.

As she waited, her mind churned. How many more of Maisie's former clients were in Jefferson or nearby? And why hadn't she pressed Elspeth for more details about that Vermont retreat?

She couldn't help but kick herself for letting the conversation slip away

The line moved quickly, and soon she was ordering a large hazelnut coffee from the barista. While waiting, she pulled out her phone to check her notifications. A cluster of unread texts and a dozen new emails greeted her.

She spotted an open table near the door and claimed it, dropping her tote bag on the floor beside her. Coffee in hand, she sat and took a long, comforting sip before scrolling through her work inbox.

One email from a brand she'd partnered with caught her eye. She skimmed the message and reviewed the list of deliverables she would be responsible for, which included short videos, social media captions, and photographs. Just as she tapped to the next message, her screen filled with updates from her agent, cookbook editor, and publicist— each one brimming with requests, questions, and looming deadlines.

With a soft sigh, she closed the app and set her phone aside. Cradling her coffee cup, her gaze landed on Talia near the exit. The assistant must have entered unnoticed, but Hope wasn't about to miss this chance to speak with her.

"Talia," she called, setting down her cup and raising a hand. The younger woman's irritation was palpable, but Hope refused to be put off. She couldn't afford to miss this opening to talk with someone who might have crucial information about the murder.

Chapter Thirteen

Talia stopped in her tracks, as if rooted to the floor, her lips parting with hesitation. Her expression tightened the moment she spotted Hope, a flash of annoyance crossing her features.

"Come join me!" Hope called out, pointing to the empty chair across from her.

Talia lingered for a moment, her eyes sweeping the coffee shop like she was searching for a way out. But after a beat, she exhaled and crossed the room, her movements deliberate. She was wrapped in a white puffer coat, a sleek black purse tucked under one arm. Up close, Hope noticed the faint redness around her eyes, subtle but telling. Talia had been crying.

"I know you're probably in a hurry, but I was hoping to talk to you," Hope said. "I promise, it won't take long."

"Sure, but I really can't stay. I need to get back to the inn. There's a lot on my plate." Talia pulled out the chair and sat, setting her coffee on the table and her purse across her lap like a barrier.

"Work?"

She closed her eyes briefly, exhaling through her nose. "What I'm doing now wasn't in the SOPs." She opened her eyes and added, "Standard operating procedures."

"I know what they are. I use them for my blog," Hope replied. They'd made onboarding assistants over the years a lot easier for her. "I'm guessing refund requests are piling up?"

"Just about every client Maisie signed in the last year has reached out." She lifted the lid on her coffee and took a cautious sip. "I'm doing my best to process them all. Even yours, if you want one." Her chin trembled, eyes glossy with fresh tears. She blinked hard, trying to keep them from falling.

"I'm so sorry for your loss, Talia," Hope said.

"Thank you." Talia's chin quivered. "It's not the first time I lost someone I was close to. My mom . . . but I can't afford to be emotional right now. There's a ton of work to do."

"I can't imagine how hard this has been, especially with everything happening so suddenly."

Talia nodded, keeping her eyes on the cup in her hands. "It feels like I'm trapped in a nightmare. First finding out who Maisie really was . . . her connection to that missing woman . . . and then the murder, the questions from the police. Honestly, it's too much. What's happened hasn't even sunk in yet."

"I get that this is a lot to process." Hope leaned back in her seat, never breaking eye contact with Talia. "But I can't seem to shake the feeling that you weren't completely blindsided by the truth about Maisie."

Talia recoiled, as if Hope's words had struck a nerve. "What? That's not fair. Maisie deceived everyone. Including me."

"No, I don't believe that," Hope said, lifting her coffee for a slow sip. "You knew who she really was all along. And you and Lorna know each other. The question is, how?"

Talia's fingers tightened around her cup. For a moment, she looked like she might deny it, but the tension in her shoulders gave her away. Her lips parted, but no words came. Finally, she exhaled, the fight draining out of her. "How did you figure it out?" she whispered.

Hope offered a small shrug, unwilling to reveal that her statement was based purely on a hunch, a guess derived from the shared look between Talia and Lorna that seemed too familiar to be mere coincidence.

Talia stared into her coffee, her voice low. "Lorna contacted me first."

Hope leaned forward eagerly, nearly sloshing her coffee as she pulse raced. At last, the puzzle pieces were snapping into place. "What did she want from you?"

"She wanted an ally," Talia admitted. "Lorna was determined to destroy Maisie, and she needed someone on the inside to help her do it."

"Exactly how had she planned on doing that?"

Talia stared into her coffee as if reading tea leaves, her words coming slow and controlled. "First, she wanted to confront Maisie face-to-face. It had been years since they'd seen each other, and Lorna wanted to catch Maisie off guard. Then, she planned to expose Maisie on social media. She was going to reveal her true identity to the world. Maisie's father was a grifter who scammed people out of money and other possessions. It appeared his oldest daughter inherited his gift for deceit."

"Why would you agree to help her do that?"

Talia met Hope's gaze, her eyes filled with a mix of guilt and resolve. "Because I found out who Maisie really was. When I discovered that Penny Foster had gone missing during the retreat up in Vermont, I couldn't just stand by and do nothing. Maisie had lied to me, to everyone. Yet she constantly talked about being your authentic self. On second thought, maybe being a lying, deceitful person was her true authentic self."

"So, you participated in a plan to take her down that ended with her death?"

Talia's head dropped in shame, her shoulders slumping under the weight of her confession.

Hope watched Talia, as a mix of emotions swirled inside of her. She was thrilled to finally have some new information, but frustration bubbled up as well. How could Talia have been so naive? Yet, as she looked at the younger woman, Hope couldn't help but feel a pang of compassion. Talia had been duped, just like so many others. There was no way she could have known Maisie was going to be murdered . . . unless that was part of Lorna's plan. The idea made Hope's skin prickle with a sudden, unsettling awareness.

"You didn't know when she hired you who she really was? You had no idea that Maisie was a fraud?" Hope asked, her voice softer now. "That a man died as a result of one of her retreats, forced to hike without being prepared? Or that a woman named Nina spent everything she had to buy into Maisie's mentorship program? Or what happened to Penny?"

For the briefest moment, something flickered in Talia's eyes, surprise, maybe, or recognition, but it vanished as quickly as it came. She shook her head, a little too firmly. "No. I swear. I hadn't followed Penny Foster's case closely when it happened, I was in the thick of finals and sending out résumés. I barely had time to sleep, let alone follow the news."

She hesitated, then added, "Looking back, that should've raised alarms for everyone. But I didn't think twice at the time."

Hope sat back in her chair, her mind processing this new information. The web of deception surrounding Maisie's identity was more tangled than she had imagined. She took a sip of her coffee, her thoughts racing as she considered the implications of Talia's revelations. Despite her frustration, Hope couldn't ignore the genuine remorse in Talia's eyes.

"Talia," Hope said, her voice steady and determined, yet gentle. "We need to find out what Lorna's plan was—and if she succeeded in carrying it out."

After a pause to let that sink in, she asked, "Have you told any of this to the police? Detective Reid in particular?"

"No," Talia admitted.

"It's time that you do." Hope stood, her expression resolute. "I'll drive you to the police department so you can speak with the detective. He needs to know all of this."

Talia looked frightened, her eyes filled with worry. "I don't want to get into trouble since I wasn't very forthcoming earlier. And I'll have to find another place to stay until this is all wrapped up, because if I tell the detective about Lorna . . ."

"There are plenty of inns here in Jefferson," Hope reassured her, reaching for her tote and grabbing her to-go cup. "The Merrifield is the nicest, but I'm sure you'll find suitable accommodations somewhere."

"You seem to have an answer for everything." Talia rose to her feet, lifting her own to-go cup. "Thank you."

"There's no need to thank me," Hope replied. "Let's just focus on getting to the bottom of this."

• • •

Hope sat in the bland interview room, arms crossed, her foot tapping a steady, irritated rhythm against the tile floor. The harsh overhead lighting buzzed faintly above her, washing everything in a sterile glare. Across the small table sat a black audio recorder, its red standby light blinking like it was taunting her. A camera in the corner was tilted just enough to make its presence obvious.

Wonderful. Surveillance and silence.

She shot it a look.

When Detective Reid had ushered her in, he hadn't bothered with pleasantries or even an explanation, just a curt "Wait here. I'll be back in a few minutes." Then the door thunked shut behind him with all the warmth of a jail cell.

A few minutes had become . . . what? Ten? Fifteen? Her phone had been left at the front desk, so she couldn't check the time—another detail that grated.

Hope shifted in the stiff metal chair and let out a quiet sigh of frustration. She hadn't done anything wrong. She'd come here to help. Talia had agreed to come clean, and Hope had offered to support her. Now they were both sitting in separate interview rooms like suspects in some crime show.

Was this necessary?

He closed the door behind him and moved across the room. He looked just as put-together as he had the last time she'd seen him— tailored suit, white shirt, dark tie. Classic detective attire. Hope tapped her fingers on the table, her patience wearing thin. She met his gaze squarely. The two of them had always walked a fine line, her relentless curiosity brushing up against the boundaries of his patience. Today, she had no intention of pretending to be agreeable.

"I've been waiting in this interrogation room for about fifteen minutes. Care to explain why?" Hope didn't give him a chance to answer. "I brought Talia here so she could cooperate, not so I could be treated like a suspect."

Sam remained standing with his arms crossed. "This isn't an interrogation room. It's an interview room, Hope."

"It certainly feels like an interrogation room," she shot back. "Locked room. Blinking red light. No explanation."

A muscle twitched in Reid's cheek, frustration maybe. Or restraint.

"I needed a few moments with Talia alone before I spoke with you," he said. "She's sharing information that is helpful to my investigation, and I need to know who knew what and when."

"Again, I'm not sure why I'm here because I knew nothing about her and Lorna's relationship and plot to reveal who Maisie really was."

"I think you have a habit of finding yourself in the middle of things. Whether you intend to or not."

Hope gave a dry laugh. "Believe me, it's not a habit I enjoy."

"You know I don't appreciate you meddling in police business," Sam said, his tone as dry as day-old toast.

"And you know I have a knack for getting people to talk, Sam." She shifted in her seat. "We're after the same thing, which is finding Maisie's killer. Isn't that worth a little . . . teamwork?"

He sighed and scrubbed a hand through his hair, a gesture that struck her as more weary than annoyed. "Fine, Hope."

She blinked. "Wait . . . fine? As in, you're agreeing?"

Sam leveled a look at her. "Unofficially. If we do this, I need you to keep me informed. No solo acts, no sitting on information. Deal?"

Hope extended her hand before he had a chance to change his mind. "Deal."

"Don't make me regret this." He shook her hand. "Now, I'm sure you have questions."

"You're right. Have you been able to match the handwriting on that *Release* I turned over? Considering what we just learned from Talia, it's probably Lorna's."

Sam's jaw tightened. "I can't comment on that. It's part of an active investigation."

Hope blinked at him. "I thought we were teaming up."

"We are," he said. "You bring me what you find, I work the case. That's the arrangement, not full access to police records."

She crossed her arms. "So, I don't get to know anything?"

"You get what I can legally tell you," he replied. "There are rules and laws to follow. But if we're smart about it, we might just get somewhere. Now, is there anything else?"

"I do have one more question. How do people like Maisie do it?" she asked, her voice low. "How do they manipulate so effortlessly? She got people to trust her. Smart people. And she never even flinched. No regret, no shame. It's like she believed her own lies." She paused, shaking her head. "In the twenty-first century, with the internet, background checks, social media . . . how does someone like that still get away with it?"

Reid didn't answer right away. He slid his hands into his pants pockets and leaned against the wall, studying her.

"They get away with it," he said, "because they know exactly what people want to believe. A good con artist doesn't push, they let you walk into the trap. They watch, listen, and mirror. They build trust by giving you just enough truth to make the lie go down smooth. It's not magic, it's psychology."

Hope swallowed hard. A wave of anger rose within her, directed mostly at herself for ever letting Maisie manipulate her.

Reid continued, his tone more measured. "And the really dangerous ones? They believe their own stories. They convince themselves they're doing what's necessary, maybe even deserved. That they're owed something. It's not that they feel no guilt. It's that they've rewritten the rules in their own mind. That makes them harder to spot and harder to stop."

She met his eyes. "Before Maisie died, she told me someone was out to hurt her. I didn't believe her. I thought it was just another part of the act."

He nodded slowly. "Could've been. Or maybe that time she was telling the truth. That's the thing with people like Maisie, you never really know what's real. And by the time you figure it out, it's usually too late."

• • •

Hope returned home and jumped on a call with her agent. With her cookbook manuscript almost ready to submit, it was time to start thinking ahead. As they tossed around ideas for her next proposal, Hope felt a jolt of disbelief—*is this really my life?* Never in her wildest dreams, back when she was a food magazine editor or writing her first blog posts, had she imagined she'd one day be a cookbook author. But here she was.

The call lasted thirty minutes, and by the time she hung up, her mind was buzzing. There were so many directions to explore, but she reminded herself to stay grounded in the brand she'd built with *Hope at Home*. She'd taken pages of notes during the conversation. After jotting down a few final thoughts, she pushed back from the table and stretched.

Princess, who had been curled up in her cat tree, leapt down and trotted over, brushing her thick fur along Hope's legs like a feline velvet rope. Taking the hint, Hope reached for the mouse teaser wand and began bobbing it back and forth. Princess pounced with gusto, batting and leaping, fully committed to the hunt.

Their playful moment was abruptly interrupted by a sharp knock at the front door. The sudden noise startled Bigelow, sending him bolting off the sofa like a furry cannonball. He charged through the living room and skidded into the foyer, his nails clicking against the hardwood floor.

Hope hurried after him, calling his name as she went. By the time she reached the foyer, Bigelow was already sitting at attention by the door, his tail wagging with anticipation. She placed a calming hand on his head before opening the door to find Amy standing on the porch, her expression a mix of determination and excitement.

"I know I'm dropping by unannounced, but that's what friends do. At least, I *thought* we were friends." Amy stood on the porch, arms crossed and a stormy expression on her face. "That is, until a *friend* started butting into my investigation."

Hope's brain scrambled to keep up. "Amy, I . . . I have no idea what you're talking about."

Amy's eyes narrowed, her voice edged with frustration. "Don't play dumb, Hope. You know exactly what I'm talking about. I've been researching and planning the Penny Foster case for months. And I'm not going to let you or anyone else jeopardize it."

Bigelow, oblivious to the rising tension, pranced in excited circles at Amy's feet. Hope placed a calming hand on his head, her gaze never leaving Amy's face.

"Amy, I wasn't trying to—" she began, but Amy cut her off with a sharp look.

"Then stop," she snapped. "Stop poking around in things that don't concern you."

"First of all, I don't appreciate your tone," Hope said. "Second, I'm not 'butting into' your investigation. I'm the person who found Maisie's body." And the one who basically hand-delivered everyone into a weekend with a con artist. But she kept that part to herself. "Now, are you here to argue, or do you want to come and talk over coffee or tea?"

Amy faltered, her posture relaxing as she dropped her arms to her sides. Now she looked more tired than angry. "Do you have any hot chocolate?" she asked, almost sheepish.

Hope tilted her head. "With whipped cream?"

"Yes, please." Amy gave a small, eager nod. "It's freezing out here."

"Well, come in then." Hope stepped back, opening the door wider.

As Amy walked inside, she shrugged off her coat. Hope took it and hung it in the hall closet, then led the way to the kitchen. The tension hadn't disappeared, but it had shifted.

Bigelow, sensing the shift in mood, gave a happy little wag of his tail and padded over to Amy nudging her leg with his nose. She reached down to scratch behind his ears, murmuring something soft, before he ambled off to his bed in the family room and settled in with a contentment huff.

Hope pulled a tin of her homemade hot chocolate mix from the cabinet. She set it on the counter and reached for the milk. Next, she retrieved two big mugs from another cabinet.

"I owe you an apology," Amy said. "I shouldn't have come at you like that. It's just . . . these past few days have been brutal."

She dropped into a chair at the table, her hands knotted tightly in front of her, looking unusually tired and worn. Her normally vibrant blond hair was flat, her eyes bloodshot, and her energetic demeanor notably subdued.

Hope glanced over as she poured milk into the double boiler and stirred in the cocoa mix. "It's okay," she said gently. "I do understand."

Amy let out a long, weary sigh and slumped forward, the tension seeming to drain from her shoulders. "This case is more complicated than I ever imagined. I've been chasing this story for months, trying to put the pieces together. But now . . . Maisie's murder, the lies, the people getting hurt, it's all gotten so twisted. So much bigger than I thought." She looked up, her expression raw. "I didn't come here to fight. I need your help."

"You know I'm always happy to help," Hope said, crossing to the refrigerator. She pulled out a container of heavy cream and moved to the stand mixer. As the cream hit the stainless-steel bowl, she flicked the switch and the wire whisk sprang to life, whipping the cream into soft peaks.

"But first," Hope said over the hum of the mixer, "I'd like to know how you came across Penny's case."

Amy sat up a little straighter, a spark of energy igniting behind her tired eyes. "I spend a lot of time at the library and online, digging through cold cases, following threads. One day, I stumbled across a newspaper clipping about Penny's disappearance. Something about it hooked me. I figured if it did that for me, it would be a great episode for the podcast."

Her voice grew stronger, edged with that unmistakable confidence Hope had seen when Amy was talking about one of her podcast cases. "A young woman, eager to launch a travel blog, goes off to a retreat that promises transformation . . . and then vanishes. No trace, no closure. Then I discovered that another participant was hospitalized after the same retreat and later died. That's when I knew I had to dig deeper. Wouldn't you?"

The mixer whirred to a stop. Hope removed the bowl and brought it to the island, where she filled the mugs with hot chocolate and then topped each with a generous swirl of whipped cream before carrying them to the table.

She set one in front of Amy and took the seat across from her. "So," Hope asked, before taking a sip of her hot chocolate, "when did Ethan get involved?"

Amy took a long sip of the hot chocolate, her eyes fluttering shut for a moment. "Okay, this is amazing," she said, setting the mug down. "Let's see, we bumped into each other at the coffee shop. I had my files out. I was knee-deep in the case. He asked what I was working on, and one thing led to another. I told him I was getting nowhere with the local police up north, and he offered to help. Said he had a connection."

"Let me guess, he knows the police chief?"

"Bingo." Amy wrapped her hands around the mug again. "He opened a few doors for me. He didn't have to, but I think he believed Penny Foster's case needed to be solved, or at least her story be told. His help has been huge."

"We all know how Ethan feels about unsolved cases. And it sounds like you're leaving no stone unturned with this story."

"This isn't just another case to me, not anymore. I owe it to them to see it through." Amy pulled out her phone from her purse and tapped the screen. "Mind if I start recording?"

Hope nodded.

Amy mouthed, "Thanks," then hit record and set the phone on the table between them.

"Once Ethan helped me get access to the police file, I started digging into the backgrounds of the other retreat attendees," she continued. "One of them was Arthur Swanson, an entrepreneur who'd been through a string of business failures. He's the one who died."

Hope felt a cold prickle creep over her skin at the thought of that fateful retreat. Hers had turned out similarly . . . with a dead body.

"How did he die?" she asked.

"The coroner said it was from asthma. When the temperature dropped suddenly he suffered a fatal attack." Amy paused. "According to the police report, the organizers were aware of his medical condition but didn't take any steps to protect him. There were no emergency protocols."

Hope shook her head, horrified. "Didn't his family sue Maisie?"

"You'd think so." Amy sighed. "But neither Drew nor I could track down any relatives. Besides, the police said there wasn't enough evidence to bring charges."

Hope frowned. "Then why disappear? Why become someone else?"

Amy leaned back, her fingers tapping absently against her mug. "The official channels might have let her off the hook, but social media didn't. A few other attendees posted about their experiences. The backlash came fast—and it was relentless. My guess? Maisie panicked. She pulled down her website, scrubbed her socials, and vanished.

Within three weeks of that Vermont retreat, Demi Covington was gone. And Maisie was born."

Hope made the universal "cut it" gesture across her throat, signaling Amy to stop recording.

Amy immediately tapped her phone screen. "What is it? Something wrong?"

"No," Hope said. "I just need to fill you in on a few things I've learned, and it's probably better if this part stays off the record."

"Oh, okay." Amy reached into her purse and pulled out a small notebook and pen. "I'm ready."

Hope started with Lorna's claim that she was Maisie's half-sister. Amy gasped, her pen pausing mid-word. Hope then went on to share what Talia had told her about their plan to expose Maisie, and finished with the news that Drew had gone up to Vermont to speak with the local police about Penny Foster's disappearance.

Amy scribbled notes as Hope talked and looked up when she had a question. "Do you think Lorna killed Maisie?"

"She definitely has a motive," Hope said. "And since you've been trying to contact people who went on that retreat, you should talk to Elspeth Higgins. She was there."

Amy's eyes widened. "Are you serious?"

Hope nodded. "This morning, I ran into her at the coffee shop and she told me about another woman, her name was Nina, who lost everything because of Maisie. You might be able to interview her for the podcast. Maybe Elspeth can help you find her."

"This is huge!" Amy snapped her notebook shut and tucked it, along with her phone and pen, back into her purse. "Thanks for the hot chocolate and for not slamming the door in my face."

Hope laughed. "Come on. I'd never do that to a friend."

"Keep me posted, okay?"

"You got it." Hope walked her to the door. She waved as Amy descended the front porch steps and got into her car.

Hope had just closed the door when her phone chimed with a text from Drew. She opened it, expecting an update on the case, but instead he was asking a favor. Could she check on Trixie? He usually went home at lunch to feed her and let her out, but since he was on his way to Vermont, he needed a substitute. The thought of a little puppy time lifted her spirits.

She texted back, *On my way.*

Chapter Fourteen

The drive to Drew's antique home was peaceful, the kind of quiet that settles in after a storm. Just days earlier, Jefferson had been gripped by harsh weather, but now the snow-covered trees and gently rolling hills shimmered under a bright winter sun. The fresh powder sparkled like sugar, turning the countryside into a postcard-perfect scene.

Hope turned onto Drew's long, winding driveway, taking in the beauty of the wooded acreage that surrounded his property. The crunch of tires on packed snow was the only sound in the stillness as the antique Cape Cod house came into view. Nestled among the trees, its weathered shingles and forest-green shutters were charming.

As she entered the home's small foyer, Hope was met by the staircase and a very pleasant surprise. The outdated floral wallpaper that had clung to the walls since the eighties was finally gone. In its place, a rich navy paint added a sophisticated touch that made the old house feel fresh without losing its charm.

A burst of playful barking pulled her attention to the left, where the living room opened from the foyer. She shrugged off her coat as she moved toward the kennel, where Trixie bounced with excitement, tiny paws scrabbling at the door.

Hope smiled. "There you are, little one. Excited to see me?"

She unlatched the door and scooped up the wiggling pup, who responded with a flurry of licks and squeaky little sounds. Hope laughed, the kind of full, happy laugh that only a puppy can bring out, and for a fleeting moment she pictured what it might be like to add a puppy to her own home.

Bigelow had joined her just after his first birthday, long past this manic puppy stage. He'd probably love the company. But then there was Princess. The cat barely tolerated Bigelow. How would she survive a puppy?

Hope chuckled again, remembering the chaos of Christmas Eve, when Trixie had turned the evening into a circus by chasing Princess through the dining room.

"Oh, you were such a naughty girl that night," Hope said, setting Trixie down with a smile. The puppy lunged for her favorite stuffed duck, pouncing on it and growling as she tugged at its worn head.

As Hope watched her play, a sudden chill swept through the room, raising goose bumps along her arms. She glanced around, half expecting to see a window cracked open or a drafty door, but everything looked just as it had when she arrived. Shrugging it off, she turned her attention back to Trixie.

"How about some lunch?" she said, giving her leg a light tap. Trixie bounded after her as she moved into the kitchen.

The space had seen better days. The dated cabinets, scuffed linoleum, and aging fixtures needed replacing, but Hope understood why Drew hadn't rushed to renovate. The house had been in his family for generations, passed down from his grandparents to his aunt Isidore Leopold, and now to him. Every room held memories. Change couldn't be made lightly, not in a house like this.

He had started carefully, beginning with the family room. He'd gutted it down to the studs and rebuilt it into an office worthy of a book lover. Floor-to-ceiling bookcases lined one wall, each filled with his impressive collection, and his desk overlooked acres of quiet woods. It was the perfect blend of past and present—classic bones with modern comfort—a reflection of Drew himself, and the deep respect he had for the legacy left in his care.

Trixie yapped happily as she watched Hope prepare her lunch, her tail wagging with excitement. Hope followed Drew's texted feeding instructions to the letter, and within minutes she set Trixie's fancy bowl on the coordinating mat on the floor. She returned the food to the refrigerator and wiped down the counter, her mind already wandering to the tasks she needed to accomplish later in the day.

As she finished cleaning up, her phone buzzed in her jeans pocket. She pulled it out, glancing at the caller ID, which displayed an unknown number. With a slight frown, she tapped on the screen and answered.

For a fleeting moment, she thought it might be Lorna Morgan calling, but the silence on the other end quickly dispelled that notion. "Hello?" she repeated, her voice echoing in the quiet kitchen.

That's when she heard it, a soft, eerie whistle that made the hairs on the back of her neck stand up. The sound was subtle yet unsettling, like a cold wind blowing through an empty house. Hope's heart raced as she gripped the phone tighter, her mind struggling to make sense of the eerie melody.

She disconnected the call instantly. A whiny bark drew her attention from the cell phone. Trixie had finished her meal and was ready to go outside, her eager eyes looking up at Hope. Taking a deep breath to steady her nerves, Hope focused on the puppy, grateful for the distraction from the unsettling call.

"Let's go outside, girl," Hope said. She retrieved her coat and led Trixie to the back door, her mind racing with questions and a growing sense of unease. As she stepped outside, she couldn't shake the feeling that someone was watching her from the shadows.

Despite the gnawing in the pit of her stomach, Hope didn't rush Trixie through her outdoor adventure. She kept a watchful eye on the puppy as she sniffed around the fenced-in area off the kitchen. When Trixie finally came trotting back, ready to escape the cold, Hope breathed a sigh of relief.

But it was short-lived. As she turned to head inside, she heard it again. The same eerie whistle, this time coming from the dense thicket of trees behind the house. Her heart leapt into her throat, and she scooped up Trixie, dashing inside and locking the door behind her with trembling hands.

She needed to leave, to put as much distance between herself and the unsettling presence in the woods as possible. But she couldn't bear the thought of leaving Trixie alone in the house, vulnerable and unprotected. With a sense of urgency, she sought out Trixie's carrier, her hands still shaking as she secured the puppy inside.

Zipping up her jacket, Hope grabbed her tote bag and the carrier and hurried out the door, her breath coming in quick, frightened gasps. She settled Trixie's carrier on the backseat of her car and was about to climb in behind the steering wheel when her phone rang again. Another unknown number.

Hope hesitated, her heart hammering in her chest as she stared at the screen. Taking a deep breath, she answered the call, her voice barely above a whisper.

"Hope, it's Melanie."

Hope exhaled, the stiffness in her shoulders softening when she heard the friendly voice. "Melanie, hi," she said, sliding into the driver's seat. She pulled the door shut and dropped her key fob into her tote.

"I hope I haven't caught you at a bad time," Melanie said, her voice strained and tense.

"No, not really," Hope replied, turning the ignition and putting the car in reverse. "I'm just leaving a friend's house. What's up?" She backed out of the driveway, scanning the woods one last time before turning onto the road and driving away, the unsettling whistle still echoing in her mind.

"I'm calling to ask a favor," Melanie said. "A big favor."

Back on the road and putting some distance between herself and Drew's house, Hope felt her muscles begin to unwind. The unsettling feeling of being watched had finally faded. Her grip on the steering wheel loosened, and she shifted her attention back to Melanie's call.

"Uh . . . sure. How can I help?" she asked.

"Detective Reid contacted me," Melanie said. "He wants me to come to the police station tomorrow. I thought I answered everything on Saturday night. I've never been called in like this before . . . I'm really nervous, Hope."

Hope could hear the strain in Melanie's voice and felt a surge of sympathy. She remembered all too well the anxiety of being summoned to the police department.

"Try not to worry too much," she said. "He's just being thorough. It's completely normal for the detective to circle back and ask more questions. It's part of how they piece things together."

She paused as she approached a four-way stop, glancing in all directions before easing through the intersection.

"I've been in your shoes more times than I'd like to admit," she added, trying to reassure her. "It always sounds worse than it is."

"I'm just worried he suspects me, and I don't want to say the wrong thing. My husband keeps telling me that if I tell the truth, I've got nothing to worry about. But . . ." Melanie's voice trailed off, heavy with doubt.

Hope understood the fear. Facing the police, especially in a case like this, could be unnerving, even when you had nothing to hide.

"It's completely normal to feel that way." Hope flicked on the left-turn blinker as she approached Old Barn Road. "Detective Reid is just being thorough. Gathering facts, cross-checking stories. That's his job. If you tell the truth, you'll be okay."

Even as she spoke the words, Hope felt the faint tug of uncertainty. She'd told the truth, too, after finding Birdie Donovan's body last year, and it hadn't spared her from being labeled a person of interest by Sam. Still, the truth had come out eventually, and the killer was caught.

A playful bark broke the silence, tugging Hope from the memory. She glanced in the rearview mirror to see Trixie pawing eagerly at the carrier door, her tail wagging in a blur of motion. A smile crept across Hope's face as the tension eased from her shoulders.

"Alright, little one," she said softly, "we're almost there."

"I was wondering," Melanie said, her voice dropping to a hesitant, almost childlike tone, "if you'd come with me to the police department tomorrow. Just for moral support?"

The request caught Hope off guard. They weren't exactly close. They were more acquaintances than friends, but she understood how daunting it must feel to face another round of questioning.

"Of course I will," Hope replied without hesitation. She slowed the vehicle as she turned onto Main Street, the familiar storefronts of Jefferson fluttering into view. "Just text me the time and I'll be there. And try not to worry too much, okay?"

Melanie let out a soft sigh, the relief clear in her voice. "Thank you, Hope. I really appreciate it."

Hope ended the call and scanned the street for a spot near her sister's shop. As she pulled into a space, a thought surfaced—agreeing to meet Melanie wasn't just about offering support. It also gave her a chance to learn more about the calligrapher, including just how much she'd invested in Maisie's coaching and whether that loss might have been motive enough for murder.

Hope found a parking space outside of Staged with Style, Claire's home décor shop. The window display showcased an array of decorative accessories. After attaching the leash to Trixie's harness, Hope scooped up the puppy and walked into the shop, the bell above the door chiming softly as they entered.

Inside, the shop revealed a curated mix of style and luxury—candles displayed in elegant jars, pillows arranged with care, and bold artwork bringing energy to the space.

Claire, dressed in tailored black trousers and a silky turquoise blouse with an exaggerated bow at the collar, looked up from her work, surprise lighting her face as she spotted Hope and Trixie. She had been carefully styling an antique armoire, its rich wood glowing under the ambient light, with an assortment of vases and candles. Beside her, a cardboard box brimming with crumpled tissue and bubble wrap hinted at the steady stream of new arrivals waiting to be displayed.

"Hope! What a surprise!" Claire exclaimed, quickly finishing adjusting a vase before rushing over to greet them. She reached out and lightly stroked Trixie's little head. "And look at Trixie! She's growing so fast. But why do you have her with you?"

Hope set Trixie down before shrugging out of her jacket and sitting at the table where Claire held her design consultations. She didn't waste any time filling Claire in on why she was at Drew's house.

"I couldn't leave Trixie alone at Drew's," Hope explained. "Something . . . strange happened while I was there. I got a call from an unidentified number, and all I heard was a low, creepy whistle."

Claire's lips pressed into a thin line of concern. She picked up Trixie, cradling the puppy in her arms, and sat across the table from Hope. "No one said anything?"

Hope shook her head. "No. Then I took Trixie outside after she ate. I felt like someone was watching me, and then I heard this eerie whistle again. It was just too unsettling to leave her there alone."

Claire reached out and placed a reassuring hand on Hope's arm. "Completely understandable. I'm glad you brought Trixie with you. You both are safe here." She paused, her expression thoughtful. "You probably should call Ethan," she suggested, as Trixie stood up on her hind legs, playfully trying to grab Claire's dangling pearl earrings.

"No, Trixie." Hope took the puppy back, setting her down on the floor with a small toy to keep her occupied. "Sorry about that. I think she's bored and looking for something to do."

Claire adjusted her earring with a smile. "She's just being a puppy." Her expression turned serious again as she looked back at Hope. "But really, Hope, you should head home, lock the doors, and call Ethan. It's better to be safe, especially after what you've just experienced. And there's still a murderer on the loose."

Hope nodded, feeling a mix of relief and determination. She knew Claire was right, and she appreciated her sister's concern and support. "I will."

As Hope gathered her things and prepared to leave, the shop's door swung open again with a cheerful chime. Elspeth Higgins burst in, breathless. "Hope! I was going to call you, but I saw you come in here."

She wore a black ruana haphazardly draped over her shoulders, as though she'd grabbed it in a rush on her way out of her own shop.

"Elspeth, whatever is the matter?" Claire asked, rising to her feet.

"Nothing urgent," Elspeth said, waving a hand. "I've just been thinking about what we discussed this morning, Hope. And I realized I should have told you that I believe the police who handled Penny Foster's case were either incompetent or . . . on the take."

"That's a serious allegation," Hope said, her brows lifting.

Claire looked between them. How do you even know about Penny Foster's case? What ties you to it?

Hope gave her sister a quick recap of Elspeth's connection to the retreat in Vermont and Penny's disappearance. The color drained from Claire's cheeks, her expression caught somewhere between disbelief and alarm.

"I'm at a loss for words," Claire said. "However, I agree with Hope, accusing the police of any wrongdoing is a serious matter," Claire said.

Hope turned back to Elspeth. "Why do you think the police were corrupt or negligent?"

"Because of how little they cared," Elspeth replied. "Only one officer came to the inn when the innkeeper called. He filled out a report and left. That was it. And when the other attendee landed in the hospital? No follow-up. Not one of them came to talk to us."

"Arthur Swanson," Hope said, remembering.

"Yes! That was his name. How did you know?" Elspeth asked.

"Amy told me. She's doing a podcast series about Maisie and the retreat," Hope explained.

Elspeth's face lit up. "Do you think she'd want to interview me?"

"I'm almost certain she would," Hope said, scooping Trixie into her arms.

Elspeth looked positively giddy. "A podcast? Oh! Do you know if it's video? Or just audio?"

Hope and Claire exchanged a knowing look—Elspeth was clearly already planning her on-air wardrobe.

"I believe she's recently added video," Hope said, smiling. "And thank you for the information about the police. I really do need to get going."

"Of course, of course, and I should get back to my boutique!" Elspeth spun on her heel and dashed out the door.

"That woman is something else," Claire said as she moved behind the sales counter. "Amy's going to have her hands full trying to keep that interview on track."

A playful yap echoed through the shop, and Hope glanced down at Trixie, who was now doing an exaggerated stretch.

"Alright, I get it," Hope said with a smile. "Somebody needs a nap, and I've got a blog post that won't write itself."

Chapter Fifteen

Hope untied her apron and set it on the countertop. She picked up the bowl of pesto chicken pasta she'd whipped up for dinner, the aroma of basil and garlic wafting through the air. This was one of her go-to meals—a no-fail, no-recipe dish that she loved for its simplicity and comfort. Leftover chicken, a couple of tablespoons of pesto with a dash of heavy cream, her favorite pasta, and a few sliced artichokes. Coupled with a slice of homemade bread, warmed and buttered to golden perfection, it was a delicious and easy meal for nights when she had no energy to cook anything more elaborate. Tonight was definitely one of those nights.

Besides, it was just her tonight. Ethan was with the girls, who were finally on the mend, and for that she was grateful. She set the bowl on the table, where cutlery and a glass of wine waited, then pulled out a chair and sat. A sip of wine, a glance around the family room, and the emptiness pressed in. The fire burned in the hearth, but its warmth did little to fill the quiet. Bigelow snored on the sofa, Princes twitched her tail from her perch, yet something felt wrong. As she lifted her fork for the first bite, the reason struck her with a sharp pang. Trixie was gone.

The moment Hope had set the puppy down on the kitchen floor earlier that day, Trixie had been off and running, a whirlwind of energy and enthusiasm. Drew had been right; the dog had no off switch. Hope chased after the puppy, trying to keep her from wreaking havoc on the house. Princess had hidden away, her feline dignity offended by the chaotic intrusion, while Bigelow had done his best to avoid the playful bites from Trixie's razor-sharp puppy teeth.

Finally, just before Drew showed up to collect Trixie, the puppy had collapsed into a tiny ball of exhaustion, snoring softly on Bigelow's bed. The house had returned to its usual calm, but now it felt almost too quiet, the absence of Trixie's boundless energy leaving a noticeable void.

Feeling a pang of loneliness, Hope reached for her laptop and turned it on, the soft hum of the machine filling the quiet room. She logged into her website and browsed through the analytics, seeking the comfort of routine and the familiarity of her work. The numbers weren't too shabby for the middle of January, though the high traffic from the holidays had long since faded. She had learned years ago not to get too caught up in the dips and flows of blogging. The graph showed that visits were picking up again, thanks to her Valentine's Day content. She had written new posts with enticing recipes and spent hours optimizing the SEO for her older posts to draw in readers. Satisfied with what she saw, she clicked off her website and navigated to the *ReadNow* website for some guilty pleasure reading.

She took a bite of her warm, buttered bread, the crispy crust crunching satisfyingly as she clicked on a post about Maisie. Her eyes scanned the comments, each one more vitriolic than the last.

Con artist! You reap what you sow.

Wondered if she'd ever come out from under that rock she hid beneath.

Too bad, we'll never know what happened to Penny now that Demi is dead.

Hope pulled her hand back from the laptop as if the screen had burned her, her appetite vanishing. She pushed her plate away, a wave of regret washing over her. Maybe Maisie had changed, like she had claimed after Hope confronted her. Maybe if Maisie hadn't stormed off, she wouldn't have gone to the sauna alone. Or maybe, Hope thought with a sinking feeling, she had fallen for a con artist who'd lied until the very end.

The weight of Maisie's actions pressed down on her, and she couldn't help but question her own judgment. Had she missed the signs of deception? The comments on the gossip site echoed in her mind, each one a harsh reminder of the public's perception of Maisie—and by extension, Hope's involvement in her story.

Hope took a deep breath and picked up her phone, dialing Ethan's number. She needed to hear his voice, to share the burden of her thoughts and the events of the day.

"Hey, Hope," Ethan's voice came through the line, and instantly she felt relieved. "Perfect timing. The girls are getting ready for bed, so I have a few minutes. How are you doing?"

She paused, weighing her words. She wanted to share what had happened at Drew's house but didn't want to worry him. Focusing on the positive first, she said, "I'm okay. I didn't find any dead bodies. But there is something I need to talk to you about."

She told him about the call she had received earlier from the unidentified number and the eerie whistle that had sent a shiver down her spine. She explained the unsettling feeling of being watched by someone at Drew's house.

As she spoke, she realized that with some space between then and now, the events of the day seemed less sinister. The call was probably a wrong number, and the sound she heard outside Drew's house was likely just her imagination playing tricks on her and not someone lurking in the woods.

Next, she told him about her conversations with Elspeth and Amy. Ethan was silent for a moment. She wondered what he was thinking. No doubt he'd wanted her to stay out of the investigation, but he knew her too well to say it. She'd hadn't listened before to his warnings. Why would it be any different this time?

Deciding to shift the focus, she returned to the more uplifting side of the day. "On a happier note, I got to spend time with Trixie. She's adorable but a handful. She wore both Bigelow and Princess out." A yawn slipped past her lips. "And me too."

Ethan chuckled softly on the other end of the line. "I'm glad you had some company, even if it was a bit chaotic."

Giggling and chatter echoed through the line, signaling that the girls were ready for bed. Hope wished she could be there to tuck them in herself..

"Sorry, babe, I better get going. If you get another unidentified call, text me right away," he said. "I wish I could come over now, but I promised I'd read them a bedtime story. I'll be there as soon as they fall asleep."

"Give the girls a kiss good night for me," Hope said before she ended the call and reached for her bowl. Her appetite had returned. When she finished dinner, she served herself a slice of chocolate mousse cake and settled back at the computer, searching for more information on Maisie Cox, aka Demi Covington.

• • •

Tuesday morning, Hope parked her Explorer in the parking lot of the Jefferson Police Department and walked along the path toward the front entrance. She soaked up the balmy twenty-five degrees with each step, relishing the absence of harsh wind. It almost felt pleasant to be outside. Her steps were quick because she wanted to have enough time to chat with Melanie before her appointment with Sam.

As she reached the entrance, she saw a man in a dark gray overcoat standing off to the side, smoking a cigarette. He noticed her approaching and quickly discarded his cigarette, rushing to hold the door open for her.

"Thank you," Hope said as she reached the door. "It's a little chilly to be standing out here."

"Don't I know it." He attempted a smile, but the corners of his lips failed to fully curl upward. His dark green eyes were ringed with heavy bags, and he looked exhausted and worried. "You'd think that would be enough to get me to stop . . . well, you don't want to hear my problems."

Hope stepped into the vestibule, greeted by a shot of hot air. She scanned the waiting area but didn't see Melanie, so she backtracked, bumping into the man, still standing just outside the door. "Oh, I'm sorry. I was supposed to meet someone and she's not here." Hope checked her watch and confirmed she was on time.

"Are you Hope?" he asked.

She nodded.

"Nice to meet you." He held out his hand. "I'm Rick Tucker, Melanie's husband."

Hope shook his hand. "Nice to meet you. Are you waiting for her?" It was possible they were arriving separately.

"She's already in with the detective. As soon as we arrived, he took her right in." He cast a disapproving glance toward the main entrance. "She mentioned last night that she asked you to come, and I'll admit, I was surprised. I didn't realize you two were that close."

Hope offered a small shrug. "We're not exactly close, but I figured she could use some support. It's not easy being called in for questioning."

Rick nodded, his expression turning somber. "No, it isn't.

Especially after what happened to Maisie. I still can't believe she was murdered in a sauna. They made her feel claustrophobic."

A loud commotion drew their attention to the waiting area, and they both rushed in. The door to the back offices had slammed open with a bang. Melanie stormed through the lobby, her breathing ragged, hair slightly askew, and her face a mask of panic.

Rick looked startled but quickly moved to Melanie's side. "What's wrong? What happened?"

"Rick, we have to *go*. Now!" she shouted. "I *can't* stay here another second."

She grabbed his arm with both hands, her fingers digging in. "We'll talk in the car. Please. *Now*."

Hope stood frozen, watching the flurry of movement unfold. "Melanie, are you alright?" she called out, her voice edged with concern.

But Melanie barely spared her a glance. "I'm fine," she said quickly, her gaze fixed on the exit. "I just need to leave. Thank you for coming, Hope. I'll call you later."

Before she could react, they had disappeared into the parking lot, leaving Hope alone in the vestibule with her mind suddenly full of pressing questions. What had just occurred? And what had caused that sudden, panicked exit

She was still piecing it together when a familiar voice cut through her thoughts, pulling her back to the moment. Sam Reid was approaching, and Hope realized she hadn't even noticed him come in.

"Hope, I didn't expect to see you here this morning," Sam said, his voice prompting her to spin around. "What do I owe the pleasure to?"

She stepped from the vestibule into the lobby, her mind still racing. "I . . . I came to offer moral support to Melanie," she explained, seeing the doubt written all over Sam's face. "Really. She called me yesterday and asked me to come here this morning. What happened? Why did she run out the way she did? What did you say to her?"

Sam held up a hand. "Hey, take it easy. I was just doing my job."

"You know, as much as I like and respect you, you don't always have the best bedside manner," she said.

Sam shifted, heading back to the door that led to the interior offices. "Lucky for me, I'm not a doctor."

Hope lurched forward, not wanting him to disappear just yet. "Wait . . . we need to talk."

Sam stopped and turned, his expression now one of skepticism. "Save your breath. I can't reveal to you what Melanie and I talked about."

Hope nodded, understanding his position. "I know." She figured once Melanie calmed down, she'd tell Hope everything that happened during her interview anyway. "We agreed that I wouldn't sit on any information."

"You have new information about the case?"

"I do," Hope said. "Do you know Elspeth Higgins? She owns EH Fashions." When Sam nodded, she continued, "Elspeth was at the Vermont retreat Maisie hosted when Penny disappeared."

Sam's mouth curved into a knowing smile. "And how exactly did you come by that information?"

"She told me when we ran into each other at the coffee shop. I told her to contact you, but sometimes she gets distracted so you may want to reach out to her."

"Thanks for the tip. Say hi to Ethan for me." He moved toward the restricted area.

"Wait. Have you found Austin Dell yet?"

Sam paused, disappointment written all over his face. "He's still unaccounted for, and so is Maisie's car."

"You think Austin stole it?"

"At this point, I can't say for sure," Sam admitted, his voice tinged with frustration. "But my gut tells me he did. Now, I really have to get to a meeting."

Hope quickly interjected, not ready to let him go just yet. "One more question. Did you get anything back on the journal from the retreat that I gave you? Did the handwriting match anyone's?"

Sam studied her for a moment, his expression softening. "Nothing yet, Hope. I promise I'll update you when I can. You have my word."

"Thank you, Sam. I appreciate it." She turned and exited the police department.

Back at her Explorer, she glanced at her watch. There was just enough time to swing by the Merrifield Inn and try to catch Lorna. She hadn't had a chance to speak with her since that awkward run-in at Matt's office. The office and Matt were now out of bounds. Hope had no intention of crossing the line, especially knowing how Ethan felt about her pressing Matt for intel. Funny how she'd assumed things would be simpler once he wasn't chief of police.

Settling behind the wheel, Hope pulled out of the lot and headed down Main Street toward the inn. She spotted a space along the street, parked, and grabbed her tote before stepping out. The day had warmed, but a sharp gust of wind swept through, practically ushering her to the front door of the inn.

Inside, Eliza greeted her in passing, balancing a tray as she headed toward the kitchen.

"Hope, good to see you," she said with a smile. "I'm afraid my aunts are out running errands."

Hope glanced into the dining room and spotted Lorna. "Actually, I'm here to talk to Lorna."

Eliza paused and gave Hope a look that said she already suspected as much. "Ah. Well, don't let me stop you." She gestured toward the dining room with an open hand.

Hope began to turn, only to hear Eliza ask, "Would you like a cup of tea or coffee?"

"Yes, tea would be lovely." She wasn't sure yet whether she'd be sipping it with Lorna or nursing it solo.

"Coming right up." Eliza vanished down the hall, leaving Hope to step into the dining room.

At a window-side table, four older women, clearly contemporaries of Jane and Sally, were enjoying scones and tea, their conversation punctuated with easy laughter. Meanwhile, Lorna sat alone at a table in the center, her back to the window. A half-eaten muffin and a delicate cup and saucer sat before her, but her attention was fixed on her phone. She appeared absorbed, eyes scanning the screen with focused intensity.

Hope approached and placed her hand on the back of the chair across from Lorna. "May I join you?"

Lorna looked up with a long, slow sigh. "If I say no, will you leave?"

"No." Hope gave a small smile. "I'm not here to cause trouble. I just have a few questions."

"Fine. Have a seat." Lorna set her phone aside and fixed Hope with a pointed look. "I've already answered plenty of questions from the police. In fact, I just had a second interview with Detective Reid *after* he learned I'm Maisie's half-sister."

The look she gave Hope made it clear—she believed Hope had tipped Sam off.

"It was going to come out eventually," Hope said evenly. "Detective Reid is thorough."

"Especially when he has little helpers." Lorna reached for her cup and took a slow sip of black coffee. "So, what do you want to know?"

"Why were you and Maisie estranged? It must've been a long time, since it looked like she didn't even recognize you."

"That picture I showed you back at the lodge, that was the last summer we spent together. Our father was larger than life. A gifted storyteller. Which, I suppose, made him a decent con man." Her mouth tightened. "But our mothers? Couldn't have been more different. Maisie's mom was his partner in crime, literally. She got arrested, and everything spiraled from there. My mother bought into his lies at first, but once she figured him out, she left him."

Lorna paused, her gaze distant for a moment.

"For a while, my mom tried to keep Maisie—her given name was Elaine—in my life. But it got harder."

"How so?" Hope asked.

"She was her father's daughter, through and through," Lorna said simply.

Just then, Eliza appeared with Hope's tea. She placed it quietly on the table and slipped away without a word.

"You were pretty confident I'd talk to you," Lorna remarked, one eyebrow lifting as she watched Hope.

"About fifty-fifty," Hope said, lifting her teacup. "I figured there was a good chance I'd be sipping this alone." As she took her first sip, she wasn't surprised to find Eliza had outdone herself once more. The tea was a subtle but intriguing blend of hibiscus and rose hips, tart yet refreshing.

"Now I understand how you've built this reputation as the town's unofficial investigator." With a slight tilt of her wrist, Lorna raised her cup and swallowed a mouthful of coffee.

Hope's expression remained neutral, not rising to whatever bait might be in Lorna's words. "I've always been curious by nature," she said simply. "But let's get back to what you were saying about when it was getting harder for you and your mom to have Maisie in your life."

"When Maisie started lying, my mom put a stop to our visits."

"You never saw her again?"

"There was a big age gap between us. I had cousins so I didn't exactly go out of my way to reconnect."

"Then why now?"

"My mom's sick. Our dad's gone. Maisie was still my sister." Lorna pushed her plate away, her fingers trembling ever so slightly. "I knew digging up the past might be ugly. But I had to try. Maybe if I'd found her sooner, she wouldn't have ended up like this. Maybe I could've helped her."

Hope took another sip, watching her closely. The words sounded right, but there was something about the delivery that felt off—too polished, too practiced. And there was something else missing: any mention of how she'd reached out to Talia and conspired to blow up Maisie's life. Maybe Lorna hadn't just inherited a troubled family history. Maybe she'd also inherited the knack for lying without blinking.

"So, you're saying Maisie didn't recognize you because it had been years since you've seen each other? And you kept your distance to make sure she wouldn't recognize you until you were ready to confront her?"

Lorna nodded.

"What's your real name?" Hope asked.

"Juliette Thompson."

"That's a pretty name." Hope folded her arms on the table and met her gaze. "I have to say that I'm not buying the heartfelt reunion."

Lorna's eyes widened. Not in surprise, but in fury. Hope saw it flare before Lorna could mask it. So that's what was under the surface.

"Because if this were really about reconciliation," Hope continued,

"I'm curious why you were so confrontational during the 'Unmasking Your True Self' session."

Lorna's head tilted. "I don't know what you mean—"

"Maisie was talking about flaws. About taking responsibility. And you challenged her on them, almost like you knew something no one else did."

"I remember the session, but—"

"And then the very next morning, after your *sister* is murdered, your first move is to consult a lawyer? To find out how to claim her inheritance as next of kin? There's also the matter of her believing someone was trying to kill her. Do you know anything about that?"

Lorna's face hardened. "I don't have to sit here and let you twist my words." She grabbed her phone, her voice rising. "You're not as nice as everyone thinks you are. You're trying to turn this on me. Maybe you're the one who killed her! After all, you're the one who found the body!"

Gasps rose from the other table. The women by the window had gone silent, their teacups paused halfway to their lips.

"Listen to me, Hope Early—mind your business, or you'll be sorry!" Lorna snapped. She shoved her chair back with a screech and stormed out of the dining room.

Hope let out a slow, steady breath, resisting the urge to slide under the table. She wasn't proud of provoking Lorna, but it had done exactly what she'd hoped. That flash of temper, that sharp edge of anger—there was no mistaking it. Paired with a motive, it seemed entirely possible she'd just had tea with a killer.

Hope stepped out of the inn, the chill in the air doing little to clear the tangle of thoughts in her head. She replayed every word of her conversation with Lorna—*Juliette*—still trying to wrap her head around why so many people at the retreat were hiding behind fake names.

She reached the parking lot, eyes scanning for her SUV, when her phone rang. Digging it out of her tote, she glanced at the screen just as she reached the Explorer.

"Hey, Amy," she said, unlocking the vehicle with a quick click of her key fob. "Good timing, I was about to call you. I just had a conversation with Lorna—"

"Hope, I need you to come to my house. Right now."

Amy's voice was high and tight, teetering on the edge of panic. Hope froze, one hand on the door handle.

"Amy? What's going on? Is everything alright?"

"Yeah . . . everything is okay . . . I just need to talk to you, and it can't be over the phone. So, are you on your way over now?" Amy's words were rushed, her usual composure notably absent.

Hope's instincts tingled with alarm. This wasn't like Amy at all. Even with the stress of the podcast, something felt off. "I've just left the inn, and I'm at my car right now. I'll be at your place in a few minutes."

"Perfect!" Amy's relief was evident in her voice. "Just come on in if I don't get to the door when you arrive."

"Why wouldn't you—" Hope began, but her question was cut off as the line went silent. She stared at her phone, a frown creasing her brow. "What the heck is going on?" she muttered to herself as she shifted her car into reverse and backed out of the spot.

Hope couldn't shake the feeling that something was seriously wrong as she drove toward Amy's house. She gripped the steering wheel tighter, her mind racing with possibilities. Whatever was happening, she knew she had to get to Amy's house as quickly as possible.

When Hope arrived at Amy's delightful Victorian house on Belmar Court, she instantly noticed that the drapes of the living room window were drawn. Amy never closed them during the day. A chill ran down Hope's spine as every fiber of her being screamed that something was wrong. She should call for backup.

She quickly grabbed her cell phone and dialed Sam's number. It went straight to voicemail. She left a hurried message, explaining the situation and asking him to call her back as soon as possible. But she couldn't wait for his reply. If Amy was in trouble, she wouldn't leave her friend to face it alone.

Hope took in a deep breath, bracing herself for whatever waited on the other side of the door. She knew walking in could mean trouble, but the thought of Amy in danger propelled her forward. Her heart pounded, each beat echoing in her ears as she approached the front steps, every sense sharpened, tuned to the unknown.

As she approached the door, she noticed it was slightly ajar, another sign that something was amiss. Amy was meticulous about keeping her doors locked, especially when she was home alone. Hope pushed the door open gently, scanning the dimly lit entryway.

"Amy?" she called out, her voice low but urgent. No answer, only a heavy, unnerving silence that wrapped around her like fog. She stepped cautiously into the house, each movement deliberate, her pulse quickening. Maybe Amy was simply overwhelmed by something she'd uncovered in the case . . . but Hope's gut said otherwise. This silence didn't feel emotional, it felt ominous.

Hope crept deeper into the house, each step measured and silent. Her gaze swept from the doorway to the shadowed corner, scanning for any trace of movement. The familiar coziness of Amy's home had vanished, replaced by a cold stillness that clung to the walls. The air felt heavy, charged with something unspoken. Her heart pounded against her ribs as she pressed forward, a single thought driving her: Find Amy. Make sure she's okay.

"Stop right there."

Hope froze, her blood running cold. She recognized that voice. It was a voice that sent a shiver of fear down her spine.

It was Austin Dell.

Chapter Sixteen

Hope froze, momentarily stunned by the sight of the man the police had been looking for. She hadn't expected to come face-to-face with him, not here, not now. Austin stood in the doorway, his expression unreadable, a mix of wariness and something rawer beneath the surface. He wasn't holding a weapon, but his presence alone carried the weight of danger.

For a beat, she could only stare. The jagged scar above his brow caught the light, a pale gash against weathered skin. His bomber jacket hung open over a faded graphic tee, his black jeans and worn boots lending him the look of someone who lived just on the edge of trouble. But there was hesitation in his eyes, a flicker of uncertainty that made him more human than monster.

Hope pushed back the spike of fear that gripped her. She couldn't afford to panic. Not now. She lifted her chin slightly, grounding herself in the moment. No sudden movements. No cracks in composure. If she was going to help Amy and get them both out of this intact, she had to stay sharp, read him fast, and choose her next words even faster.

"Where is Amy? I want to see her now," Despite the fact that anxiety twisted like wire beneath her skin, she managed to sound composed.

Austin shifted his weight, avoiding her gaze. "She's fine. I didn't hurt her or anything." He motioned toward the kitchen. "She's in there."

His hand shook slightly as he gestured, a small tell that didn't escape Hope's notice.

She paused, every instinct on edge. This could be a trap. But Amy needed her, and standing still wouldn't bring answers. Hope gave a small nod and stepped forward, moving deliberately, her eyes sweeping the hallway for any other sign of danger.

The kitchen felt like it belonged in another decade. Faded tiles lined the countertops, chipped and dulled by time. A low-hanging light buzzed overhead, casting yellow-tinted shadows that bled across the cracked linoleum. Hope's heart clenched. Amy adored this space. Its vintage charm had always been one of her favorite things about the house. Now, any sense of that was gone.

Hope spotted her friend seated at the kitchen table, her face pale but her eyes defiant. She rushed forward.

"Are you okay?" Hope quickly scanned Amy for any injuries. There didn't appear to be any but just to be sure, she asked, "Did he hurt you?"

Amy shook her head. "No, he didn't hurt me. But he barged in while I was bringing in my groceries." Her gaze drifted to the back door, where a canvas tote of groceries lay toppled over, its contents scattered across the floor. "Then he made me call you."

A surge of anger rippled through Hope as she turned her attention back to Austin. He was leaning against the counter, his arms crossed. Unfortunately, he had the upper hand. While Hope didn't see a weapon, she couldn't be sure he didn't have one hidden. And his size alone was intimidating; given his muscular frame, he could easily overpower them both.

"What's going on? Why did you force your way in? What do you want from us?" Hope asked, her voice thin though she fought to keep it level. "You should leave, Austin. Now."

He uncrossed his arms, his hands clenching into fists at his sides. "Oh, no. I'm not going anywhere. Not until you both help me clear my name."

Hope's eyes widened in disbelief. "Help you? How on earth do you expect us to do that?"

Austin took a step closer, his eyes darting between Hope and Amy. "I figure between her podcast"—he nodded toward Amy—"and your track record of solving murders, you can help me convince the police that I didn't kill Maisie."

Hope's mind raced as she tried to process Austin's request. She glanced at Amy, who sat silently at the table. Her expression gave nothing away. Hope turned her attention back to Austin. "And what makes you think we would help you?"

"Because I didn't kill her." Austin pulled out a chair across from Amy and dropped onto it, the wooden legs creaking under his weight. "I swear I didn't kill her." His gaze flicked between them, desperation etched into every line of his face.

Hope and Amy exchanged a wary glance, but Hope sensed an opening, an opportunity to de-escalate. If Austin believed they were listening, they might have a chance to call for help without tipping him off.

"We'd like to help you," Hope said. She sat at the table, folding her hands on the table ready to listen.

Amy shot Hope a look of alarm. "We would?" she whispered.

Hope gave a subtle nod, silently willing Amy to go along with her. "Do you know who killed Maisie?" she asked, keeping her eyes locked on Austin.

He shook his head with conviction. "No. I've got no clue. But it doesn't surprise me. She made a lot of enemies. Too many people felt burned by her. That's why she was always worried about her identity being found out."

"You mean the people she conned," Amy said. "The ones who thought she was going to change their lives."

Austin acknowledged with a nod.

Hope swallowed her distaste for Austin. He might be awful, but he had information she needed. "You knew her a long time. You must've known about the different names she used."

A weary sigh escaped his lips as he dragged a hand through his hair. "Yeah. I met her when she was going by Demi. Back then, I bought into everything she was selling. She had this pull . . . like, this magnetic charm. But once I saw behind the curtain . . . it was different."

He paused, the edges of his voice roughening. "Her childhood was a mess. She grew up surrounded by lies and schemes. It was all she knew how to do. And for a while, we actually had something good. But that retreat in Vermont? That was the beginning of the end."

Amy's brow knit with confusion. "What do you mean, *you had something good?* You were part of the scam, weren't you?"

Austin's expression darkened, a flicker of indignation flashing in his eyes. "Was it really a scam? She gave people what they wanted, hope and guidance. The only thing she faked was her name. She didn't hurt anyone."

"She took their money under false pretenses," Amy shot back.

"That's more than just a name."

Hope watched him closely, searching for cracks in his composure. "Amy's right. People were hurt, Austin. People like Penny Foster. All those people who spent too much money on her services because they believed she could help them. And now Maisie's dead. If you didn't kill her, then who did?"

Austin slumped in his chair, the bravado slipping from his shoulders. "I don't know. I swear I don't. But I need you both to believe me."

"Then help us understand. Tell us everything. No filters, no holding back. Can you do that?" Hope asked.

Austin nodded, the fight in him dimmed but not gone. "Yeah. I'll tell you everything."

"Start with the retreat in Vermont," Amy said. "What happened to the man who died because of the hike. And what about Penny? She didn't leave the retreat on her own, did she? She was murdered. Maisie did it, right?"

"She didn't kill Penny Foster." Austin paused letting the silence stretch before confessing, "It was me. I did it."

Hope's breath caught, the shock knocking her off balance. "You did?" She was seated across from a man admitting to murder, just the sort of situation Ethan and Sam had warned her to avoid. Since there was no backing away now, she had to stay sharp, keep him talking, and think a step ahead so she and Amy could get out of the situation unscathed.

"I didn't mean to hurt anyone, I swear. But Maisie told me to deal with Penny, and I did. I just wanted to calm her down, get her to back off. She was threatening to go public—say Maisie was a fraud, that she caused that man's collapse." His voice cracked. "She came at me. Slapped me. I pushed her. She hit her head on a rock. It happened so fast . . . I didn't mean for it to go that far."

"So it was an accident," Hope said, reaching across the table to rest her hand over Amy's, signaling to stay calm.

Amy's gaze snapped to Hope's, disbelief and fear swirling behind her eyes. Hope gave her hand a reassuring squeeze, urging her to hold it together.

Austin nodded, desperation rising in his voice. "Yes. It was an accident. I never meant to hurt her. And I didn't touch Maisie, I swear. I loved her. I would've done anything for her."

"You loved her," Hope repeated softly. "We believe you, Austin. But it's time to tell Detective Reid what happened to Penny. Let him hear it from you."

She purposefully avoided the word *murder*.

"Amy will share your story on her podcast. People will know it wasn't intentional. That it was an accident. But we need to call the detective. Is that okay?"

Austin nodded. "Yeah, you can call him."

• • •

After the officers left with Austin in custody, the house settled into an unnatural quiet. The immediate danger had passed, but a charged energy seemed to cling to the air, leaving Hope feeling unsteady.

In the kitchen, Amy handed Hope a glass of water, her hands still shaking, the adrenaline not yet worn off. They stood together in the silence, the weight of what had just happened pressing in around them.

"Oh. My. Word. Did that really just happen?"

"It most certainly did," Hope said, taking a sip of water as her thoughts raced. She turned to Amy, her gaze full of concern. "Are you okay?"

Amy shook her head slowly, her face pale and drawn. "I don't know. I'm terrified . . . and weirdly exhilarated. And mad at myself for letting him get the drop on me."

She crossed the kitchen and sank into a chair, her movements weighed down by exhaustion. "How do you do this, Hope? You've come face-to-face with killers before. How do you stay so cool?"

"I hope it's the last time," Sam said as he stepped into the kitchen through the back door, his face lined with concern. "Austin's on his way to the station. Sounds like he's ready to unburden himself."

"About Maisie's murder?" Hope asked. "He said he didn't do it. That he loved her."

"That's what he told us," Amy added, lifting her glass for a sip of water. "They were together for years. Honestly? I believe him."

Sam gave a slow nod, his gaze distant. "Maybe. But according to Austin, Maisie didn't exactly return the sentiment. He claims she was seeing someone else."

Hope and Amy exchanged a surprised glance. "Who?" they asked in unison.

Sam shook his head. "He didn't say. But if it's true, it gives him a motive. We've got a lot to unravel." He looked between them. "We'll need official statements. Can you both come down to the station later today?"

Hope nodded. "Of course."

"Yeah," Amy said, setting down her glass. "Just tell us when."

Sam studied them both for a long moment, his expression softening with concern. "Are you sure you're both okay? You don't want to get checked out at the hospital?"

Hope shook her head. "We're not hurt. Just rattled. We'll be alright."

"Yeah, we're okay," Amy added.

Sam nodded slowly, though the worry didn't entirely leave his face. "Alright. But if that changes, don't wait. Get medical attention. I'll see you both at the station later."

With that, he turned and let himself out, the back door clicking shut behind him.

The kitchen fell quiet. The adrenaline had ebbed, leaving only exhaustion and disbelief in its wake. Hope and Amy met each other's eyes, no words needed. They were safe. Shaken, but safe. And for now, that was enough.

• • •

Hope returned home, the day's events weighing heavily on her mind. In the kitchen, she filled the kettle with water and set it on the stove, the familiar routine providing a small measure of comfort. As she waited for the water to boil, she dialed Ethan's number, steeling herself for the conversation she knew was coming.

"Hope, are you okay?" Ethan answered on the first ring, his voice threaded with concern, undercut by a hint of irritation.

She squeezed her eyes shut. He already knew what happened. Darn his contacts at the police department.

"I am." She poured the hot water into her favorite mug, preparing a cup of vanilla almond tea, and recounted the harrowing experience at Amy's house. As expected, Ethan was not happy. "I'm home now."

"You should never have gone into Amy's house, Hope," he admonished. "You had no idea what you were walking into. You're lucky that Austin wasn't armed and that you both made it out alive."

Hope sighed, cradling the mug in her hands. "I know, Ethan. Believe me, I've been thinking about that ever since I left Amy's. I'm grateful it turned out the way it did." In hindsight, she saw how it could have gone sideways.

After enduring Ethan's lecture, Hope hung up the phone and glanced at the barrage of text messages that had come in while she was talking. Drew had been blowing up her phone, clearly having caught wind of the incident and wanting details. His messages were followed by concerned texts from Jane and Melanie.

Hope took a sip of her tea, deciding who to reply to first. But before she could choose, an incoming call from Claire had her tapping the speaker button.

"Hey, I was going to call you," Hope said, dropping onto the sofa in the family room. Bigelow, sensing her distress, rested his head on her lap.

"What on earth happened?" Claire's voice was high-pitched and frantic, her words tumbling out in a rush. "Is it true you and Amy were held at gunpoint by that Austin guy?"

Hope rolled her eyes, a small smile playing at the corners of her mouth despite the circumstances. The speed and inaccuracy of Jefferson's gossip mill amazed her. "No, no, we weren't held at gunpoint. Where did you hear that? Never mind. I assure you that Austin didn't have any weapons. Look, I'm tired, and I just want to drink my tea and decompress a bit. Can I call you back?"

Claire's voice softened, her relief palpable. "Well, that's a relief. How about I come over for dinner? I'll pick up something on the way so you don't have to cook."

Hope felt a wave of gratitude wash over her. "I'd love that, Claire.

Thank you."

The call ended, and Hope quickly responded to messages from Drew and Jane before setting her phone to airplane mode. For a moment, she allowed herself to relax completely, running her fingers over Bigelow's velvety ears. The rest of the world could wait.

When her mug was empty, Hope stood, making sure not to disturb Bigelow's peaceful slumber. She moved into the kitchen, the antique pumpkin pine floorboards creaked under her steps as she approached the island. The mug made a gentle clinking sound as she set it down, the noise seeming loud in the quiet room. She bit back a chuckle, knowing that only the crinkle of a snack bag or the rumble of a delivery engine would rouse her sleeping dog.

Now it was time to address the other messages waiting for her attention, but first she wanted to touch base with Amy. Hope unlocked her phone and navigated to her contacts, her finger pausing over Amy's name. She tapped the speaker icon and placed the phone on the counter, leaning forward slightly as she waited for the call to be answered.

"Oh, hi, Hope," Amy answered after the first ring, her voice surprisingly upbeat given the day's events. "How are you doing?"

"I was calling to ask you the same question," Hope said. "I made a cup of tea and relaxed a bit with Bigelow. Ethan wasn't pleased when I told him what happened."

Amy chuckled. "Got a lecture, huh? Sorry about that. I didn't want to call you, but Austin made me."

"I know," Hope replied quickly, not wanting Amy to feel guilty. "Don't worry about it. Ethan will calm down. Soon."

"Well, fingers crossed he doesn't listen to the gossip in town. I just heard that we were held at gunpoint!"

"I know. Claire shared that with me a little while ago." Hope stepped away from the island. "I was wondering if you wanted to come over for dinner tonight? I thought it might be nice for us to unwind together after everything that's happened. Claire is coming over. She's picking up dinner."

"Oooh, that sounds fabulous," Amy said, her voice brightening at the invitation. "And then I can fill you in on my meeting with Kit."

"Meeting? When?"

"Like now," Amy said, her voice muffled by background noise, as if she was getting out of her car. "I just arrived at the lodge. I called her after you left and told her we needed to talk. I want to get her reaction to Austin's confession and arrest for the podcast."

Hope admired Amy's tenacity, but a niggling feeling of doubt began to grow in the pit of her stomach. "Amy, are you sure that's a good idea? Maybe you should wait until—"

"Sorry, Hope, I have to go," Amy interjected, her voice hurried. "I'll text you when I leave, and then you can let me know what time to arrive for dinner. Thanks!"

Before Hope could protest further, the line went silent. She stared at her phone, her mind racing with concern. While she admired Amy's follow-through, something didn't feel right. She couldn't quite put her finger on it, but she knew she didn't want Amy to be alone with Kit. Even though Austin had confessed to Penny's murder, he maintained his innocence in Maisie's death. And Kit, along with others, had a motive to kill the self-help guru.

Hope wasted no time leaving her house and getting into her Explorer to drive to the lodge. As she navigated the snow-packed driveway, her tires occasionally slipping on icy patches, she left a voicemail for Ethan, detailing her plan to join Amy in her meeting with Kit. She wanted to ensure that someone knew exactly where she was and what she was doing, just in case.

As the lodge came into view, Hope's worries began to lessen. Perhaps she had overreacted when Amy told her she was going back there. The sight of the rustic building, draped in a serene winter landscape, looked anything but sinister. Then again, she knew looks could be deceiving.

She spotted Amy's car parked in front of the lodge's main entrance, so she pulled up next to it. Hope got out of her car, her breath misting in the cold air as she looked around. There were no shoveled paths leading to the deck, but a set of footprints trailed around the side of the building.

Amy must have entered through the side door, Hope thought, her eyes following the tracks. She hesitated for a moment, her instincts still buzzing with a low-level alarm. But she pushed aside her lingering nervousness and followed the footprints, her boots crunching softly in the snow.

The side entrance was ajar. Hope paused, listening for any sounds from within. Hearing nothing, she pushed the door open wider and stepped inside, her heart pounding in her chest.

The lodge was quiet, the only sound the faint hum of the heating system. Hope looked around, her eyes adjusting to the dim light. She saw a flicker of movement down the hallway and strained to listen, her breath shallow in her chest.

"Amy?" she called out softly, taking a cautious step forward. "Are you here?"

There was no response, only the echo of her own voice in the empty hallway. She moved farther into the lodge. There was no one in sight. The registration desk was empty. But the door to Henry's office was cracked open.

She hesitated for a moment before walking behind the registration desk and approaching the office. While she knew that the police had done a thorough search of the property and the likelihood of any evidence being left behind was slim, she couldn't resist taking a look for herself.

She pushed open the office door wider, the hinges creaking in protest. The room looked sterile, cluttered, and cold. Stacks of paper teetered on the desk, and the bare walls gave nothing away. The air was heavy, tinged with the scent of dust and something stale.

Hope scanned the room. Something small and dark caught her eye beneath the desk—a USB drive. She dropped to her knees, the chill of the floor seeping through her jeans. Reaching under, her fingers brushed the plastic casing, and she grasped it, heart quickening.

But as she started to rise, she froze.

A tense ripple crawled up her neck. She wasn't alone.

Before she could turn, quick hands yanked a hood down over her head. Darkness swallowed her. She thrashed instinctively, kicking and trying to scream, but her voice was muffled by the coarse fabric, her movements restrained by a crushing grip.

A voice muttered something close to her ear—low, unintelligible.

Familiar? She couldn't tell.

Panic surged through her.

She'd walked straight into a trap.

As she was dragged across the floor, her mind spiraled with questions. Who had found her? What did they want? And how the hell was she going to get out of this alive?

Chapter Seventeen

"Hello? Is anyone here?" Maretta's voice echoed through the foyer, sharp and commanding, cutting through the silence. "Hello!"

The mayor's unexpected arrival gave Hope the opportunity she needed. Her captor froze, startled by the sudden intrusion.

"Kit? Are you in here?" Maretta's voice rang out again, her footsteps growing louder as she moved through the lodge. "Where is everyone?"

Hope seized the moment. Fueled by a surge of adrenaline, she clawed at the arm pinned across her chest, wrenching it with all the strength she could summon in her frightened state.

Her attacker snarled in frustration and retaliated with a sharp, brutal knee to her lower back. Pain flared hot and immediate, stealing her breath. She cried out, but the sound was smothered by the thick fabric of the hood.

Then, just as suddenly, the grip slackened. She was shoved away, landing hard on the cold floor. Disoriented, she barely registered the hurried footsteps pounding away from her, growing fainter by the second.

She lay on the cold floor, gasping for breath, her body throbbing from the struggle.

"What on earth is going on?" Maretta called, alarm rising in her voice. "Stop! Stop right now!"

Hope heard the mayor crossing into the office. She tried to call out but her voice came out in a rasp.

"Maretta . . . help . . ."

"Hope!" Maretta gasped, dropping to her knees beside her. Her hands fumbled to remove the hood, and light poured in, harsh against Hope's eyes. "My goodness—what happened? Who did this?"

Hope blinked, trying to focus on Maretta's face. "I . . . I don't know," she croaked. "But they're gone. I heard them leave. Did you see who it was?"

Maretta's expression hardened. "No. Whoever it was nearly knocked me over running out of the lodge," she said, voice low with fury. "We're getting you help. Then we're finding out who's behind this."

The next hour was a blur of flashing lights and urgent voices. Police cars arrived in a rush, casting red and blue patterns across the snowy lodge exterior. Inside, Hope sat in the library where she gave her statement to Officer Stanton while other officers fanned out, scanning every corner of the lodge for any sign of her attacker.

Amy and Kit soon appeared, their faces tight with worry as they took in the chaotic scene.

"We were in Kit's cabin recording a segment for the podcast. We only realized something was wrong when the police showed up," Amy said, settling beside Hope on the sofa. "If only we were here maybe this wouldn't have happened. Or we might have seen who it was."

Hope gave a faint nod. She wanted to believe that was enough to rule Kit out—wanted to—but her mind refused to let go of the possibility. Just because someone vouched for Kit didn't mean she was innocent. And yet . . . Amy wouldn't lie for her. Would she?

Kit hovered in the library doorway, her shoulders tense as she watched the scene unfold. She stepped forward carefully, balancing a glass of water in one hand and an ice pack in the other. Hope gratefully accepted both, pressing the cold compress onto the sharp ache in her back.

"Would you like anything else?" Kit asked, her voice careful.

Hope looked up, studying Kit's face. There was concern there but something else, too. Fatigue? Or just the aftershock of another terrifying event at the lodge?

"No, thank you," Hope replied, taking another sip from the glass. She adjusted the ice pack, wincing slightly at the lingering pain.

Maretta sat across from Hope, her eyes narrowing. "What on earth were you doing in Henry's office? Your snooping never fails to get you into trouble. It's a good thing I came along when I did."

"It was." Hope offered a faint smile, genuinely grateful for Maretta's timing. "Thank you, Maretta. Honestly, I'm not sure what I was hoping to find. We know Henry knew that Maisie and Austin were involved in Penny's disappearance because he took the bag of her belongings. But I don't think he knew Austin killed her."

"That is quite an accusation," Maretta said.

"It's true," Hope said firmly, even as a dull ache flared in her lower back. "Austin confessed to me and Amy."

"When?" Maretta demanded.

"A few hours ago, at Amy's house," Hope said. "He barged in, made her call me. We were able to alert the police, and he's in custody now. But he swears he didn't kill Maisie."

"I should've been informed of an arrest." Maretta pulled out her phone, thumbs tapping furiously. "Since Ethan left, the whole department's gone off the rails. I didn't always approve of his methods, especially when it came to indulging your sleuthing, but at least he kept things orderly."

Hope caught the flicker of something that might have been praise and tucked it away with a mental note to share with Ethan.

"Now, what is this about Henry knowing something about that poor girl's disappearance?" Maretta looked up from her phone.

Kit stepped closer, her voice even. "He found Penny's bag after they got back from the hike and assumed she left voluntarily. But he never turned it over to the police."

"The Henry I knew wouldn't have done that," Maretta assured.

Hope leaned forward, her voice clear. "That's the point, Maretta. He isn't the man you knew in high school anymore."

"Maretta, sometimes people change in ways we don't want to believe." Amy's words earned her the infamous Maretta glare and had her leaning back into the sofa.

Kit remained still at the edge of the room, watching the exchange. Hope felt it again, that tickle of doubt, like something was off but too fleeting to name.

"If you three are correct about Henry taking that bag, don't you think it's unlikely he'd leave it in his office? That would be a reckless, if not stupid, place to hide evidence," Maretta asked.

Hope adjusted the ice pack against her sore back before taking another sip of water. "Honestly, I don't know what I was looking for. When I saw the USB on the floor, I went to pick it up. That's when I was attacked from behind."

Kit stepped away from the doorway, her arms no longer crossed.

"That was probably Henry's backup drive for his financial records."

With a decisive movement, Maretta stood from her chair. "Hope, you need to go home and get some rest after what you've been through. And I need to find out why I wasn't notified about Austin Dell's apprehension. That's a conversation I need to have with Chief Ackerman immediately."

As the discussion concluded, Kit excused herself and disappeared from the library. Maretta marched toward the door, clearly spoiling for a confrontation with the police chief. And Amy came around to help Hope up from her seat, carefully supporting her as they walked slowly toward the parking lot and Hope's parked Explorer.

"Are you sure you don't want me to drive you home?" Amy asked, concern etched across her face. "You still look a little . . . pale."

Hope reached the door to the driver's side and turned to face Amy. "I'm okay to drive. Just a little sore."

"You should go to the emergency department. You could have internal bleeding."

Hope grimaced at that possibilty, her hand brushing her back. "If I don't feel better, I promise I'll see a doctor."

Amy nodded reluctantly. "Sorry, I just . . . I listen to too many podcasts. You probably don't want the medical details."

Hope gave a half smile. "I'll pass, thanks." She hesitated, frowning. "Austin's in custody, but I was just attacked. That means Maisie's killer is still out there."

Amy's eyes widened. "Or . . . Austin had help."

Hope nodded. "Either way, I can't stop now. I need to figure out who did this."

Amy squeezed her arm. "Be careful. And keep me updated."

"I will."

Hope slid behind the wheel and started the engine. In the rearview mirror, the lodge grew smaller behind her as she pulled out she drove away, but the weight of the day's events clung to her. There was something she was missing.

She just hoped she figured it out before it was too late.

• • •

When Hope arrived home, she saw Ethan's pickup truck parked in the driveway. Her heart swelled with a mix of relief and apprehension. More rattled than she cared to admit, and fatigued to the core, she didn't even bother pulling her Explorer into the garage. As she reached the mudroom door, it swung open and Ethan stepped outside, his arms open wide.

He gathered her into his arms, his hold steady and full of love, exactly what she needed in that moment. Hope let out a shaky breath as tears welled in her eyes. She pressed her face against his chest, the solid weight of his arms grounding her in a way nothing else could. A soft sob escaped as Ethan's hand traced slow circles along her back, his presence wrapping around her with the quiet strength of something that would never falter.

After a moment, Hope pulled her head from his chest and looked up at him. The worry in his eyes was unmistakable, and it made her heart ache. She wondered how much he knew about what had happened.

"Are you okay?" he asked.

Hope nodded as she pulled away from him and offered a small, reassuring smile. "Now I am. Can we go inside? It's cold out here."

Ethan's lips curved into a grin. "What, my body heat wasn't enough to warm you up?" he teased softly.

Her smile grew wider, and she playfully nudged his shoulder. "We can try again later," she flirted lightly. She entered the mudroom, shedding her coat and tote bag as Ethan followed her inside.

"Are the girls here?" she asked, glancing around the kitchen.

"No, they're still at Heather's." Ethan leaned against the counter. "The flu is not something to mess around with. Both are feeling better, though."

Bigelow came bounding toward Hope, his tail wagging furiously. She knelt to greet him and scratched behind his ears. "It's good to be home," she murmured, her voice filled with warmth and contentment.

Ethan watched her, his eyes reflecting the love and concern he felt for her. "I'm glad you're home too, Hope. Let's get you settled in and comfortable. You've been through a lot today."

Hope stood and walked over to Ethan, taking his hand in hers.

"Thank you for being here. It means the world to me."

He squeezed her hand gently, his voice soft and reassuring. "Always, Hope. Always."

"Go ahead. I'm ready. And I probably deserve it," she said.

"Deserve what?" Ethan asked as he walked to the refrigerator. He took out a beer, unscrewed the cap, and took a drink before turning back to her. "A lecture?"

Hope pressed her lips together, steeling herself for what she expected to be a stern talk. After all, she had just been through a harrowing experience, a hood had been pulled over her head, and someone had been dragging her off to who knows where. If Maretta hadn't shown up . . . She quickly shook off the thoughts, not wanting to dwell on the what-ifs.

"Babe, I'm not going to lecture you," Ethan said softly, setting his beer bottle on the kitchen island.

"You're not?"

Ethan shook his head. "No. When I got the call and Sergeant Brooks shared the details, every worst-case scenario ran through my mind. I know Maretta stopped the incident, but what really happened was that you got lucky. *Again.*"

Hope blinked, her mind racing. She couldn't help but wonder how many more times luck would be on her side. The gravity of the situation settled over her, and she felt a shiver run down her spine.

"I know how important it is to you to find out what really happened," he said, his voice filled with admiration. "But I worry about you getting in over your head."

She looked up at him. "I know you worry about me. And I'm grateful for that." She paused, her fingers tracing patterns on the countertop. "But I can't just stand by and do nothing. Not when it's becoming clear that what happened to me is tied to Maisie's murder." A shiver ran through her as the chilling thought took hold—the person who attacked her was probably the one who killed Maisie.

Ethan's hand covered hers, stilling her nervous movements. "I understand, Hope. And I'll be here for you, no matter what." His thumb brushed over her knuckles. "Just promise me you'll be extra careful. I need you to look out for yourself too."

"I promise, Ethan. I'll be careful."

His expression softened, and he gave her hands a gentle squeeze before releasing them. "Good. Now, what's for dinner?"

Hope rolled her eyes, a small laugh escaping her lips. Of course, he was thinking about food. But they both knew that cooking was one of the ways she coped with stress.

"Something hearty would be perfect for this chilly night," she decided aloud, already feeling better at the thought. Because of what happened at the lodge, she canceled the dinner plans with Claire and Amy, but cooking still appealed to her. The familiar routine would help settle her nerves. "What do you think about Salisbury steak with mashed potatoes?"

Ethan's eyes lit up. "Sounds amazing. Need any help?"

Hope shook her head. "No, I've got this. You just keep me company."

"I can do that." He took another swig of his beer.

As she gathered ingredients, Hope began to hum, the rhythm of the kitchen reassuring. The scent of sautéed onions mingled with herbs as she folded them into the ground beef and breadcrumbs.

"You know, I've always admired your resilience. No matter what happens, you find a way to bounce back and keep going," Ethan said.

She glanced over at him, her smile soft and full of gratitude. "Having you here, supporting me, makes all the difference."

Ethan reached out and tucked a lock of hair behind her ear. "You've got me in your corner, no matter what."

They shared a quiet kiss, the kind that spoke of comfort and certainty. Then Hope turned back to the stove. As she shaped the meat mixture into patties and placed them into the sizzling pan, a savory scent began to rise, curling through the kitchen like a balm. With each task, her thoughts slowed, giving her a rare moment of peace and space to appreciate the quiet comfort of Ethan nearby.

She glanced over at him. "You know, sometimes the best therapy is just being in the kitchen, creating something delicious."

Ethan nodded in agreement. "And you're really good at it. I can't wait to taste them."

"They'll be ready soon. In the meantime, how about you set the table? We can make it a cozy dinner for two."

"Sounds like a plan." Ethan pushed off from the island and began gathering plates and utensils. "And maybe we can open a bottle of wine to go with it?"

Hope looked up from pan. "That sounds perfect."

As they worked together to set prepare dinner and pour the wine, Hope felt a deep sense of contentment, knowing that she was in her happy place, surrounded by love and the simple pleasures of home.

Chapter Eighteen

On Wednesday morning, Hope stepped out of the chicken coop, the soft clucks of her hens fading into the quiet hush of a snow-covered yard. Her breath puffed in the frosty air as she tugged on her gloves, her boots pressing into the packed snow. Bigelow bounded at her side, kicking up powdery flurries as they crossed to the mudroom. Sunlight crept over the horizon, casting a pale gold light that made the icicles hanging from the eaves glint like glass ornaments.

The serene quiet was broken by the sound of tires crunching over the icy driveway. Hope turned just as Drew's red sports car pulled in, its bright color jarring against the muted winter landscape. The engine hummed for only a moment before he cut it off and threw open the door, stepping out with urgency etched into his features.

Bigelow, sensing only the chance for fun, let out an enthusiastic bark and dashed toward Drew. His paws scrambled in the snow as he made tight, playful circles around Drew's legs.

"Easy there, big guy!" Drew chuckled, trying to settle the overexcited dog. Then he looked at Hope, pulling her close in a firm hug. "Oh. My. Goodness! Are you okay?"

"Drew," she said, breath caught, "you're hugging me too tight."

He pulled back immediately, guilt flashing across his face. "Sorry. But really, how are you?"

"I'm okay," she said with a nod. "Still a little sore from where I got kicked, but it's manageable." She hesitated, the urge to tell him about the nightmares pressing at her throat. But she held it back. No need to add to his worry.

"Come inside," Hope said with a small smile. "I made banana bread this morning."

She led Drew inside, where he shrugged off his parka and joined Bigelow by the fireplace. The dog was already sprawled out, blissfully soaking in the contentment of the moment. Drew held his hands out to the flames, rubbing them together.

"I didn't think it could get any colder," he said, "but I was wrong."

At the kitchen counter, she poured the coffee, then sliced the banana bread, its sweet, fruity aroma filling the kitchen and making her stomach rumble.

She then set the mugs on the table followed by plates of banana bread.

Drew joined her at the table, hands curled around the mug, as though the heat might thaw the chill from his bones. "I couldn't believe it when I heard about the attack at the lodge," he said, his expression tight with concern. "What a day. First you and Amy were held captive by Austin . . ."

"I wouldn't exactly say we were held captive," she said, before taking a sip of her coffee. "He didn't have a weapon, but he forced his way into Amy's house. He was angry. Intimidating."

Drew tore off a piece of banana bread and popped it into his mouth, his eyebrows lifting in appreciation. "Still sounds like being held captive to me," he said after he swallowed. "And this? Incredible. You really do make the best banana bread."

"Thank you for saying that." She broke off a piece and popped it into her mouth. After swallowing the bite, she asked, "Have you talked to Amy about what happened yesterday?"

Drew nodded, reaching for his mug. "I did. She gave me a rundown and then said she was meeting with Kit. Later, I'm going to listen to the recording of that conversation." He took a drink of his coffee before continuing, "I haven't had the chance to ask you about meeting with Melanie yesterday morning. How did that go?"

Hope opened her mouth to respond, but the chime of the doorbell interrupted her. Bigelow, who'd been dozing by the fireplace, sprang to life and raced toward the hallway, his tail wagging in a blur of excitement. "I wonder who that could be?" Hope murmured.

"Maybe it's Mitzi, or one of your other neighbors, just checking in on you. I'm sure word's gotten around about what happened at the lodge." Drew pushed back his chair and stood. "I'll get it. You stay here." He walked out of the family room, his footsteps echoing down the hall. Moments later, he returned with Jane and Sally in tow. "We have company," he announced with a smile.

Jane rushed over to Hope, enveloping her in a hug. The scent of fresh gardenias, Jane's signature fragrance, filled the air. "Good to see you up and about, dear," Jane murmured, her voice filled with genuine concern. "We heard what happened."

"It's all over town," Sally added, dropping onto a chair across from Hope. "Is it true someone put a bag over your head?"

Hope hesitated, the memory of the terrifying moment rushing back to her. She took a deep breath, reminding herself that she was safe in her home with her friends. "Yes, it was a fabric bag," she conceded, her voice steady despite the lingering fear.

"Dear, are you okay? You look a little pale," Jane said.

"I'll pour the coffees and bring the banana bread to the table," Drew interjected from the kitchen island, sensing Hope's uneasiness. "Hope baked this morning, and it's delicious."

Hope offered him a grateful smile and then looked at Jane, "I'm fine. Just a little tired and sore."

"I can imagine you are," Sally said, standing up to help Drew. She poured the coffee into the mugs he had set out and returned the carafe to the coffee maker. "I'll take these. Could you get us some cream?"

"Don't forget the sugar," Jane called after Drew.

Hope caught the trace of amusement—and just a hint of exasperation—on Drew's face. He wasn't exactly used to playing server, but he managed it with his usual charm.

"I'm glad you both stopped by," Hope said. "I was just about to call and fill you in." She turned slightly. "Oh, Drew, would you grab my notebook and a pen? Top left drawer in the island."

Drew's shoulders slumped, but he nodded. "Is there anything else I can get for you?" he asked with a playful sigh.

A smile played on Hope's lips. "Not at the moment, but I'll let you know."

As Drew retrieved the notebook and pen, Hope turned her attention back to Jane and Sally. "Where should we start?" she asked, her mind already racing with possibilities.

Jane accepted the sugar bowl from Drew, her eyes thoughtful. "I think we should begin with our victims," she said, stirring a spoonful of sugar into her coffee. "That's where I started plotting my novels." As a former mystery writer, Jane's analytical mind was still as sharp as ever, even in retirement.

"Good idea," Drew agreed, setting down the creamer, a platter of sliced banana bread, and Hope's notebook on the table. He dashed back to the island to grab more plates and returned to the table. Helping himself to another slice of banana bread, he continued, "Let's start with Maisie and Henry."

Hope opened her composition notebook to a blank page and scribbled the name Maisie Cox at the top. Beneath it, she wrote "Demi Covington." She tapped the pen against the page, her brow furrowing in thought. "The one question that has been nagging at me since Amy told me that Maisie and Demi were the same person is how she managed to keep her real identity hidden."

Sally nodded, her expression serious. "That's a valid point. In this digital age, it's incredibly difficult to maintain a secret identity, especially if you're running a business online. There are so many trails and traces that can lead back to you."

"Maybe she had help," Jane suggested. "Someone tech-savvy who could cover her tracks and make sure her real identity stayed buried."

Hope's eyes widened at the possibility. "That's a good point, Sally. It would explain a lot. But who would have helped her, and why? The first person that comes to mind is Austin. But he didn't strike me as being tech-savvy."

Drew swallowed a bite of banana bread, his gaze thoughtful. "We need to look into her past, see if there's anyone she was close to who had the skills to pull this off. And we should also consider who might have benefited from her deception."

Hope nodded, jotting down notes as she spoke. "Agreed. Let's start by digging into Maisie's background."

"There's her assistant, Talia," Jane said. "Though she hasn't worked for Maisie for very long."

Hope jotted down Talia's and Austin's names. "You know, I really had a hard time getting a read on Talia."

"I was able to get some basic background on her," Drew said. "Nothing that stands out. Before she worked for Maisie she worked for an online financial coach."

The doorbell rang again, and Hope glanced at Drew. He held up a hand. "I've got it," he said, already heading toward the front door.

A moment later he reappeared, this time with someone neither of them had expected to see.

"Maretta," Sally exclaimed. "What on earth are you doing here?"

"Exactly my question," Drew echoed, already fetching another mug. He filled it to the brim with coffee, knowing Maretta took hers black, no sugar. "Here you go," he said, handing her the mug.

Maretta accepted the coffee, looking slightly awkward. "I . . . I wasn't expecting you to have company, Hope. I apologize for coming over without calling first."

"Maretta, you know none of us stands on ceremony," Jane reassured her with a warm smile. "We didn't give Hope a heads-up that we were coming over either."

"Me neither," Drew added, gesturing to an empty chair at the table. "Come on, sit down and join us. We were just visiting with Hope."

"Drew is right. Join us." Hope was surprised by Maretta's visit but also touched. Despite Maretta's occasional disapproval and her claims that Hope was a "murder magnet" in town, it was clear that the older woman cared for her. After all, Maretta had known Hope and Claire since they were children.

"Thank you." Maretta took a seat and lifted the coffee mug for a sip.

Her gaze landed on Hope's composition notebook, and her eyebrows rose in curiosity. "A composition notebook? Are you all still trying to solve Maisie's murder despite what happened to you yesterday?"

Hope nodded, her eyes meeting Maretta's. "Yes, we are. We were just discussing how Maisie managed to keep her real identity hidden. It's a puzzle that's been nagging at me."

Sally helped herself to another slice of banana bread before saying, "We concluded that she had help."

"As we were discussing earlier, we need to investigate her past," Drew said. "See if there's anyone she was close to who had the skills to pull this off."

"I've been doing some digging of my own and came to a similar conclusion," Maretta announced, drawing surprised looks from everyone at the table. "Maisie, or rather Demi, had a complicated past.

Our technology director suspects someone used advanced techniques to wipe out any trace of Demi Covington online and manipulated search engines to bury whatever might have remained deep in the results."

Hope's brows lifted. Of all the things she'd expected Maretta to say, this wasn't it. It was clever—shockingly so—and she never would've guessed Maretta had been quietly investigating on her own. "That actually explains a lot," she said, her words slow as she worked it through. "It's the only way she could disappear so completely . . . and come back as someone else."

"Add a change in her physical appearance, like a new hair color or colored contact lenses, and voilà, you have Maisie Cox," Drew said, nodding in agreement. "Nice job, Maretta! You've really done your homework."

Maretta flushed at the praise. "It helps to know who to talk to," she said with a modest shrug. "And we should keep in mind that Demi had a pattern of reinventing herself. Remember, she was born Elaine Thompson. That first transformation was subtle, but this time she went all in. She made sure every part of her old life was wiped clean."

Hope's thoughts churned as she processed the new revelation. "So, we need to figure out who helped her and what they stood to gain."

Maretta gave a small shake of her head. "If she used a digital forensics expert, it's not likely anyone close to her was involved. Those kinds of professionals are discreet and expensive."

Jane's fingers tapped against her mug, her eyes gleaming. "I do love a mystery and Maisie Cox was definitely one."

Hope smiled back, bolstered by the shared energy around the table. "Let's get to it. Every clue brings us closer to the truth, and I think we're finally getting somewhere."

By the time their conversation wound down, Hope had scribbled a list of suspects: Melanie, Talia, Austin, Henry, Lorna and Kit.

After Hope waved goodbye to Drew—he was the last to leave—she returned to her notebook at the table. She tapped her pen on the open book repeatedly as she reviewed the list of suspects.

Talia was the only person in Maisie's life who could have either had the technical skill to pull off such a reinvention or been capable of finding someone who could. But why kill Maisie? Below Talia's name, Hope jotted down, *Not sure she has a motive.*

Could Lorna have been hurt so badly by her half-sister that she killed her? Maybe her threats to reveal who Maisie really was didn't go the way she hoped, and instead Maisie met her with indifference, or worse, contempt. Or maybe Lorna was simply looking for an inheritance. She wrote below Lorna's name, *Has motives but not sure she did it.*

Austin had sworn he hadn't killed Maisie and that he loved her, but from what Hope had seen, it hadn't appeared that Maisie felt the same way. Plus, Austin seemed to have lacked the tech skills needed to pull off the reinvention. But he could have had a connection to someone who did. Hope added a note next to Austin's name, *Possible accomplice?*

As for Kit, the motive was obvious, Maisie was responsible for her sister's death. Hope wished she knew where Kit was at the time of Maisie's murder. She made a mental note to follow up on Kit's whereabouts. Then she added a note next to Kit's name, *Too obvious of a suspect?*

As for Melanie, was her frustration with Maisie enough to warrant murder? Even if she had spent thousands of dollars on coaching she felt was useless, would she have killed Maisie? Maybe in a state of rage when she learned Maisie was a con artist. Hope underlined Melanie's name, her pen hovering over the page as a new thought struck her and had her writing another name below Melanie's.

Rick Tucker. Melanie's husband.

Fragments of thoughts flew through Hope's mind. Earlier, during her discussion with the Merrifields, she had recalled the terrifying moment of having a fabric bag put over her head. She felt like she couldn't breathe, felt claustrophobic. Claustrophobic. That's what Rick had said about Maisie—she always hated saunas because they made her feel claustrophobic.

Hope's eyes widened as the realization hit her. She quickly scribbled the question next to Rick's name, her heart racing with the implications, *How would Rick know that?*

Chapter Nineteen

Hope got busy once her company left and she whipped up a batch of brownie cookies, the rich scent of chocolate curling through the kitchen like a promise. Once they were cooled and carefully packaged, she grabbed her coat and headed out, the question burning in her mind—how did Rick Tucker know Maisie hated saunas? It wasn't the kind of detail she would've broadcast online. It was too personal, too specific.

Hope had gotten Melanie's address from Jane, promising to fill her in on her plans later. Jefferson, nestled in the northwest corner of the state, was known for its graceful farms and a thriving antiques scene. As she wound her way through snow-blanketed pastures and over gentle hills, Hope passed elegant barns and sturdy fencing, where horses stood in quiet clusters, their blankets bright against the white landscape.

Despite the slick roads and the light fall of snow, she couldn't help but notice the beauty around her. Jefferson had always been home, and navigating its wintry back roads felt second nature. The winding drive, bordered by bare trees and the occasional pine dusted in white, brought a gentle stillness she hadn't realized she'd been craving.

At last, she pulled up to Melanie's house—a picture-perfect Cape Cod tucked onto a wooded area and enclosed by a low stone wall.

Hope parked and reached for the package of brownie cookies on the passenger seat.

Cookies almost always guaranteed an invitation inside, and she doubted Melanie could turn down such a tempting treat.

She stepped out and made her way toward the house. Before she reached the door, it swung open to reveal Melanie, looking confused.

"Hope, this is a surprise." Melanie's voice was far from welcoming, her eyebrows furrowed. "What are you doing here?"

Hope offered a friendly smile as she extended the tin of cookies. "I made some brownie cookies and thought you might like a few. It's been a rough week and I figured we could all use a little pick-me-up."

"That's kind of you," she said, her voice softening. She took the tin but didn't move aside to let Hope in.

Cold air nipped at Hope's cheeks as she shifted her weight. "It's a cold one today, isn't it?" she said, casting a hopeful glance toward the house. When Melanie didn't answer, Hope tried a more direct approach. "I was also hoping we could talk, if have a few minutes."

Melanie glanced over her shoulder, then back at Hope. After a beat, she nodded. "Sure, come on in. I was working on a project and I could use a break. Let's go to the kitchen."

Hope stepped inside, unzipping her jacket as she followed Melanie to the kitchen. The space was modest but functional, with high-end appliances that hinted at serious cooking, a hanging pot rack over the center island, and a scatter of small gadgets on the counters showing the kitchen had been well-loved and often used. She slipped her jacket off and draped it over a chair at the island, taking a moment to appreciate the space.

"Your kitchen is lovely," Hope commented, her hands clasped on the countertop. "Do you enjoy cooking?"

Melanie shrugged noncommittally. "Yes, it's a passion of mine. I have a pot of coffee brewed. Do you take milk and sugar?"

"Just milk, please," Hope replied with a grateful smile.

Melanie gave a small nod and turned to the counter, pouring two cups of coffee. She placed one in front of Hope, then picked up her own.

"I'm sorry I rushed out of the police department yesterday." Melanie stirred a spoonful of sugar into her coffee. "I was waiting for you, and then Detective Reid came out and called me in. It all happened so fast."

Hope raised her cup for a sip. "Actually, that's not what I wanted to talk about."

Melanie's eyebrows raised in curiosity. "Oh? What then?"

Hope set her cup down gently. "I wanted to talk to you about something your husband said."

Melanie's expression shifted to one of nervousness. "Rick? When did you talk to him?"

"Yesterday, at the police department. Honestly, I'd forgotten about it. Until just a little while ago, I remembered and it got me thinking about what he said."

Melanie stirred her coffee again, as if gathering her thoughts. "He didn't say anything about talking to you," she replied. "What exactly did he say?"

"He said that it was odd that Maisie was found in the sauna because she didn't like them. She was claustrophobic."

The color drained from Melanie's cheeks.

"How would your husband know that?"

Melanie gripped her coffee cup tighter. "I . . . I don't know," she stammered. "Maybe he heard it from someone else?"

"Maybe," Hope said, her voice thoughtful. "But it's an interesting detail to know about someone, don't you think? Especially since Maisie didn't share that on her social media. So, who would he have heard it from? You maybe? Did you know?"

Melanie looked away, her discomfort evident. "I had no idea."

"Then my guess is that he found out from her. How well did Rick know Maisie?" Hope asked.

"Too well."

"They were having an affair, weren't they?"

Melanie shook her head. "I guess there's no point in denying it. The detective knows all about it and apparently you do too. Rick and Maisie had an affair but it ended last summer."

"That's why you were so rattled yesterday," Hope said gently. "Sam questioned you about the affair and it hit , didn't it?"

"You have no idea."

"How long have you known?"

Melanie let out a slow breath, her fingers absently circling the rim of her coffee cup. "Since Detective Reid told me about it. It . . . knocked the wind out of me."

Ouch. Hope's heart ached for Melanie. She could only imagine the pain and humiliation of learning about a spouse's infidelity, especially during a police interview. "I'm so sorry, Melanie," she said softly. "That must have been difficult for you."

Melanie looked up, her eyes filled with a mix of sadness and resignation. "It was. But I've had time to process it. I just . . . I never thought Rick would do something like that. And now, with Maisie gone, it's all so complicated."

"It's a lot to deal with, but you're not alone. And maybe talking about it will help. Do you know how Rick and Maisie met?"

Melanie's gaze was distant as she recalled the details. "They met at one of her retreats. Rick was there for a work event, and they just . . . clicked. At least, that's what he told me."

"He attended a retreat she ran?"

Melanie's shoulders hunched slightly inward, as if she could shrink away from the question. But she couldn't. "No, he did not. However, they met at the hotel and had drinks . . . Anyway, he told me that the affair ended right after he got back home. He swears it was the first time he ever did anything like that."

"Do you believe him?" Hope knew firsthand that once trust was broken in a marriage it was almost impossible to regain. That's why she'd had to walk away from her first marriage.

"Right now, I don't know what to believe," Melanie said. "All I know is that because Rick and Maisie had a fling months ago, I'm a suspect."

"Weren't you a suspect before that interview with Detective Reid?" Hope asked.

Melanie shot Hope a sharp look, her fragility from moments ago replaced with a flash of defensiveness. "What are you talking about?"

Hope met her gaze steadily. "You threatened Maisie. I heard you."

Melanie's expression hardened. "You don't know what you're talking about."

Hope pressed on. "You were angry at Maisie because your business hadn't taken off like you thought it would after her coaching. What I don't understand is why you went to the retreat if you didn't believe she was helping you."

Melanie huffed, her shoulders tensing. "Because it was nonrefundable. I figured I might as well go and see if I could get anything more substantial out of her. But all I heard was that canned self-help nonsense. The more she talked to us, the more I began to realize we'd all been swindled."

Hope nodded, remembering her own impressions of Maisie. By the end of the first workshop, she had realized that Maisie wasn't as authentic as she'd appeared online. "I don't disagree with that assessment of Maisie."

Melanie's voice trembled. "I was desperate for help."

"Why?" Hope asked.

Tears welled in Melanie's eyes as she confessed, "Because we have no money. Not only did my husband cheat on me, but he gambled away most of our savings. I didn't know until I booked the retreat how bad our financial situation was." She took a deep breath, her voice quivering. "It looks like there were a lot of things I didn't know."

A quiet ache stirred in Hope as she registered the hurt in Melanie's voice. "I'm so sorry, Melanie. That's a lot to deal with."

Melanie wiped away a tear, her voice now filled with bitterness. "Yes, it is. And now, I'm left picking up the pieces of my life, trying to figure out how to move forward."

"You'll find a way. I did." Hope offered a supportive smile. She waited a beat before asking her next question, knowing it would be hard but unavoidable. Given Melanie's motives, she had to ask. "Did you know that yesterday afternoon I was attacked at the lodge?"

Melanie's hand flew to her heart, as if physically pained by the news. "What? No, I didn't hear that. Who would do that to you?"

Hope took a deep breath, the memory of the attack still fresh in her mind. "I don't know. They put a hood over my head and started to drag me away, but luckily Maretta interrupted, and they ran off."

"How awful!" Melanie exclaimed and then a second later, realization dawned on her face. "You don't think I did that to you, do you?"

Hope met Melanie's gaze. "Where were you yesterday afternoon?"

Melanie's expression turned thoughtful as she recalled her whereabouts. "I was here, working on a project. I've been trying to find ways to salvage our finances. I didn't leave the house all afternoon."

"Was anyone here with you?" Hope asked, her voice steady but probing.

"You can't really think I attacked you?" she asked, her voice laced with indignation.

"Honestly, I don't know," Hope admitted.

Melanie's expression darkened, her voice taking on an unsettling edge. "Then it would be a very foolish thing for you to come here alone, wouldn't it? Putting yourself in a precarious situation since it would be so easy to finish the job I started yesterday, wouldn't it?"

Hope's back stiffened, a shiver running down her spine. She hated to admit it, but Melanie was right. She had put herself in a vulnerable position.

"Melanie! Stop it!" Rick's voice echoed through the room, startling both women. How long had he been standing there, just out of sight?

Melanie whirled around to face her husband, her voice rising in defense. "We were just talking . . . about you and Maisie."

Rick's cheeks flushed. He turned his attention to Hope, his expression stern.

"Where were you yesterday, Rick?" Hope asked.

He scoffed. "I'm not answering your questions. In fact, we're both done with your intrusiveness into our lives. You should go now."

"I understand that this is difficult, but I'm only trying to find the truth. Someone attacked me, and Maisie is dead. If you have nothing to hide, then there's no reason to be defensive."

Rick stepped closer to his wife, placing a hand lightly on her shoulder. "We have nothing more to say. Leave."

Hope stood, gathering her tote and jacket. "Thank you for your time, Melanie. I'll see myself out."

Hope rushed out of the house and into the safety of her car. Once inside, she pulled her phone from her tote and quickly texted Drew: *Just left Melanie's house. Meet me at the diner.*

A second later, he replied, *I'm swamped. Can it wait?*

She sighed. *No. I think I just had a conversation with the killer.*

Less than a second later came Drew's text: *Leaving now.*

Hope set her phone down and backed out of the driveway, her fingers tight around the steering wheel. Even back on the road, she couldn't shake the unease that had settled between her shoulder blades when Melanie had called her foolish for coming alone.

• • •

By the time Hope made it to the Village Diner, she realized just how much she needed the break. The familiar clatter of dishes, the hiss of the coffee machine, and the scent of burgers on the grill felt strangely soothing after everything that had happened.

Seated across from Drew in a booth, she recounted her run-in with Melanie over glasses of soda and plates of cheeseburgers and fries.

"She really said that to you? 'It would be so easy to finish the job I started yesterday, wouldn't it?'" Drew picked up a French fry, his eyes wide with disbelief. "It's almost like she was taunting you."

Hope leaned back. "Melanie certainly took a dark turn there. Up until then, it had been civil, at least."

Drew raised an eyebrow. "Until you asked her for an alibi," he pointed out before popping the fry into his mouth. After swallowing, he continued, "Do you really think she's capable of murder?"

Hope reached for her soda. "I had doubts until she turned all creepy and threatening. Now, I think she needs to be considered a suspect. According to her, Sam is already doing that." She went on to share the rest of her visit with Melanie and how she got asked to leave.

Drew nodded, his gaze serious. "What's also weird was how Rick suddenly appeared. He got angry too, right?"

"Exactly. If they're innocent, they have nothing to hide. Besides, I'm the one who was attacked yesterday." She set her glass down and picked up her burger. "Then again, his affair has been revealed and so has his gambling problem."

"So far, we have not one but two motives for why Melanie could have killed Maisie. But really, why didn't she just off her husband? He seems to be the problem here."

Hope couldn't help but chuckle at Drew's comment. "What I have to figure out is why I was attacked yesterday. And if it was Melanie, why would she want to hurt me? Up until a few minutes ago, I didn't think she had a solid motive to kill Maisie."

Drew took a bite of his burger and swallowed before asking, "Who else was there?"

Hope's mind raced as she recalled the events. "When I arrived, I saw Amy's car, but she wasn't in the lodge. After Maretta showed up and scared off the attacker—"

"She does have that effect on people," he joked.

"Be nice. I don't know what would have happened if she hadn't shown up when she did," she said.

"You're right. I'm sorry."

"As I was saying, after Maretta showed up, Amy and Kit came to the lodge."

Drew wiped his mouth with a napkin. "Were they together the whole time?"

Hope nodded slowly, her thoughts whirling but not quite connecting. "Yes, I think so. That's why Amy went to the lodge—to talk to Kit." She sighed, feeling like she was grasping at floating puzzle pieces that refused to fit together.

Drew's phone buzzed, and he retrieved it from his jacket pocket, reading the text message. "Good news, Henry is awake."

"That's wonderful news. Now he can tell the police what happened. Maybe he knows who the killer is, and he can explain why he held onto evidence in Penny's case."

Drew typed a quick reply, his gaze still on his phone. "The bad news is that he's not able to communicate just yet."

"So, he can't tell us who attacked him."

Drew shook his head.

"That's not helpful." Hope picked up a French fry and dipped it into ketchup. "Guess we're still on our own for figuring out who did."

Chapter Twenty

By the time Hope returned home—after running a few errands following lunch with Drew—the sky had deepened into a heavy winter darkness. She turned onto her quiet, unlit driveway, the shadows thickening around the familiar outline of her house. Her thoughts churned with unresolved conversations, unsettling moments, and too many loose ends she needed to untangle with Amy. She guided her Explorer into the garage, the door rumbling closed behind her with a final, echoing thud.

The garage was a testament to her organizational skills. Shelving units lined the walls, filled with labeled bins and containers for car supplies. Her motto, *everything in its place*, was emblazoned above the workbench, a quiet reassurance in a chaotic world.

She reached for her tote and stepped out of the vehicle, only to feel something foreign beneath her foot. Glancing down, her breath hitched. A journal lay on the concrete floor. Not just any journal—the same kind distributed at the Limitless Living retreat.

For a second, she wondered if it was hers. But that was impossible. The police had taken hers as evidence. Brow furrowed, she bent to pick it up, her pulse quickening. Inside the front cover, a handwritten message leapt off the page:

> *There's a limit to your living, Hope.*
> *And you've reached it.*

A wave of dread washed over her, prickling her skin like a sudden drop in temperature.

She scanned the garage, her senses heightened. The space that once felt familiar now felt like a trap.

She gripped the journal, her fingers digging into the edges. Who'd left it? How did they get in?

Swallowing hard, she fumbled through her tote for her phone, her hands trembling. When she finally pulled it free, the screen illuminated with a new text from Drew: *Kit wasn't the only one with a relative at the retreat in Vermont. Nina had a daughter. Call me.*

Nina? Of course. The woman who'd attended the retreat with Elspeth, the one who spent all her money on Maisie's coaching.

Before Hope could answer Drew, a sharp voice cut through the quiet like a knife.

"Put the phone down, Hope."

She froze. The cold now wasn't just in the air—it rooted deep in her bones.

Turning slowly, she saw Kit standing close by, her face blank, yet the threat in her stance was unmistakable.

"Welcome home," Kit said, nodding toward the side entrance. "You really should lock your doors. But hey, I appreciated you made it easy for me."

Hope's pulse hammered in her ears. She tightened her grip on the phone.

"What are you doing here?"

Kit's smile was small and sharp. "You're a smart woman. You've read the journal. You already know why I'm here."

Hope swallowed the knot in her throat. "You killed Maisie."

Kit's eyes glittered with something far too close to satisfaction. "I waited years. Then one day—bam—there she was. All that talk about manifesting finally paid off. Funny, isn't it? Her own philosophy got her killed."

"The police will arrest you," Hope said, forcing strength into her voice. "Detective Reid's not going to let you walk away from this."

Kit scoffed. "Reid's chasing shadows. Melanie's practically gift-wrapped for him. Who knew she had so many reasons to want Maisie dead? And Austin? Talk about guilty as sin for one murder, so it's not hard to believe he didn't commit a second one." Her tone hardened. "Now, stop stalling. I said drop the phone. We need to deal with my problem. Which is *you*."

Hope didn't move.

Kit stepped forward, menace radiating off her like heat from a flame. "I won't say it again. Drop. It."

As Hope shifted, she discreetly pressed the SOS button on her phone, praying her emergency contact would see the alert. Then she slid the phone into her tote and raised her hands in surrender.

A car rolled up outside. And the a door slammed shut.

Hope's breath hitched. *Ethan?*

The side door creaked open, and for a moment relief sparked in her chest.

But it wasn't Ethan.

It was Talia.

"Talia! Call the police!" Hope shouted.

She didn't move. Instead, she stood frozen, her face guarded—cool and unreadable, but with something darker flickering beneath.

"Talia!" Hope cried again, desperation cracking her voice. "Call the police!"

But Talia stepped forward instead. "Come on," she said. "We have to go."

Hope went still. Her thoughts clicked into place, sharp and sudden.

Drew's text echoed in her mind: *Kit wasn't the only one with a relative at the retreat.*

Talia's mother was Nina. The woman who'd lost everything.

Talia wasn't there to help. She was in on it.

Hope stared at her, the truth sinking like lead in her stomach. Her blood turned to ice.

"Nina was your mother," she said slowly. "You planned all of this, didn't you, Talia? You got the job with Maisie, wormed your way into her world. And when Lorna showed up, you latched onto her. You would do anything to destroy Maisie."

Talia's smile was cold. "No. Not destroy her. Kill her," she said. "My mother was destroyed after she'd been scammed and lost all of her money! Her world, my world, fell apart."

She glanced at Kit. "We're wasting time. Let's get this over with." She looked back at Hope. "I'm really sorry you got involved in this."

A sharp glint flickered in Talia's eyes—was it regret, or something far colder? Hope didn't have time to decide. Something hard slammed into her head. Pain exploded behind her eyes, sharp and blinding, and the world tilted violently. Her knees buckled, the floor surging up to meet her as everything dissolved into darkness.

• • •

When she came to, Hope was sprawled on the cold garage floor, her head throbbing. The air was heavy with exhaust fumes, each breath searing her lungs. She blinked, vision swimming.

Panic surged as she tried to stand. Her strength faltered, but she forced herself toward the car door, fumbling at the handle. It didn't budge—Kit and Talia had made sure of that.

She scanned the space through stinging eyes. The SUV's engine still rumbled. The key fob was missing. She pounded on the window, fists aching, to no avail.

Gasping now, she lunged for the garage door opener and slammed her hand against the button. Nothing. She followed the wire up with her eyes. The cord had been cut.

A new wave of fear surged through her. She had to think—fast.

She frantically searched for the emergency release cord, but it was jammed tight. No escape. Hope's mind raced for another way out, but the fumes were thickening, stealing her strength.

A loud bang shattered the haze. The side door burst open, a rush of cold air slicing into the garage.

"Hope!" Ethan's voice, raw with urgency, broke through the suffocating air. He coughed as the fumes hit him but pressed forward. "Hope!"

She turned from the garage door, vision swimming, and saw his figure cutting through the fog. "I'm here," she croaked, her voice barely a whisper. Her legs gave way, sending her sliding to the concrete.

Strong hands found her. Ethan scooped her up in one swift, careful motion. "I've got you," he murmured, his breath catching as he carried her into the night.

The instant they hit the open air, Hope coughed violently, her lungs clawing for oxygen. Ethan knelt with her on the frozen ground, his arm a steady brace as she gasped and heaved against the bitter cold.

"Just breathe, Hope," he said, voice rough but steady. "Nice and slow."

She squeezed her eyes shut, fighting to steady her breathing, to flush the poison from her body. When she finally looked up, Ethan's face came into view, brow furrowed, jaw tight, but a flicker of relief softening his features.

"It was Kit . . . and Talia," she rasped.

Ethan smoothed her hair back with a soft touch. "Shh . . . Don't talk. Breathe for me. Slow, deep breaths."

• • •

Flashing red and blue lights painted the driveway in frantic pulses. The wail of approaching sirens had grown louder and drawn Hope's neighbors out onto their front yards. They watched as police cars zoomed onto the street, followed by an ambulance that skidded to a halt in the driveway.

Hope blinked up at the sky, the stars spinning overhead, as a medic's voice broke through the chaos. "You're going to be okay, Hope. We're taking you to the hospital to be checked out."

"Hope!" Drew's voice cracked across the night. He stumbled toward her, his face pale with shock as he reached for her hand.

"She's okay," Ethan reassured.

"Oh, my goodness! Is it true?" Drew gasped, glancing between Ethan and the officers. "Was it really Kit?"

Ethan nodded grimly, his jaw tight. "Yes. And Talia was in on it too."

Hope squeezed Drew's hand and then let go. She wanted to say something, but the world tilted around her. She caught only glimpses—the swirl of uniforms, Ethan giving his statement to an officer, Drew jogging alongside the gurney as the medics wheeled her toward the ambulance.

Just before they lifted her inside, Ethan leaned close, his hand brushing hers.

"They caught them both," he said. "Talia and Kit are in custody. You're safe now."

Hope nodded, glancing past him at the cluster of neighbors gathered on their lawns, wide-eyed and whispering.

Never a dull moment on Fieldstone Drive, she thought faintly, and tonight would give them something to talk about for years.

Chapter Twenty-one

The sun shone for the first time in what felt like ages, its faint warmth reaching the sidewalks of Jefferson and softening the chill in the air. Hope made her way toward the Merrifield Inn, where snowbanks along the curb had begun to shrink into messy, slushy heaps.

As she stepped inside the inn, the familiar blend of cinnamon, coffee, and friendly chatter wrapped around her, instantly putting her at ease.

"There she is!" Eliza called from behind the reception desk, pressing her hands together. "We've been waiting for you! I set out a tray with one of my special tea blends. I call it Comfort in a Cup and I guarantee you'll love it."

"That sounds like exactly what I need." It had been one week since Hope had been ambushed in her garage by Kit and Talia. After an overnight stay at the hospital for observation, she'd been released. The memory of that night still lingered, but with each passing day its grip on her seemed to loosen.

Eliza rose from her chair, but before she could come out from behind the desk, her aunts rushed in from the dining room, fussing like mother hens over Hope.

"You poor thing." Jane pulled Hope into a quick but fierce hug. "You had us scared to death."

"You gave us all a fright." Sally embraced her next, then stepped back to straighten Hope's scarf. "You're sure you're feeling all right?"

"I'm fine," Hope said with a smile. "Better than fine, actually. It's good to be out."

"The photo shoot for your cookbook is coming up, isn't it?" Eliza led Hope and her aunts into the parlor, where a tea tray waited on the coffee table.

"Tomorrow." Hope draped her jacket over the back of a chair and settled onto the sofa. "It's both exciting and terrifying."

"Terrifying? You're used to being photographed in your kitchen." Jane joined her on the sofa.

"I'm usually the one taking the pictures," Hope said with a small laugh. "And when I worked at the magazine, I oversaw the shoots. I'm not used to being the one in front of the camera. I'm probably overthinking it. I know the photographer, and he's very good."

Things were moving quickly with her cookbook publication. The title had been finalized—*Simply Delicious: Comfort Food Recipes from Hope at Home*—and a release date set. Tomorrow's photos would be for the cover, interior spreads, and publicity. The process shots were already complete.

"While I'm a little nervous about tomorrow, I'm very grateful I'm even able to do the shoot, considering . . ." Hope's voice trailed off.

"No need to dwell on what could have happened," Sally said, handing her a cup of tea. She poured another for Jane and then settled across from them.

"Here, let me finish," Eliza offered, taking over the pouring for her aunt.

"When we heard about Kit and Talia, we couldn't believe it," Eliza said. "They were working together the whole time?"

"That's how Kit had an alibi when you were grabbed in Henry's office," Jane said, sipping her tea. "Talia was there, and she's the one who attacked Hope."

"Yes, she was." Hope nodded.

She'd gotten an update on the case from Sam earlier that day. Talia was, in fact, Nina Finch's daughter. Like Maisie, she'd assumed a new identity to hide the connection. Maisie never knew—not until it was too late. Talia's plan to get close enough to take her down had worked perfectly. Then Lorna came along. Though she'd kept her own identity a secret, she and Lorna conspired to ruin Maisie's carefully constructed life. What Lorna didn't realize was that Talia had also aligned herself with Kit. Their plan went far beyond public humiliation. Lorna had no idea they intended to kill.

"Talia's motive was revenge?" Sally asked.

Hope nodded again. "Her mother put everything she had into Maisie's programs. When she realized she'd been conned, it was too late. She lost her home, and Talia ended up living with her father, who wasn't exactly Father of the Year. Not long after that, Nina spiraled.

Last year, she passed away. Talia blamed Maisie."

"It's amazing how devious and dangerous people can be." Eliza handed Sally her cup before pouring one for herself. "Then again, Talia and Kit lost someone because of Maisie. It sounds like Lorna carried a lot of anger from childhood, too."

"That may be true, dear, but it doesn't excuse what they did." Jane's tone was firm. "Especially trying to harm Hope!"

Hope offered a small smile. "And they were willing to let Melanie or Austin take the fall for Maisie's murder."

Sally set her cup and saucer on the end table and reached for a shortbread cookie. "Speaking of Austin, was it him who attacked Henry?"

"It was." Hope's finger moved absently along the rim of her teacup as she recalled her conversation with Sam. "Sam told me Austin confessed to hitting Henry in the back of the head when he stepped outside for more firewood. They'd argued, and Henry refused to hand over Penny Foster's bag." Even now, her mind spun at the sheer deceit that had unfolded at the retreat.

"Did the police ever find the bag?" Jane asked.

"They did." Hope picked up a cookie of her own. "Henry hid it in the basement."

"Henry," Maretta said as she stepped into the parlor. "Now there's someone who's changed more than I ever imagined. I thought I knew him, but clearly I didn't know him at all."

"Maretta, join us." Sally patted the sofa cushion beside her.

"I'll get another cup." Eliza sprang from her chair and hurried out of the room.

Maretta shrugged off her coat and draped it over the arm of the sofa before sitting down, placing her black purse beside her. "It's good to see you out and about, Hope. I'm sure your neighbors are still buzzing about all that commotion on your street last week."

"I imagine they'll forgive the disturbance, considering the police caught two killers." Hope sipped her tea. Over the past week, neighbors had dropped off meals and flowers—some truly concerned, others clearly fishing for gossip.

"Any updates on Henry's condition?" Jane asked.

"He's been released from the hospital," Maretta replied.

"More good news." Eliza returned, a fresh cup and saucer in hand. She poured Maretta's tea and handed it to her before settling back into her chair. "Will Henry be facing any charges for holding onto Penny Foster's belongings?"

"I don't know yet." Maretta took a sip of tea, then smiled. "This is delicious."

Eliza's cheeks blossomed with color. "Thank you. It's one of my special blends."

"Well, I think Henry should be held accountable." Sally reached for another cookie. "If he'd turned over Penny's things when she first went missing, the police might've seen through Maisie's lies and found justice for Penny. And maybe Maisie would still be alive."

Maretta gave a small shrug. "That's for law enforcement to decide. Either way, Henry will have to live with the choices he made."

"Have you spoken to him?" Hope asked. Once upon a time, Henry had meant a great deal to Maretta—perhaps even been her first love, though Hope had never heard her say it outright.

"We've spoken." Maretta paused, as if she'd rather steer the conversation elsewhere, but added, "Once he's feeling stronger, he'll be coming to dinner."

"How does Alfred feel about that?" Hope asked.

"He's fine with it. Why wouldn't he be? Henry and I are barely acquaintances at this point," Maretta said before taking another sip of her tea.

"No reason at all," Jane said briskly, sensing the tension and steering the conversation elsewhere. "Speaking of changes, have you heard about Melanie and Rick?"

"They've separated." Hope set her teacup down. During her visits with neighbors, she'd heard the news more than once. "It's always sad when a marriage falls apart."

"Maybe they'll work through their troubles." Eliza's tone carried a note of optimism.

"They've got a lot to work through." Sally didn't sound as hopeful.

Hope didn't want to linger on the topic of the Tuckers' crumbling marriage. Too many good things were happening around her now, and there was no sense dwelling on heartbreak.

For a few moments, they sat quietly, sipping tea and nibbling buttery cookies. Then Maretta broke the silence.

"I must say, Hope, it's a wonder how you always manage to land in the middle of trouble. You've got more lives than that cat of yours." She gave a small shake of her head, her smile teasing.

Laughter bubbled through the room, warm and familiar.

Hope lifted her teacup to hide a grin. Somehow, trouble did have a way of finding her—whether she went looking for it or not.

• • •

The next day, Hope's kitchen was awash in natural light from the window over the sink and the wide bank of windows that overlooked the patio. Still, her photographer, Nate Sherman, had set up a few soft, diffused fill lights to perfect the atmosphere as his team moved briskly through the shoot.

Carol, the food stylist, was someone Hope knew well from her magazine days, meticulous to a fault and a little bossy, but an undeniable pro. The petite redhead was now fussing over the final touches on a platter of meat loaf slices, tucking parsley sprigs neatly around the roasted vegetables.

Hovering nearby was Lily, the project manager, tablet in hand and a constant eye on the clock, working to keep the packed schedule running smoothly.

The counters were crowded with cooling racks holding roasted potatoes, trays of cookies, and glossy, picture-perfect pies, all awaiting their close-ups. Bigelow lay sprawled across the floor, his turn in front of the camera finished for now, while Princess perched regally atop her cat tree, still casting imperious glances at the lens as if she owned the set. The kitchen buzzed with quiet energy—the soft click of the camera, the low hum of the team discussing angles, and the occasional bark from Bigelow when he thought he deserved another treat.

"You're doing great, Hope," Nate said, peering over his high-end DSLR camera. He wore dark jeans and a fitted henley, his light brown hair tousled like he'd been running his hands through it all afternoon.

"Tilt your head a little to the left and lift your chin just a touch."

They continued shooting until the final photo was snapped. Hope's cheeks ached from smiling and her feet throbbed from hours of standing, but from the few images she'd glimpsed on Nate's camera screen, it had all been worth it. She could finally exhale. The cookbook was done. No more recipe testing, no more styling sessions, no more last-minute tweaks. It was official.

Her moment of relief, however, was short-lived. The real challenge loomed ahead, selling the book to foodies across the country. Leave it to reality to drain the sparkle from a hard-earned victory.

"Hey, you okay?" Nate asked, stepping into the mudroom with his camera bag slung over his shoulder. His voice was gentle, almost hesitant. "Worried about the photos? Don't be. They're fantastic. Your editor's going to have a tough time picking the cover."

Hope mustered a smile. "I'm fine, just tired."

"I can imagine," he said, pulling on his leather gloves. "I heard what happened last week. Didn't want to bring it up and mess with the vibe today, but . . . I'm glad you're okay. You showing up like this? That took guts." He gave her arm a light tap, warm and sincere.

"Nate!" Lily's voice rang out from their rental. "Let's go!"

He laughed and tossed Hope a grin. "Duty calls. Thanks for today and for feeding us so well." He patted his stomach. "Tomorrow, it's nothing but cardio."

With a wink, he disappeared out the door.

Hope watched the team pile into the SUV, their gear barely fitting, and back out of the driveway. She was about to step inside when Amy's car pulled into the now-empty spot.

"Oh, my goodness! Today was your photo shoot!" Amy's eyes darted over the array of styled plates and platters like a kid in a candy store when she entered the kitchen. "Hope, this is huge! It's your moment. I'm so proud of you."

"We just wrapped," Hope said, filling the kettle and setting it on the stovetop. "And congratulations are in order for you, too. The podcast is blowing up, and you were right in the middle of the story when Austin barged into your house."

Amy grinned, hovering near a tray of buttery Madeleines. "I sure was. And so were you. Can I have one of these?"

Hope, reaching into the cabinet for mugs, gave her a quick glance and a nod. "Help yourself. Plate a few and bring them to the table. Everything's edible." She paused, glancing over. "There's still a lot about Maisie's story that people want answers to."

"Oh, they're going to get them." Amy plucked a few Madeleines and arranged them with exaggerated care. "Episode three drops Monday. And let's just say . . . I went deep."

"How deep?" Hope asked, intrigued.

Amy leaned in, eyes gleaming. "I kept digging when I found out Maisie died broke. So, the question is, where did all the money go?"

Hope blinked. "You're not going to leave me hanging, are you?"

Amy gave a sly shrug.

"Oh, come *on*," Hope said. "You're seriously doing this?"

When Amy didn't answer, Hope swiped the plate from her hands. "Then no Madeleines for you."

"Hey!" Amy reached for it. "That's blackmail."

Hope held the plate just out of reach. "Spill it."

"Fine. Talia cooked the books. Built herself and Austin a cozy little nest egg behind Maisie's back."

Hope's mouth dropped. "No way!"

"Now give me the Madeleines."

Hope handed over the plate and Amy made a beeline for the table like a victorious thief. "So Talia and Austin were in it together? What about Kit?"

"My theory? They were going to cut her loose once they wrapped things up with . . ." Amy hesitated, then gave Hope a look. *"You."*

"Wait, let me wrap my head around this. Talia and Austin were embezzling funds from Maisie, meanwhile Talia was plotting to kill her and got Kit to go along with it. All the while, Maisie was trying to get Penny Foster's belongings from Henry. What about Austin's claim that he and Maisie were in love?"

"Another lie. As for the rest, talk about crazy! I can't believe we were going to spend a whole weekend with those people."

The kettle whistled, and Hope pulled it from the burner. "Talk about a tangled web of betrayal and murder."

Amy bit into a Madeleine and moaned in delight. "Honestly? These alone are worth the price of the cookbook."

Hope poured the hot water into their mugs and dropped in two tea bags. "That's so sweet of you to say."

Before Amy could answer, a loud knock at the front door echoed through the house, followed by a bark from Bigelow, who bounded out of the kitchen like a four-legged cannonball.

Hope glanced at Amy, confused. "Hmm…I wonder who that could be. I'm not expecting anyone."

"Maybe the crew forgot something?" Amy asked as she stood.

Together they walked to the front door with Bigelow trailing behind them. Hope pulled opened the door and found a small crowd gathered on her front step—neighbors, friends from the garden club, and even a few members of the food pantry board. At the front was Claire, holding a bouquet of bright flowers and grinning from ear to ear.

"We heard the cookbook photos wrapped today," Claire said. "And we thought it was time for a little toast."

Someone popped the cork on a bottle of sparkling cider, and Bigelow barked again, as if in agreement.

Hope's eyes welled with tears. "You guys . . ."

Amy elbowed her gently. "Told you this was your moment."

Hope stepped aside, laughing as the group poured in with warmth and laughter trailing behind them. "Come on in. I'll make tea and there's plenty of food."

• • •

Sunday afternoon Hope's house was full of people and food. The aroma of simmering minestrone soup floated in the air, blending with laughter, the low rumble of a football game from the family room, and the occasional bark of excitement from Bigelow. From where she worked at the kitchen island, she could see Ethan, Matt, and Alfred Kingston, each with a beer in hand, sitting on the sofa watching the football game. Molly and Becca were on the floor giggling as they played tug-of-war with Bigelow, who was thrilled to see his favorite little humans again.

Hope and Claire moved in sync, one slicing pickles, the other arranging sandwiches on a platter. The energy was cozy, familiar and just the right amount of chaotic.

The mudroom door eased open, and Drew stepped inside cautiously, cradling Trixie in his arms. "Where's Princess?" he asked, scanning the room.

"Don't worry. She skedaddled as soon as she saw Molly and Becca. She's probably tucked away in a laundry basket upstairs." Hope grabbed a towel and wiped her hands.

Drew set Trixie down, and she immediately tore across the room, joining the fun on the floor with the girls and Bigelow. Amy followed Drew in, cheeks pink from the cold, still glowing with excitement over her smash podcast episode.

"You should see the podcast numbers," she said to Hope with a grin. "Episode two is officially my most-listened-to episode *ever*. I'm killing it this season!"

"That's amazing," Hope said, giving her a quick hug. "And you deserve it."

"And," Drew added, "my editor *loved* my piece on Maisie. Called it one of the most compelling things I've written."

"Well, look at you two," Claire said with a wink. "The media darlings of Jefferson."

Just then, Jane and Sally arrived with their arms full. Sally carried a plate of cookies, while Jane held a bottle of wine.

"Jeffrey sends his apologies," Sally said. "He's up in Boston visiting his son."

"No worries," Hope said, ushering them inside as Claire took the cookies and wine. "We're glad you both could make it."

"I see Matt's here," Jane observed. "Everything good between you two? I heard you threatened to withhold your Christmas cookies from him."

Hope chuckled. "Of course I didn't mean it."

Maretta appeared from the hallway, smoothing her sweater. "It looks like everyone's here."

"Yes, they are." Hope motioned for Claire to join her into the family room, Maretta trailing after them. Crossing straight to Ethan, Hope slipped her arm through his. Hope drew in a breath, ready to make the announcement—but Maretta clapped her hands, claiming the room's attention before she could speak.

"Since we're all gathered, this feels like the perfect time for an announcement." Her gaze bounced between Hope and Ethan. "Don't you agree?"

All eyes turned to them.

"You've got another surprise?" Claire asked, raising her eyebrows. "The last time you surprised us was with your engagement!"

Hope nodded toward Ethan. "This one's all his."

Matt stood from the sofa and crossed to Ethan, giving him a congratulatory slap on the shoulder. "It's a good one, too."

Ethan wrapped his arm around her shoulders. "Changes are happening," he said, smiling at the group.

Amy leaned forward in her chair, brimming with anticipation. "You've finally set a wedding date!"

"Well, it's about time," Sally murmured.

Drew cupped his face in his hands. "Finally. I can't wait for the bachelor party or the bridal shower."

"Don't keep us in suspense," Jane urged.

Hope laughed and shook her head. "No, that's not the announcement. Sorry." She glanced up at Ethan with a look that said *soon, though.*

"Okay, here it is. I'm going back to the Jefferson Police Department." Ethan let the words settle a beat before adding, "As chief."

The room erupted in cheers and applause.

"That's wonderful!"

"Fantastic news!"

Claire clapped loudest of all. "It's about time!"

"I'm sorry to lose the best investigator I've ever had," Matt said, returning to the sofa, "but I'm thrilled Jefferson is getting its best chief of police back on the job."

"This is wonderful news," Sally said. "Though, I'm curious, why are you going back?"

"The truth is that I miss the job, and I my officers." Ethan looked over at his daughters. "Things are good with the girls and Heather now so I can devote the time necessary to being the chief."

Hope nodded. She'd supported his decision to leave the Jefferson Police Department when he needed to focus on his family. Being chief meant always being on call. But now, after a few months, he'd told her that Molly and Becca were more settled, and Heather was thriving in her post-rehab life. He also admitted he missed police work. And, truth be told, she kind of missed seeing him in uniform.

"Now I can stop interviewing substandard candidates," Maretta said. "Honestly, I don't have time to keep wasting."

Hope laughed, taking in the moment. Friends and family clustered together, laughter bubbling from every corner.

She felt Ethan's hand slide gently into hers. When she met his gaze, he gave her fingers a reassuring squeeze.

No, things weren't perfect. But they were moving in the right direction.

And soon, it would be time to start planning a wedding.

Recipes from Hope's Kitchen

Salisbury Steaks

When I'm craving comfort food, it's hard not to think of something smothered in rich, savory gravy, and for me, that usually means Salisbury steaks. I've been making this recipe for over a decade now, tweaking and adjusting along the way to create a version my family and friends absolutely love.

These steaks are the perfect comfort food and they're so easy to make. Pair them with buttery mashed potatoes or homemade risotto to elevate them. I love serving them with roasted carrots and homemade biscuits.

For the steaks:

1½ lb. ground beef (80/20)
2 tablespoons Worcestershire sauce
2 tablespoons ketchup
1 teaspoon light brown sugar
1 large egg, beaten
½ cup breadcrumbs
1 teaspoon mustard powder
¾ teaspoon seasoned salt
½ teaspoon ground black pepper
1 tablespoon vegetable oil

For the gravy:

8 ounces sliced baby bella mushrooms
1 small yellow onion, finely chopped
2 tablespoons unsalted butter
2 tablespoons all-purpose flour

½ teaspoon seasoned salt
1½ cups beef stock
3 tablespoons heavy cream
1 tablespoon ketchup
1 teaspoon Worcestershire sauce
1 teaspoon Dijon mustard
Chopped parsley, to serve

For the steaks:

In a large bowl, mix together the ground beef, Worcestershire sauce, ketchup, brown sugar, egg, breadcrumbs, mustard, seasoned salt, and pepper until fully combined. Divide the mixture into 6 equal portions, about 4 ounces each. Shape each portion into a 1-inch-thick oval patty. For a classic "steak" look, press a few lines across the top of each patty with your finger.

Heat a large skillet over medium heat and add the oil, swirling to coat the bottom. Place the steaks in the skillet and cook for 6 to 8 minutes, until golden brown. Flip and cook the other side for another 6 to 8 minutes, or until the internal temperature reaches 160°F. Remove the steaks from the skillet and set aside

For the gravy:

In the same skillet over medium heat, add the mushrooms and onion. Cook, stirring occasionally, for about 6 minutes, until the onions are softened and the mushrooms are lightly browned.

Add the butter and stir until melted. Sprinkle in the flour and seasoned salt, stirring until the flour is fully incorporated and no streaks remain, for about 1 minute.

Increase the heat to medium-high and pour in the beef stock, scraping the bottom of the skillet to loosen any browned bits. Stir until smooth and bring to a simmer. Reduce the heat to medium-low and cook for 6 to 8 minutes, stirring occasionally, until the gravy has slightly thickened.

Stir in the heavy cream, ketchup, Worcestershire sauce, and Dijon mustard. Allow the gravy to return to a gentle simmer, stirring occasionally. Return the steaks to the skillet, spooning the gravy over the top to coat. Let them cook for 2 to 3 minutes to warm through. Garnish with parsley before serving.

Banana Bread

If you're picky about banana bread, this recipe is for you! It's moist, tender, perfectly sweet with just a hint of tang—everything we want in a slice. The flavor only gets better by the next day (if it lasts that long). Toast it up, add a little salted butter, and enjoy it with your morning coffee or as an after-school treat. This easy, foolproof recipe fills your kitchen with the most irresistible aroma and just might become the only banana bread recipe you'll ever need.

½ cup melted unsalted butter or vegetable oil, plus more for greasing pan
1¾ cups all-purpose flour
1 cup toasted pecans, chopped (see cook's note)
½ cup granulated sugar
1 teaspoon baking soda
1 teaspoon ground cinnamon
½ teaspoon fine salt
¼ teaspoon freshly grated nutmeg
2 large eggs, lightly beaten
¼ cup buttermilk, sour cream or yogurt
½ cup light brown sugar, lightly packed
1 teaspoon pure vanilla extract
4 soft, very ripe, darkly speckled medium bananas, mashed (about 1½ cups)

Preheat the oven to 350°F and lightly butter a 9-by-5-inch loaf pan.

In a large bowl, whisk together the flour, pecans, granulated sugar, baking soda, cinnamon, salt, and nutmeg. In a separate medium bowl, whisk together the eggs, melted butter, buttermilk, brown sugar, and vanilla. Stir in the mashed bananas. Gently fold the banana mixture into the flour mixture until just combined. It's fine if the batter is a little lumpy.

Pour the batter into the prepared loaf pan and gently tap the pan on the counter to level it out. Bake for about 1 hour, or until the top is golden brown and a toothpick inserted into the center comes out clean. Allow the bread to cool in the pan for 10 minutes before transferring it to a wire rack to cool completely.

Cook's Note: For nut-free banana bread, leave out the pecans.

Brownie Cookies

Calling all chocolate lovers—these Brownie Cookies are your ultimate fix! With a chewy, fudgy center and perfectly caramelized edges, they combine the best parts of brownies and cookies into one irresistible treat. Baked jumbo-sized (thanks to a ¼-cup scoop), these cookies are ooey, gooey, and downright impossible to resist.

2⅔ cups 60% cacao bittersweet chocolate baking chips
½ cup unsalted butter, cubed
4 large eggs, room temperature
1½ cups sugar
4 teaspoons vanilla extract
2 teaspoons instant espresso powder, optional
⅔ cup all-purpose flour
½ teaspoon baking powder
¼ teaspoon salt
1 package (11½ ounces) semisweet chocolate chunks

Preheat the oven to 350°F. In a large saucepan over low heat, melt the chocolate chips and butter, stirring until smooth. Remove from heat and let the mixture cool slightly until just warm.

In a small bowl, whisk together the eggs, sugar, vanilla, and espresso powder (if using) until well combined. Stir this into the warm chocolate mixture. In a separate bowl, whisk together the flour, baking powder, and salt. Add the dry ingredients to the chocolate mixture and stir until fully combined. Gently fold in the chocolate chunks. Let the dough rest for about 10 minutes, until it thickens slightly.

Drop the dough by ¼-cup portions onto parchment-lined baking sheets, spacing them about 3 inches apart. Bake for 12 to 14 minutes, or until the cookies are set. Allow to cool on the baking sheets for 1 to 2 minutes before transferring to wire racks to cool completely.

Bakes about 1½ dozen cookies.

Acknowledgments

Writing this book has been an absolute joy, and I am deeply grateful to everyone who has contributed to its creation and success.

To my dear author friends—Jenny Kales, Linda Reilly, Lena Gregory, Holly Danvers, and Darci Hannah—your encouragement and unwavering support have been a constant source of strength and inspiration. Whether through your thoughtful advice, shared experiences, or simply cheering me on, your friendship has meant the world to me.

A special thank-you Lt. Michael Confield for answering my procedural questions with patience and clarity. I am deeply grateful for your help.

To my editor, Bill Harris, and the wonderful team at Beyond the Page, your expertise, patience, and hard work have shaped this book into something I am truly proud of. Your guidance and vision have been instrumental in bringing this story to life.

To my agent, Jill Marsal, who has not only believed in my work but has championed it. Thank you!

Lastly, and most importantly, to my readers—thank you. I'm truly thrilled that you've spent time with this story, and I hope you enjoyed reading it as much as I enjoyed writing it.

About the Author

Debra Sennefelder lives and writes in Connecticut, where she shares her home with her family and slightly spoiled Shih Tzu. An avid reader across a range of genres, mystery fiction is her obsession. Her interest in people and relationships is channeled into her novels against a backdrop of crime and mystery. She's the author of the Food Blogger Mystery series, the Resale Boutique Mystery series, and the Cookie Shop Mystery series. When she's not writing, she's either baking or reading. To learn more, visit her on the web at www.debrasennefelder.com.